DEATH
ON A WINTER'S DAY

BOOKS BY VERITY BRIGHT

The Lady Eleanor Swift Mystery Series

DEATH
ON A WINTER'S DAY

VERITY BRIGHT

Bookouture

Published by Bookouture in 2021

An imprint of Storyfire Ltd.
Carmelite House
50 Victoria Embankment
London EC4Y 0DZ

www.bookouture.com

ISBN: 978-1-80019-573-8
eBook ISBN: 978-1-80019-572-1

To my readers, for continuing to believe one day Eleanor will get her man, and Gladstone will get his sausages!

Murder is terribly exhausting – Albert Camus

1

'They've cancelled Christmas!'

Lady Eleanor Swift stared at her butler's reflection in the gold-framed mirror above the telephone table. He looked back at her, his face as inscrutable as ever.

'Indeed, my lady. Most unfortunate.'

He turned to go, but she shook her head.

'Wait, Clifford. Don't go anywhere. I might need you.' She held the handset back to her ear, instantly wrenching it away again as the loud crackles and hisses threatened to pierce her eardrum. 'Botheration! I've lost him again.' She spun round, her unruly red curls flying out from their last few restraining pins. 'Clifford, can you believe it? The Ashleys have cancelled Christmas!'

'Indeed, my lady. Most unfortunate, as I believe I said.'

'But they had guests invited and everything. It was all arranged. It's unthinkable to cancel now.'

'A most unexpected turn of events, my lady.'

She listened again at the handset and then shook her head. 'This is hopeless, I can hardly hear Clarence when he's speaking. And then he just disappears completely for a random number of minutes. Can't we upgrade something so one can converse without risking one's eardrums?'

Clifford shook his head. 'I suspect the problem is, in fact, at the other end. Castle Ranburgh is not known for being located in the centre of modernity.'

She grimaced. 'Draughty corridors and icy bedrooms? Bit eighteenth century, is it?' She held up a hand before he could reply. 'Ah! Clarence, you're back. Please be quick, I fear I might lose you again.'

A familiar clipped English tone came through the crackling on the line. 'Wilhelmina is so upset. This was to have been her fairy-tale Christmas. Out of London, up in the wilds of the Scottish Highlands in that old pile of stones my uncle bought in his later years.'

'Then why have you cancelled Christmas at Castle Ranburgh?'

A deep sigh reached her ears as the line cleared. 'I haven't. The... the staff have.'

In the mirror, Eleanor saw her butler stiffen in horror as he caught the words.

'Your staff!? Even with my limited knowledge of how to be a lady of the manor, Clarence' – she ignored Clifford's pointed cough – 'I do at least know staff aren't supposed to dictate things like when their employers have Christmas, are they?'

'Indeed not!' Clifford muttered.

She flapped her hand at him. 'Clarence, why are you allowing your staff to ride roughshod over your plans? I don't understand.'

The baron's vexed voice came back on. 'Because, Eleanor, they are extremely devout Presbyterians, like most of the population up here. And, it seems, they frown on celebrating Christmas for reasons I cannot pretend to understand but need, it seems, to respect. Which is why I can't quickly rally some temporary staff together to stand in for them. No one will countenance working for us during the celebrations. And any staff further afield who might have been for hire were engaged elsewhere weeks ago. I've never spent any time up here at Christmas before, so I had no idea. It's hit me like the proverbial brick. What? Oh yes, darling. Hold on, Eleanor, Wilhelmina is desperate to speak to you.'

The young baroness' voice came on the line. 'Eleanor?'

'Hello, Wilhelmina.'

'Eleanor, it's so awful!' She sounded genuinely distressed. 'This is so important to Clarence. And me. This will be my first Christmas as hostess at the castle. Cancelling would be such a terrible faux pas. And it will scupper Clarence's chances for sure.'

The crackling started up again in even greater earnest.

'Chances of what?' Eleanor swung around to her butler. 'This is impossible!' She returned to the phone. 'Wilhelmina. I think I have an idea. Give me half an hour and I will try and telephone you back. Pardon? I can't hear you, I'm afraid.'

She dropped the handset onto its cradle. Or meant to. It fell to the marble floor, where Clifford collected it and handed it to her with a pained expression. She shook her head again.

'No idea what Wilhelmina was trying to say at the end there. They really must get a better line. I can't believe they may have to cancel! Such a shame!'

Her butler cleared his throat.

'Yes, Clifford?'

'Shall I assemble the staff, my lady?'

She stared at him in confusion.

'Y-e-s. In the kitchen. But... but how did you know I was about to ask?'

'Sober experience, if you will forgive the observation, my lady.'

His coat-tails swished around the corner of the corridor, leaving her alone. She stared at her reflection and wondered for the hundredth time how her butler managed to be so respectful and yet, at the same time, so disrespectful.

She wandered over to the full-length portrait of her late uncle, Lord Byron Henley. He had not only taken her in as his ward when she was nine after her parents' disappearance, he had also left her his estate, Henley Hall, on his death the previous February. A high-ranking official in the army, he'd spent most of his time stationed in India, although he'd travelled the world in between. After he'd resigned his commission, his other interests kept him abroad. That they had never spent more than the odd day or two together her entire childhood still made her sad. Whenever she stared at his picture a part of her regretted spending so much of her life overseas as well. She smiled up at the portrait.

'I realise now why you put up with Clifford as your butler, wingman, confidante and, as the years went on, your very good friend, Uncle. He really is the most loyal, devoted and intelligent man one could ever hope to know. He is also, however, the cheekiest butler on the planet!'

She made her way to the kitchen where her staff were standing to attention in a smart line. With Clifford at the head, Mrs Butters, her diminutive, comfortably rounded and ever-genial housekeeper was next. Flanking her was Henley Hall's warm-hearted but no-nonsense cook, Mrs Trotman, her perfect English-pear hips making her flour-covered apron stick out sideways. Eleanor's young maid Polly, jiggling nervously on her long willowy legs, completed the ensemble. *I think she might be fifteen now, Ellie. How time flies!*

Eleanor's bulldog, whom she'd inherited along with the staff and Henley Hall itself, lumbered out of his quilted bed by the range and presented her with a soggy leather slipper. She bent to greet him.

'Thank you, Gladstone. A lovely, if rather revolting, welcome.' She straightened up and regarded the line of attentive faces. 'Oh gracious, this wasn't meant to feel like an inspection. No need to be quite so formal.' She caught Clifford's pursed lips. 'Ah, but perhaps there is. Right, straight in is probably the best approach, then. Some good friends of mine, Lord and Lady Ashley, are in a terrible bind. There's been mutiny afoot.' She looked along the ladies' faces, which registered only confusion. She glanced at her butler. 'Clifford, since you have clearly already deduced what I want to ask, would you be kind enough to explain?'

'As you wish, my lady.' He turned to the three women. 'Her

ladyship is asking if we will accompany her to Castle Ranburgh in Scotland for Christmas to act as staff to Lord and Lady Ashley.'

'Oh my stars!' Mrs Butters' eyes shone with excitement and curiosity. 'How can it be they lost their entire staff? Not a terrible illness, I hope?'

'Not at all,' Eleanor said. 'In fact, it's the unthinkable. Insurgency!'

Her staff gasped in horror, except Clifford who cleared his throat pointedly.

'Perhaps, "religious observance" might be a more accurate description, my lady. We do not wish to plant the seed this end of the British Isles that such things as insurgency among staff ever occur. After all,' he shuddered, 'this isn't France!'

'Lord, no!' Mrs Butters said, crossing herself. 'May it never come to that!'

Mrs Trotman, the cook, sniffed. 'Devout Catholic and Anglican staff usually celebrate Christmas and still manage to fulfil their duties to my knowledge, so why can't them up north?'

Clifford nodded. 'That may be, Mrs Trotman, but we must be equally tolerant of the views of all religious groups, as his late lordship would insist. The full explanation would, regrettably, delay preparation of her ladyship's luncheon to an unforgivable degree. Suffice to say, the Presbyterian Church was largely responsible for celebrations being banned by law around 1640. The overriding authority in the area of Ranburgh is Presbyterian. And their church still frowns on such activities.'

The ladies shared a look. Mrs Butters spoke up. 'But what did they ban, Mr Clifford? And what do they frown on still?'

'Christmas, Mrs Butters.'

The three ladies' jaws fell. The young maid shook her head in disbelief.

'No Christmas tree, dinner or... presents?' she whispered.

Clifford nodded. 'Quite, Polly. In fact, Christmas Day is not even a public holiday in Scotland. It is a normal working day.' He turned back to Eleanor. 'My lady, did Lord Ashley explain how he originally intended to make arrangements for entertaining a castle's worth of guests in secret?'

'No, Clifford, as you know, he didn't get the chance.' She turned to the rest of her staff. 'Ladies, I'm afraid I don't have all the facts and can't answer the raft of questions you might have, but would you be willing to help out? It really is a fearful ask on my part. Such short notice and it will disrupt your normal Christmas here. Please understand, you are not obliged to agree.'

Mrs Trotman pointed towards the pantry. 'I'm ahead on the preparations for the Henley Hall Christmas Eve luncheon for the villagers, m'lady. I know Reverend Gaskell is already booked to play host in your absence, but he'll have no one to help with the clearing up if we all go. I can't be coming back to my kitchen all stacked with week-old washing-up being licked half-clean by the mice.'

'Don't be daft, Trotters.' Mrs Butters nudged her friend in the ribs. 'The reverend will treat Henley Hall with all the reverence he lavishes on his beloved Saint Winifred's Church. And you forget, he can ask the Women's Institute for help.'

Clifford sniffed sharply. 'And all but the ballroom, kitchen and restroom facilities will be firmly locked.'

'Besides, Trotters,' Mrs Butters said. 'Scotland is known for its whisky. You might learn a few new recipes for your home-brewing concoctions while you're up there.'

Mrs Trotman tutted. 'Concoctions? Cheeky mare. They're fine distillations, they are. Years of handed-down family knowledge. I'll be teaching them Scottish folk more like. Polly'll need to take care not to break Lord Ashley's delicate china, mind.'

The young maid looked aggrieved. 'I haven't broken nothing for weeks, honest. Well, only one thing and you said it was already cracked.' She looked pleadingly at the cook. 'I would be ever so careful, Mrs Trotman, if it means Christmas in a castle! I've never ever even seen one afore.'

Mrs Trotman ruffled the young girl's hair. 'We'll see. Now, Butters, are you sure you'll cope with all those rugged Highland types in tartan skirts, flashing their knees at you?' The two women giggled as they bumped hips and then coloured at Clifford's sharp cough.

Eleanor bit her lip to hide her amusement.

'It looks like you have the deciding vote, Clifford. And for once, please don't be pressured into agreeing. This has to be unanimous. Christmas is too precious a time for everyone.'

'Thank you, my lady. Sincerely appreciated. I do, as it happens, hold some reservations. One graver than the others.'

'Go on.' She gestured that he had the floor.

'Might I enquire, if we do not accompany you to Castle Ranburgh, what would you do?'

'Well, I would find some temporary staff somehow to take up to Scotland with me. I can't not help. This is too important to the Ashleys. I could barely hear Wilhelmina, but I could sense the desperation in her voice.'

Clifford nodded. 'Then, if anyone is to deliver on your kind intentions, my lady, it would be your own staff.' He turned to the rest of the line. 'Ladies, it appears we will all be spending the festive season in Scotland being uncharacteristically unseasonal.'

Two hours later, Eleanor was once again doing battle with Castle Ranburgh's crackling phone line.

'Clarence? Finally, I've got through to you. Listen, it's all sorted. I'll bring my staff. Yes, that's right. They've all agreed. The ladies will arrive by train the day before and Clifford and I will follow in the Rolls.'

His muffled reply made her frown. 'I missed that. A few what remaining? "Crook?" "Woodman?" "One spade?"' She raised her voice even higher to carry over the constant noise. 'Clarence, this is hopeless! Just do what you need to do and let Wilhelmina know she can have her dream Christmas. We'll sort out whatever it is you're saying when we arrive. Goodbye.'

Sensing Clifford's presence, she made a show of hanging the

handset back on its cradle as delicately as if she were placing a newborn in its cot.

'One really ought to treat this type of apparatus with great care.' She smiled at him in the mirror. 'The Ashleys are immensely grateful.' She wrinkled her nose. 'But I can see you aren't keen on the idea, Clifford, even though you agreed to come. Maybe I put you on the spot in front of the ladies? I could call the Ashleys back?'

He left that hanging for a moment, but then the corners of his lips quirked.

'The Cliffords never go back on their word, my lady.'

She laughed. 'Neither do the Swifts!' Then a thought struck her. 'But if you knew Christmas was all but banned in that part of Scotland, why didn't you say when I received the Ashleys' invitation?'

He looked at her as if she had fallen and hit her head. 'Because I am a butler. Commenting on the actions of a baron and baroness and the response of a lady would have been beyond inappropriate.'

She laughed. 'Of course. Well, it's going to be a lot of fun. Up in Scotland. All of us together.'

He gave his customary bow from the shoulders. 'My lady, at the risk of offering a contrary opinion, no – it is going to be woefully disagreeable.'

She looked at him in confusion. 'But why, Clifford?'

'Because, my lady, as Scotland's national poet, Robert Burns, noted, "The best laid schemes o' Mice an' Men, Gang aft agley. An' lea'e us nought but grief an' pain, For promis'd joy!" But your luncheon is ready. Shall we?'

2

'Seventeen!' Eleanor pointed triumphantly through the drizzle sliding down the side window of the Rolls. From inside the car, the rain made it almost impossible to see anything except vague outlines of distant cloud-wrapped hills and waterlogged heather- and gorse-covered moors. 'That windswept slate barn affair there is not only the loneliest building I've seen so far, it's also the most melancholy. And I claim "bleak grey" to describe its colour.' She slapped the dashboard. 'Ha, finally I win!' She turned to Clifford, who seemed unmoved by her enthusiasm. Ruffling her bulldog's ears where his heavy head lay in her lap, she continued on undaunted. 'But I have to confess that, even given the seventeen different hues of grey I've trumped you with, the wilds of Scotland have a definite beauty in their bleakness. Especially on such a minor, twisty track as this one. We seem to have been following it for hours. Is there no main road?'

Clifford eased the stately car round yet another tight bend. 'This *is* the main road, my lady. And if we are to make the castle with any chance of my being prepared for the guests, one would hope it will soon start acting like one.'

She glanced at her butler. For him, he sounded almost... annoyed?

'Chin up. No one likes a sore loser, Clifford. You chose the colour theme for the last game. Besides, I've only beaten you at one game once the entire way, despite driving for' – she leaned over and peered at the Rolls' clock – 'nineteen hours!' She couldn't stop a yawn escaping. 'Nineteen torturously long, back-stiffening, rear-end-numbing hours!'

He gave a sharp tut at her mention of anatomy. 'You insisted, my lady, on journeying to Castle Ranburgh by car to see the parts of Britain you've never seen before. And we have endeavoured to ease the voyage by stopping for, not one, but four picnics of unladylike proportions, two of which were in far from suitably salubrious coaching inns.'

Suddenly aware that she had inadvertently added to his worry over arriving at Castle Ranburgh with insufficient time to prepare, her own testiness at the long trip dissipated.

'Oh golly, I'm sorry, Clifford. I should have realised how much you'll need to orchestrate things. And in a castle you've never even seen, with only our ladies to somehow make up a comprehensive-enough complement of staff. No wonder you politely insisted we set off in the middle of the night. I really have been thoughtless.'

His uncharacteristically taut expression softened.

'Not a term I would ever countenance being appropriate for you, my lady. To experience something new should never be missed and no pauses at all would have been foolhardy, I'm sure. Especially since we have been negotiating rain, squalls and' – he gripped the steering wheel as the inadequate windbreak of straggly trees ended abruptly at the edge of an enormous loch – 'high winds for most of the journey.'

She leaned back in her seat and glanced appreciatively at the man who had been the much-loved linchpin in her uncle's life. And was becoming so in hers, though she still knew so little about him.

'I love the image of you and Uncle Byron driving along elegantly together for hours, playing games on the move, competing like gentlemen.'

Clifford slowed the car to negotiate another particularly sharp bend. 'I confess, to our shame, perhaps not always exactly like gentlemen, my lady. The competition did become heated on occasion.'

She chuckled. 'Aha! You see, that's something else you have in common with the Swifts. You like to win!'

'And on that note,' he said, the corner of his lips twitching upwards, 'eighteen.' He brought the car to a smooth stop.

'No!' She slapped her leg. Gladstone woke up with a confused woof. 'Sorry, boy.' She patted his head. 'Where's this extra shade of grey then, Clifford? I think you're making it up.'

'The face of the gentleman with a dead deer slung across his shoulders, my lady.' He lifted a leather-gloved finger from the steering wheel and gestured to her side window.

'Where? Agh!' She clutched her chest as a gnarled man in head-to-toe dark-green worsted rapped on her window with the handle of a shotgun. 'You win, Clifford,' she whispered. 'What description would you say best fits though?'

'Thunderously grey, my lady,' he whispered back as she wound her window down.

'Good afternoon.' She winced at the horizontal rain that poured in. 'Although, it is a rather soggy one.' She shrunk back into her seat as the man leaned into the car, causing the deer's lifeless head to swing inside. His thick grey-white hair stuck out at all angles around his weather-beaten face.

'Yer'll be expecting me boat ready and all, m'lady,' he said in a thick Scottish burr.

She looked at him in confusion. 'Oh, I shouldn't think so. But thanks awfully for the offer, Mister?'

'Suit yerself, m'lady. Mighty frozen yer'll be then when yer reach yonder castle since yer'll have to swim. If the monster does nay get yer first, mind.' He held her horrified stare with a rheumy eye.

'Swim? Monster?' She spun around, her eyes wide. 'Clifford?'

'He is correct on both counts, my lady.' Clifford wound down his window, and the man shuffled to the other side of the Rolls, seemingly oblivious to the wind and rain. 'Actually, my good man' – Clifford leaned out of the car – 'as you have rightly supposed, her ladyship is a guest of Lord and Lady Ashley. And thus we would be most grateful for your services. As rapidly as you are able to manage without inconvenience.'

The man sucked on his teeth for a moment. 'Gratitude is nay gonna buy me supper, though, is it?'

Clifford pulled his leather wallet from his inside pocket and extracted some change. The man took it and nodded down the road.

'Once yer've parked this lorry of a car in the stone barn o'er there, you can come aboard and sit either side of him.' The man slapped the deer's rump. 'Save me the bother of strapping him down.'

'Delighted,' Eleanor said weakly.

With the Rolls finally stored and secured to Clifford's satisfaction and their cases unloaded, Eleanor left the barn. Pulling the hood of her thick winter coat over her head against the icy rain, she followed the man towards a flimsy-looking wooden jetty that was protruding out into a dark mass of water. Gladstone loped deject-edly alongside, clearly hankering after the dry warmth of the Rolls.

'It's a tiny ancient rowing boat,' she hissed to her butler, who, as usual, was walking two paces behind her. 'I pictured something significantly more substantial.'

'How fortunate that you remembered to pack your sea legs then, my lady,' Clifford whispered back. 'As long as the monster does nay climb aboard and bite them off halfway o'er, mind.'

'Oh, stop it!'

Having been brought up by bohemian parents who spent their time between international postings sailing most of the world's seas and oceans, she had indeed gained her sea legs at the same age most children were learning to walk. Now, however, only a few brief minutes into the unexpected ferry ride, her stomach was far from happy. Perhaps it was that their captain seemed to slam the tiny craft into every inky-black wave, or perhaps it was the dead deer's head lolling in and out of her lap. She gripped the side with her one free hand, the other holding tightly to Gladstone's collar.

If she hadn't been so focussed on the opposite shore, which still looked a hideous distance away, she might have laughed at Clifford. He sat perched ramrod straight on the other end of the single plank that served as a seat, swinging like a displaced metronome with each lurch of the boat.

As they took a wild turn to the right round a small rocky headland, her hand flew to her chest in awe. The foreboding stone keep of Castle Ranburgh loomed out of the drizzling sky, towering over the adjoining castellated sections of equally austere buildings. Once brutishly designed for defence, the sprawling citadel now looked to be more crumbling in dejected surrender. *How could anyone want to call this home, Ellie?*

'Oh gracious, look! Castle Ranburgh is on an island.' It was only then she realised her teeth were chattering as she tried to yell over the icy wind whipping the back of the boat round.

'Indeed, it is, my lady,' Clifford said in his usual measured, if slightly raised, tone. He was now valiantly wrestling to keep their cases from sliding over the side. 'The only route in or out is by boat, since the stone bridge was swept away by a violent storm over thirty years ago, I believe. Loch Vale is a sea loch, my lady.'

'No wonder the Ashleys usually reside at their London address,' she yelled back.

This brought a loud snort from their rower as he heaved on the oars.

The ordeal seemed to be coming to an end as they reached a narrow channel between two rows of formidable-looking rocks, which constantly disappeared and re-emerged as the waves crashed over them.

'Ah, look, there's Clarence,' Eleanor said with relief, pointing at the tall, slim figure in a black suit standing on a stone promontory.

She leaned forward, blinking the water from her eyes. 'No, it isn't him. But it can't be he sent a guest to meet us, that wouldn't do.'

Her butler pursed his lips as he let a pair of field glasses she hadn't spotted him pull out fall on their straps against his chest.

'I think you will find from his attire and his height, my lady, that he is the first footman.'

She stared at the figure in confusion and then back at Clifford.

'But... but the staff are all supposed to have left?'

'Quite!'

Once safely disembarked on the island, they negotiated the uneven stony path to the castle, followed by the footman carrying Eleanor's bags. The man's manner was surly in the extreme. *Not a good omen*, Eleanor thought as she stopped in the courtyard. She stared up at the forbidding tower, which loomed menacingly over the rest of the buildings like an ugly bully, making her subconsciously shrink back, like a cornered rabbit.

'Eleanor! A happy Christmas to you!' a clipped English male voice called from an arched oak door as thick as a bookcase, the dim light from beyond cutting across the cobbles.

'Clarence! And a happy Christmas to you. We've had quite the trip across the loch.'

Baron Ashley strode over to her with a welcoming, if somewhat haggard, smile. His tall frame seemed more angular than the slim build she remembered, his face rather drawn and pale against his black evening wear and white bow tie. He ran a hand down his long, pointed nose. 'Ah, yes, apologies, that was Drummond, from the village. I hope he wasn't too, erm...' He tailed off, seeming to notice that the footman was clearly listening in.

'He was perfectly charming.' She let him lead her a little way forward before whispering, 'But perhaps your loch's monster might have been a more genial choice for ferryman. I feel I may have just survived crossing the river of Styx.'

'Oh dear. I'm so sorry. He's all I could rustle up, given the recent contretemps with the staff, I'm afraid. Come, you must be soaked. And frozen. Wilhelmina is so looking forward to seeing you again. But do mind the uneven stones.' He pointed to a section where two of the steps up to the entrance had cracked, leaving a running gap perfect for turning both ankles at once.

'I'm just a bit chilly,' she fibbed, stepping carefully. 'Oh, but, Clarence, wait.' She spun round and gestured to her butler, the sleety rain already settling in thick white flecks across his smart black wool overcoat. 'This is Clifford. He is a master of' – she smiled fondly at him – 'well, everything, actually.'

'Most kind, my lady.' Clifford gave Baron Ashley a deferential bow from the shoulders. 'My lord, it will be a pleasure to assist in any way I can.'

Baron Ashley nodded. 'Good. Dinner is at eight.' Turning away, he muttered, 'Rather you than me,' which Eleanor's sharp ears heard. She was about to ask about the unexpected presence of the footman but the front door swung back revealing a line of more staff waiting. Spotting three familiar faces, she bounded over the thick stone lintel and beamed at her cook, housekeeper and maid from Henley Hall. 'Ladies, how was your train journey?'

'That part was just fine, thank you, m'lady,' Mrs Butters said noncommittally.

Eleanor dragged her gaze from the positively medieval interior of the castle – an endlessly high-ceilinged hallway festooned with all manner of swords and shields, all cheerfully decorated rather incongruously with a variety of Christmas decorations. She scanned the three faces of her staff in front of her. 'Everything alright, ladies?'

They all exchanged a look before nodding slowly.

'Yes, m'lady,' they chorused unconvincingly.

It was then that Eleanor noticed the short, older woman standing at arm's length along the line from Mrs Trotman, her face set in a fierce scowl. Her angry grey curls were pinned under her white cap, her red-knuckled hands clasped across her cook's uniform. There was no mistaking the confrontational set of her broad shoulders, nor the intimidating stare of her sharp amber eyes.

What the—!? A footman and now another cook, Ellie? That can't be good.

'So, you've met Henderson,' Baron Ashley said, gesturing at the footman who dropped Eleanor's cases on the long, high-backed ebony settle. The footman made a show of walking to the head of the line where he stood poker straight. Baron Ashley cleared his throat. 'And this is Mrs McKenzie. Castle Ranburgh's, erm... wonderful cook for many years.'

'Mrs McKenzie.' Eleanor smiled at the cook. She shivered at the glare that accompanied the curt curtsey this received. She spun round to the maid whom Baron Ashley had failed to introduce. The young girl glanced in terror at Mrs McKenzie before curtseying.

Eleanor smiled along the line of staff.

'Thank you. What a splendid team you will all make.'

'Good.' Baron Ashley clapped his hands. 'Eleanor, Wilhelmina is on total tenterhooks and the other guests are hankering to meet you. Once you've changed, of course. Oh, and Clifford?'

'My lord?'

'As agreed, you are head of the staff at Ranburgh for the duration of Lady Swift's stay.' Baron Ashley avoided his footman's eye. 'Now, Eleanor, Henderson will show you your room.'

As she followed the churlish footman up the main staircase, she glanced back down into the hall where Clifford was leading out the staff.

Oh, Ellie! Perhaps it would have been better if Christmas truly had been cancelled!

3

Up in the room she'd been shown to, Eleanor peeled off her soggy clothing. A quick scan round revealed only a heavy wooden chest and wardrobe, a small marble washstand and an ancient four-poster bed. However, the room was suitably cosy thanks to a crackling fire in the massive grate. Three flickering oil lamps provided enough light for Eleanor to dry herself on the fabulously fluffy towels before putting on her favourite evening gown – after all, it was Christmas! It had been her mother's, grey silk with bluebirds embroidered on the bustier and delicate peonies set amongst patterns of grasses swirling up from the skirt's base.

She had concluded there was no hope for her rain-frazzled red curls, when Polly, her maid, appeared. That Clifford had sent her with a glass of warming Dutch courage and an egg cup of almond oil to tease Eleanor's hair back into shiny soft waves meant the world. Despite having less than two hours to coordinate Christmas Eve dinner with fractious staff, unseen facilities and an unknown wine cellar, he'd put easing her nerves at formal social affairs above everything. As always.

Thus, she trotted down the sweeping black-oak staircase with more of a spring in her step than she'd expected, poking her tongue out at the carved gargoyles leering down from the elaborately vaulted ceiling. On the first-floor landing a noise caught her attention. She glanced along the gloomy corridor. A man with his back to her was closing one of the doors leading into what must be more bedrooms, Eleanor guessed. He turned and looked up and down the corridor. For some unknown reason, Eleanor froze, hidden by the shadows. Satisfied no one was there, the man hurried off in the opposite direction to her, towards the staff stairs.

Eleanor frowned for a moment and then shook her head. All these gloomy stairs and corridors were starting to make her jumpy. The man was obviously just a guest getting something from his room. Even when he'd turned, she hadn't been able to see his face, but she figured she'd meet whoever it was soon enough.

She carried on down the next flight of stairs, a sprinkling of bright modern paintings among the usual dark oils catching her attention. Pausing to adjust her beaded green shawl, she again drank in the arresting view of the grand hallway, with its series of intricately fluted archways leading in every direction. In one corner a Christmas tree fit for a fairy tale reached almost to the distant ceiling. She detected the baroness' creative hand in the festoons of silver and purple satin bows, peppered between intricately cut-out paper lace angels. Standing majestically either side of the tree, a life-sized woven-willow stag wore a crown of flickering tea lights. The whole scene made her breath catch in her throat.

Her Mary Jane heels clicked against the pale-grey flecked flagstones. Six enormous cartwheels, each bearing sixteen candles, hung from thick chains above, casting a long shadow down the corridor. The sound of raised voices emerged from a partially open door in front of her. She recognised Baron Ashley's among them.

'But I think you've misunderstood, old man. We've just got our communications muddled, that's all. Give me some more time and—'

'Nope. Heard loud and clear the first time. Just as you heard my answer. Underhand tactics are for desperadoes. I repeat. No survey! No deal! You can't pull the wool over the eyes of Eugene

Randall the Third. Thought you would have realised that by now, Clarence.' The man's voice was undeniably American, but from what part Eleanor wasn't sure.

'Underhand! Now, just back right up there... Oh, Eleanor, it's you.' Baron Ashley emerged from the room as she tried to slip away unnoticed.

She spun around, noting the short, impatient-looking man who had come out with him.

'Hello, Clarence.' She held her hand out. 'And good evening and a happy Christmas to you, Mister?' The sharp cut and too-bright blue shade of the man's double-breasted suit confirmed that the twang she'd detected was from the other side of the Atlantic. And likely from the far west too.

Baron Ashley clapped a tentative hand on the man's shoulder. 'Eugene, meet Lady Eleanor Swift. Eleanor, this is Eugene Randall.'

'The Third,' his guest added, patting his wide chest and glancing at the baron. 'It doesn't take a castle to have heritage and ancestors, *old man!*' He looked Eleanor up and down. 'And the season's greetings to you. You're the intrepid traveller our lady hostess has regaled us with so many tales about. Late, but well worth the wait, I'll bet.' He winked and then looped her still outstretched hand over his arm, before pointing to the oak door across the hallway. 'The much-needed liquor is this way, I believe.'

The first thing that struck her on entering the room was the warmth. No heating system on earth could heat the castle's rambling corridors, but here two roaring fires at opposite ends had taken the chill out of the vast space. Soft shades of strawberry pink and gold dotted through the otherwise ivory furnishings made it the most welcoming space she'd seen so far. Though more subdued than the decorations in the grand hall, the lush garlands of red-berry holly along each fireplace gave the space an instantly festive feel. Nestled in the alcoves, porcelain figurines dressed in glittering gold silk held out beautifully wrapped gifts. The positively modern electric lighting made her blink as she smiled at the six heads that had turned at her arrival.

Baroness Ashley leaped up from the tall velvet-upholstered chair that made her dainty frame seem almost childlike.

'Eleanor, so wonderful of you to come. Happy Christmas!'

Eleanor nodded appreciatively at the gentlemanly way Mr Randall handed her over to their hostess before he hotfooted it to the drinks table.

'Happy Christmas to you, Wilhelmina. What a positively delightful setting for Christmas. Castle Ranburgh is as extraordinary as it is exquisite.' She scooped up the young woman's hands, genuinely pleased to see this epitome of the delicate English rose once again. Aware that Clifford making the rounds with a tray of champagne had caught the rest of the room's attention, she leaned in and whispered, 'How is it all going?'

Baroness Ashley's hand strayed to the silk flower clip loosely holding her honey-blonde curls and stared up with haunted deep-blue eyes.

'Rather nerve-racking, if I'm honest. Thank you so much for coming to lend me support. You know that my family and, well, most of Clarence's wouldn't come, so you being here means the world to us both. And thank you for loaning your staff,' she added as Clifford started in their direction.

Eleanor frowned. 'Happy to be able to help, Wilhelmina. Only... I thought all of yours had mutinied?'

'But Clarence told you on the telephone, surely? Oh dear, was it when the line went dead for a moment? So sorry. Three of them stayed on begrudgingly, you see. Secretly, I think it might be because they had nowhere to go. Well, except for Lizzie, she's simply terrified of Mrs McKenzie.' She shivered. 'We all are. Clarence promised me he'd asked if your staff would be happy to work with ours, though?'

'I didn't hear any of that,' Eleanor said, feeling guilty for dragging her treasured staff along now. 'But it was a terrible line.'

'Oh, Clarence!' Wilhelmina muttered.

Clifford materialised beside Eleanor, his tray bearing two filled champagne flutes. Eleanor caught his eye and fluffed her perfectly tamed curls as a silent thank you for his earlier thoughtfulness. He nodded imperceptibly as both women accepted a glass. Eleanor took a sip and tried to think of something to help ease Baroness Ashley's evident nerves.

'I've always found playing hostess feels much more daunting than the episode ever turns out to be.'

Only she spotted the amusement her comment gave Clifford as he stepped away. The truth was, she had still yet to hold so much as a formal tea at Henley Hall, even though she'd inherited it well over a year ago. Not that she was antisocial; she often attended events at other estates, after all. It was just that having spent a lifetime abroad, she may have been perfectly comfortable tackling dangerous animals, and equally dangerous locals in far-flung places, but tackling the social niceties of England in her own home was a far more daunting prospect.

Maybe in the new year, we could give it a whirl, Ellie? Invite some of the notable names in the area and practise the art of polite conversation? Got to master being a society lady sometime, after all. If only to prove Clifford wrong.

But watching Wilhelmina trying not to peer anxiously round at her less than animated guests, while turning her glass repeatedly in her hands did nothing to shore up Eleanor's resolve. She looped her hand through her hostess' arm, receiving a grateful squeeze in reply.

'How about some one-on-one introductions? I've only met Mr Randall so far.'

'Oh, Eugene, yes. He is a particularly significant member of our party for Clarence. Unfortunately,' she ended in a mutter.

Eleanor followed Baroness Ashley's gaze over to where the American was talking animatedly to a strapping older man with an impressive ginger moustache. Resplendent in a broad-shouldered black velvet jacket and red tartan cravat, the second man exuded quiet confidence. Baron Ashley looked uncomfortably stiff as he joined the other two. His efforts to appear relaxed by hanging one arm over the mantelpiece and one shiny evening dress shoe crossed over the other, seemed a tad forced to Eleanor.

Oh, Ellie, Clarence is obviously too caught up in important boys' business to realise how much his wife needs his support.

The problem was, Baron Ashley had married his wife for love, not duty, something that Eleanor thoroughly approved of. However, most of his family – and his wife's – disapproved and had refused to attend Christmas at the castle, as Wilhelmina had said. She was not only half his age but also untitled and from distinctly working stock. Not that her father didn't have money, it was that it was the wrong kind of money, made through hard labour, grit and other unsavoury activities the titled classes found thoroughly distasteful. Eleanor had championed the couple when she'd first met them at a friend's luncheon party, and now she felt it her duty to help.

'Who's the chap talking to Mr Randall?'

Baroness Ashley glanced across the room. 'That's Robert Cameron, Laird of Dunburgh. Hugely influential in the area. Owns a hundred square miles and all the villages around Loch Vale and more. Between you and me, I was terrified of meeting him, but he's actually ever so easy and genial. His son is here too. Plus the doctor. Oh, and the only relatives of Clarence's who deigned to show up.'

Eleanor frowned. 'I thought... you know...'

Baroness Ashley sighed, weary before the party had even begun. 'I know. But for some reason two of them *did* decide to grace us with their presence. I've really no idea why. I'd best brave introducing you to them.'

'Have a glug of bubbles first,' Eleanor whispered, taking a long swig herself. 'Fizzy fortification works wonders I find.'

4

'Sir Edward and Lady Fortesque, may I present Lady Swift?'

At that precise moment Eleanor's stomach let out a loud and unladylike gurgle. The gaunt woman turned her head of thinning grey-brown hair with a poorly disguised sniff.

The man bowed stiffly. 'Lady Swift. Pleased to meet you, I'm sure. Happy Christmas.'

'Happy Christmas to you both,' Eleanor said. 'Delighted to meet you. I wonder, Lady Fortesque' – she glanced over at Baron Ashley – 'do I detect a most fortunate family resemblance?'

The woman hesitated, then tilted her chin graciously as if to emphasise the length of her elegant, powdered nose. 'Clarence is my cousin. On my mother's side. And happy Christmas to you, Lady Swift.' She ran a finger over the three strings of pearls that hung over her prominent collarbones.

'How wonderful to spend Christmas with family,' Eleanor said with an unexpected croak, feeling a little wistful. After the disappearance of her parents, her uncle had been her only remaining relative. Now he was gone, she sometimes felt alone in the world. She did have a sort of beau hovering on the horizon. She hoped she did, at least. He was, however, a detective who split his time between Oxford and London. They only met often enough to be awkward with each other. She shook her head and looked around the room for a glimpse of Clifford's reassuring presence, but his coat-tails were just disappearing around the door frame.

Baroness Ashley hurried Eleanor on to the next guest.

'May I introduce Doctor Connell, the area's highly respected physician and surgeon.'

Eleanor accepted the proffered hand thrust out from the more modest black suit than the others in the room, noting his immaculately groomed nails and scrubbed slender fingers. The doctor's fair hair brushed his collar as he tilted his head, his other hand adjusting his small round spectacles. There was something in the way his steel-grey eyes scanned her face that suggested his many years in practice had made instant health assessments an automatic habit. However, his appearance confused her. He didn't look a day over forty-five.

'Fifty-six, Lady Swift,' he replied to her unspoken question after they had exchanged season's greetings, highlighting that her face gave her thoughts away all too often. 'Hard work and an extremely hardy constitution, combined with a passion for climbing our Munros. Or mountains, as you'd call them. Nothing like strenuous exercise to build superlative health.' He released her hand. 'As you are all too aware.'

Eleanor looked questioningly at Baroness Ashley.

'Oh, I might have mentioned your exciting cycling adventures,' her hostess said apologetically.

'Been quite the unusual dinner conversation,' Sir Edward remarked, his top lip curled.

His wife tittered. 'Of course, such things used to be deemed unseemly in certain circles. But perhaps one is behind the times.'

Doctor Connell glanced at them sharply and then smiled at Eleanor. 'I, for one, was captivated and astounded by your travels, Lady Swift. We could do with more women like you. In the medical profession, especially. Although there are some pioneering women already challenging this male bastion.'

'Really?' Sir Edward laughed curtly. 'I, for one, wouldn't be seen dead visiting a medical practice that employed women doctors.'

The uncomfortable silence was broken by the step of heeled boots on the stone floor. She turned to see a powerfully built ginger-haired man in his mid-thirties dressed in an impeccable evening jacket matched with a deep-pleated red kilt that ended just above his square knees.

'Lady Swift, I presume,' the man said with a bear-like growl, putting both hands behind his back.

'Oh goodness.' Baroness Ashley flustered over. 'So sorry, both. Very remiss of me. Erm, this is Gordon Cameron, Master of Dunburgh, the Laird's son. And, as you cleverly spotted, Mr Cameron, this is indeed Lady Swift.'

Eleanor couldn't miss how he was staring at her fiery red curls.

'Pleased to meet you, Mr Cameron. And a happy Christmas!' She pointed to her hair. 'I believe we may share a Gaelic connection.'

'Aye? How so? I'm nay aware of any Swifts among the clans.'

With his wide-legged stance and pointed gaze, she wondered if he was hiding his battle sword up under his kilt. Surely that could be the only explanation for the razor-edge to his tone and his lack of seasonal greeting?

'Ah, now that's easily explained. You see, my Gaelic ancestors were Irish, not Scottish.'

'Lucky them, Lady Swift,' he said drily.

They all turned as a fractious noise erupted at the drinks table. Eugene Randall was waving an empty whisky glass at his host.

'To heck with tradition, Clarence, it's drier than a desert round here.'

Baron Ashley rubbed his forehead. 'Just while the ladies are present, there's a good chap. Billiards and scotch a-plenty later, what?'

'Later, my eye,' Randall grumbled. He thrust a pointed finger at Clifford, who had stepped up behind them. 'Double scotch. Double quick.'

'Perhaps you might like to try the renowned Ranburgh dram, sir?' Clifford said in his usual measured tone, picking up a crystal decanter from the rear of the table. 'A perennial favourite during the festive season.'

'Don't give a fig about its pedigree. Just pour, man.'

Lady Fortesque slid up to Baroness Ashley. 'Is that rather loud man staying the entire week?'

'Ask Clarence,' Baroness Ashley said with a huff. 'He's his guest.'

Eleanor watched as Randall took a hefty swig of his new drink and then held the glass up to the light. 'Mighty flavoursome. Keep that one coming.'

To ease her hostess' obvious discomfort, Eleanor clapped her hands and smiled at Gordon Cameron. 'Perhaps I should meet your father before dinner?'

He glanced over to the fireplace where the Laird was slapping a genial hand on Baron Ashley's sagging shoulders. At that moment the Laird turned and caught his son's eye. A frown flashed across his face. His son scowled back and strode from the room, his kilt swishing around the back of his knees.

'Oh dear,' Baroness Ashley muttered.

Lady Fortesque wandered back to her husband, a smirk playing round her lips. The Laird put down his drink and came over.

'Lady Swift, what a pleasure. Please forget all that title stuff on my side, it's Robert.' He shook her hand warmly. Up close, she couldn't miss the smile lines around his eyes and was instantly drawn in by his affable and informal manner. Baroness Ashley excused herself, before grabbing her husband's elbow and dragging him to the far corner of the room.

'And it's Eleanor.' She smiled at the Laird. 'Happy Christmas to you. I hear you are a close neighbour of the Ashleys?'

Unlike his son, he returned her season's greetings, and then lowered his voice. 'Fine pair. Rare to meet true love playing out. Even rarer to see it bloom so when the establishment has gotten sniffy. What does age or lack of a title matter in our progressive times?'

She felt her shoulders relax, even though she wasn't sure just how progressive times were. 'I couldn't agree more.' They looked over at the Ashleys, deep in discussion.

'Quiet backbone of pure steel, that one,' the Laird muttered.

'Clarence? I'm sure he has.'

This brought on a chuckle that made the Laird's ginger moustache tickle his cheeks. 'I meant Wilhelmina, the lady of the house. Underneath, our baroness is quite the new bairn that not only survived the hillside night but was standing ready to fight the dawn.'

She fought the frown of confusion that threatened, deciding Clifford would be able to explain what she guessed was a local expression to her later. Her butler had an unfailing knack of seeming to know everything about the local culture and language, no matter where they went. She nodded towards their host.

'Poor Clarence, though, I was hoping he might relax a little over Christmas, but he seems to be rather caught up in important discussions with Mr Randall.'

'Oh, he'll get his chance.' The Laird tapped his nose with a grin. 'There's nothing like Scottish whisky to soften a man's objections to parting with his money. Will you excuse me a moment, dear lady? I imagine we'll be called to eat soon.'

Left alone, Eleanor took in the view that was as far from the expected Christmas Eve party as she could have anticipated. The Ashleys were trying to play down what was clearly a disagreement between them. Baroness Ashley kept looking uneasily over at Eugene Randall, who seemed to be struggling to focus on the row of portraits along the furthest wall. The Fortesques were sitting watching them with haughty expressions, and Doctor Connell had the air of a man who wished he was anywhere but where he was. As the Laird reached the door to leave, his son swept in past him without a word.

Sensing Clifford behind her, Eleanor turned and pretended to be perusing the drinks table. 'Maybe I'd better try some of that fortifyingly strong whisky,' she whispered. 'The one you're saving for the already slightly pickled Mr Randall.'

'I shouldn't bother, my lady,' he whispered back, as he poured her a small Oloroso sherry. 'I prepared it especially for the gentleman after noting the way he attacked his third brandy.'

She cocked a questioning eyebrow.

'Mr Randall is entirely ignorant that the "enhanced flavour" is merely the "opening up", as is the official term, due to the precisely measured dilution with water I instigated.'

She laughed. 'Top-notch, Clifford.'

His tightly pursed lips told her, however, that he was far from his usual spirits.

She turned back to the less than convivial atmosphere in the room and muttered to herself, 'Oh golly, how long until this torture ends?'

Clifford adjusted the perfectly aligned seams of his white gloves. 'Only until we return to Henley Hall, I should imagine, my lady.'

She watched him step over to the door and pick up the gong from the walnut side table. He raised the beater and brought it down, announcing dinner. Eleanor squared her shoulders and followed her hosts and the other guests towards the door.

Well, it can't get any worse, can it, Ellie?

5

Despite Eleanor's best efforts, after a year or more back in England, she was still confused by the mysterious intricacies of aristocratic etiquette. Brought up abroad in far-flung locations, she was as used to dirt floors as marble ones. Even her years in a stiflingly traditional girls' boarding school hadn't drummed the niceties of formal society into her. And the minute she could, she'd left the school and England and resumed travelling, although this time without her beloved mother or father.

Now she hung back and watched Lady Fortesque's polite but aloof reaction as Baron Ashley offered his arm to lead the procession into dinner. This only highlighted the marked contrast of the Laird's genial smile as he took Baroness Ashley's arm, then patted her hand in a grandfatherly way. Eugene Randall brought up the rear with a loud whoop.

'Food. Finally!' Dropping his empty glass into Clifford's hand as he passed, he walked unsteadily after the two couples, calling over his shoulder. 'Top that up, chummy.'

To his credit, Clifford displayed none of the disapproval she knew would be surging under his immaculate morning suit. Throwing him an understanding look, she made to follow the others but was pulled up short by his discreet cough.

Oh, dash it, Ellie! He's right. Time to pretend you know your etiquette. With horror, however, she realised the only gentlemen left to escort her were the sniffy Sir Edward, the sullen Gordon Cameron and the somewhat bored-looking Doctor Connell. Plumping for the longest of the short straws, she smiled at the doctor, hoping he would be the first to play gentleman. Instead, he blinked back at her from behind his spectacles and tugged on the cuffs of his jacket.

She quickly turned away to ease his embarrassment. *What were you thinking of, Ellie? Of course, you need someone of similar standing. A mere doctor would never do!* She shook her head at what she felt were ridiculous and outdated rules of etiquette. *During the war no lord's wife complained that their husband's life had been saved by a mere doctor, did they, Ellie? And yet now they're not even good enough to escort a lady into dinner.*

With a resigned grunt, Sir Edward marched over and offered her a begrudging elbow.

'How lovely,' she said as he escorted her stiffly past Clifford.

Even in the middle of a tropical heatwave – something Eleanor doubted very much had ever occurred in this part of the world – Castle Ranburgh's dining room was never going to be hot. This was because it was the castle's great hall. Close to eighty-feet long, the stone walls rose fifty feet to a vaulted ceiling. The enormous fire-places at either end, however, had each been filled with half a forest of crackling and glowing logs that gave the room a welcoming warmth. Luckily, the fires also gave out a fair amount of light as the weakly glowing electric torchlights, however suitably dramatic for the grandiose setting, were singularly useless as actual lighting.

It wasn't the subdued lighting, however, that caught Eleanor's breath. She paused halfway across the centuries-worn flagstone floor, too entranced to notice Sir Edward release her arm with a snort. An oak table that could have seated fifty or more had been prepared for a proper Christmas Eve dinner. Draped in a spotless ivory tablecloth, five enormous candelabras blazed along the table's

length, interspersed with sprays of silver spruce, offset by individual arrangements of striking, red-berried holly. An exquisite
handmade paper cracker sat at each setting. The glassware
sparkled, and the silver shone. Eleanor smiled to herself as she
detected Clifford's meticulous hand having artfully disguised the
odd number of place settings. Holding onto the chair at the head of
the table, Baroness Ashley beamed as she looked it over in
surprised delight.

'Crackers as well. So beautiful!'

Once the three ladies were seated, the gentlemen adjusted
jacket tails and trouser legs and settled into their allotted places.
Eleanor tried not to stare to her left at Gordon Cameron to see if
he would arrange the pleats of his kilt under him. He didn't. Dropping into his seat, he looked the table over with a deep frown. With
the Ashleys at either end, Eleanor was surprised to note that
Eugene Randall had not been placed next to either. Baron Ashley
clearly wanted something from his American guest, although quite
what, and how, after she'd overheard Randall refuse so vehemently
in the grand hallway, she couldn't imagine. The American,
however, was in the central seat facing the fireplace with Doctor
Connell to his left and the Laird to his right. Equally, she did not
expect to see Lady Fortesque at the end of the line of four guests,
leaving her at Baroness Ashley's left. Wouldn't the most senior
lady expect to be seated to the right?

*Ah! Ellie, by the repeated huffy glares thrown at our hostess by
Lady Fortesque, I'd say you're correct on that score!* Eleanor could
only assume Baroness Ashley had insisted on the seating arrangement in the hope it would somehow bring more harmony to the
proceedings.

Baron Ashley held up his glass. 'Merry Christmas and
welcome to Ranburgh, one and all.'

She raised her glass. 'Hurrah! Here's to a Christmas Eve spent
in an enchanting setting with friends, old and new!'

Clifford, who was dispensing a lap blanket to each of the ladies
to ward off under-table draughts, discreetly dropped an object into

her hand underneath her rug. Without needing to look, she knew it was one of her late uncle's wonderful inventions. A silver-cased hand warmer that gave off the perfect amount of heat for hours. Her uncle had got the idea during the war when several soldiers under his command had used old tobacco tins filled with lit tinder. Eleanor smiled and mouthed a 'thank you'. Despite being an outdoor girl, she felt the cold, especially in her fingers. Something, it seemed, she'd inherited from her mother.

With now warmed hands, she applauded the arrival of the first appetiser. Until, that is, it was sitting in front of her. Three opaque pastry swirls were oozing a pungent dark-green filling that was congealing in lumpy puddles on the stone-cold plate. She took a sip of champagne, trying to work out how to tackle the unappetising mess without her disgust showing on her face.

Lady Fortesque's sharp voice cut into her thoughts. 'So unconventional to have an uneven number for Christmas Eve dinner. Audacious planning, Wilhelmina. I'm sure you are to be congratulated.'

Baroness Ashley's smile was colder than Eleanor's plate. 'As Clarence has explained several times, Fanny, we are fortunate to be able to hold any kind of Christmas celebration. So, we are sincerely grateful to have the opportunity to share it with our guests, uneven numbered or not.'

'That's because Christmas is a lie!' Gordon Cameron looked around the table as if challenging the assembled company to disagree.

The Laird laughed but held his son's gaze. 'It's no crime that's being committed here, laddie.'

Eleanor nodded to herself. So that was why the Laird's son hadn't returned her festive greeting when they'd first met. Like the locals, he was obviously against the whole idea of Christmas. *Then why did he come to Christmas Eve dinner, Ellie?*

A few minutes later, her musings were interrupted by Henderson's arrival with a giant tureen. Wondering what on earth the muddy bowl of greyish liquid was meant to be, she took hold of the ladle. She blanched as several unidentifiable brown lumps surfaced momentarily before sinking slowly, leaving a large bubble of scurf winking at her. Peeping sideways at Clifford holding an identical tureen for Baron Ashley, she saw him swallow hard as a thick curl of grey steam rose and assaulted his nose.

Thankful she had been able to serve herself, and hence having only taken the polite minimum, she took another long swig of her wine to line her throat first. A unified round of silent wincing followed as soup spoons were cautiously sipped by all. Except Eugene Randall, who threw the contents of his to the back of his throat and smacked his lips loudly.

'Tastes better than it looks, folks, wouldn't you say?' He slurred his 's's noticeably.

The Laird hurried to quell Baroness Ashley's blushes at the unintended rude remark. Even Eleanor knew you never remarked to your host on the quality of the food served unless it was to compliment it.

'A creative variation on our traditional regional broth, I think you'll find, Eugene. Rather, er, bracing. Just right for warming one in such cold, but festive, weather.'

Eleanor bit back her smile as, despite his defence of the broth, the Laird hurriedly took a hearty tong's worth from Clifford of what smelt like her cook's delicious Stilton straws. When the chance came, Eleanor too took an unladylike portion to help get the soup down.

'Yes, Eugene,' the Laird continued as the soup was cleared away, 'what a great treat for you. Visiting at this wonderful moment when Scottish and English festive cultures meet.'

'Perhaps the treat is on your side, sir,' the American said drily.

Sir Edward smirked as he was served his next course clumsily by Henderson. Eleanor noted Clifford's disapproving glance at the footman as he began serving the second wine.

Eugene Randall laughed as he stared round at the table.

'Truth is, only reason I came all the way out here when Clarence told me of his scheme was because I thought, hey,

Eugene, a little razzle-dazzle from over the border could go a long way in brightening the underdevelopment up here. Old glories are a poor meal to survive on for long, I imagine.'

Gordon Cameron rapped his spoon hard against the table.

'Tread carefully, Randall. It only takes twelve Highlanders and a bagpipe to start a rebellion! And only one to teach a blackguard like you a lesson he'll nay forget!'

6

The awkward silence that greeted the Laird's son's remarks was in stark contrast to the festive cheer of the surroundings. Before Eleanor could jump in to help save Baroness Ashley's dream Christmas from sliding into the icy loch outside, Randall waved his almost empty glass at his host.

'So much for your supposed meeting of interests, old man. It seems your guests are as far from reaching an accord as you and I!'

Baron Ashley cleared his throat. 'Do keep an open mind until we've had another chance to sort out this... misunderstanding, Eugene. And perhaps a, ehm, clear head.'

Lady Fortesque sniffed. 'If it isn't too late for that.'

Eleanor noted Baroness Ashley nodding. It seemed the two women were united over something at least, albeit a shared antipathy for the guest they were both clearly struggling with. *To be fair, Ellie, his behaviour does seem to be declining as rapidly as the level of his glass.*

Baron Ashley waved a hand to gain Randall's attention again. 'Really, Eugene. I mean, we were interrupted earlier.' He shot Eleanor a glance. 'There's more you need to hear. No one likes a wasted trip all the way across the Atlantic, after all.'

Randall shrugged, but it seemed Baron Ashley's words had hit their mark.

'Alright, I'll listen. But from what I've seen so far, urbane glamour would be as welcome here as an icebox in the Arctic.' He leaned towards Gordon Cameron. 'Tell me, what'll it be for Christmas morn, my Highland friend? Haggis shooting at first light?'

Chuckling at his joke, he swigged the last of his drink, then spluttered and clutched at his throat as it went down the wrong way. He continued to splutter, while turning a worrying shade of puce. Doctor Connell rose to go to the man's aid, but the Laird was already standing behind the American. Pushing him forward by the shoulder, he gave him a series of hearty slaps on the back. Clifford materialised with a tall glass of water.

'A prop of some nature too, man.'

The Laird waved the water under the choking man's nose with a quiet force that meant declining was not an option. As Clifford reappeared with a thick red velvet cushion, the Laird pushed it down hard behind the American's back, adjusting it to keep the inebriated man upright.

The table returned to politely picking through their food. Conversation was sporadic and Eleanor struggled to interject much that met with any enthusiastic response. The weather as a topic was quickly abandoned since it was as dismal as the third course, although the Laird promised them the ever-present rain and sleet was forecast to turn to snow in the night, much more in keeping with the festive season. Eleanor imagined the surrounding hills covered in a pristine layer of white. She really had to get out for a good tramp on Christmas Day. Maybe some of the other guests would be up for it too. She crossed her fingers that, like the weather, the food would improve as well.

The next course, however, gave her little room for hope. Undercooked grouse liver and overcooked rissoles were accompanied by haggis squares, all three only made palatable by the addition of what tasted like Mrs Trotter's irresistible port and red onion chutney. Thankfully, the crackers provided a much-needed reprieve and everyone got into the festive spirit, even the Laird's son, outwardly at least. She crossed arms and pulled a cracker with him and Sir Fortesque, either side of her.

A beautiful emerald-green velvet wristband with a pearl-coloured button fastener fell from hers. She picked it up, feeling quite choked up as she ran a finger over the exquisite beadwork spelling out her initials. Like the crackers themselves, it was clearly a work of love made by her housekeeper. She looked up to see the Laird smiling across at her. He pointed to the wristband.

'So delightful to see the simple things still bringing such heart-felt joy. That's what Christmas should be, in my mind.'

She smiled back and nodded, resolving to thank her house-keeper later.

Looking around the table, she smiled. Everyone, except Gordon Cameron, was sporting a jolly Christmas hat. *It seems as if Wilhelmina might still get her dream Christmas, Ellie.* Then the fifth course arrived and her face fell. She peered at her plate. Was that a leg or a wing? Or a section of something's... neck? She shud-dered over the realisation that it might have been none of those, given the way the cut of what she hoped was meat lay limply on a bed of over-boiled cabbage and carrots. Again, Mrs Butters came to the rescue bearing two jugs of delicious-smelling gravy, which she poured liberally over Eleanor's food with a look of deep sympathy. Eleanor managed a discreet pat of her housekeeper's hand by way of gratitude for her cracker present.

Those served by Henderson fared less well as he dispensed only a mean trickle of gravy, casting a black look at Mrs Butters as he did so. Lizzie followed behind him with a bowl of swede and parsnip cubes, her eyes rimmed red, Eleanor noted in concern. She glanced at Clifford, who was minutely adjusting the seams of his gloves, the telltale sign that something was very much wrong.

Eleanor hurried through her plateful with only the minimum of grimacing and then excused herself, catching her butler's eye on her way out.

Out in the corridor, she beckoned him over.

'What on earth is going on in there?' she hissed.

'I believe it is the Castle Ranburgh Christmas Eve dinner, my lady.'

'Oh, stop it. Something is very wrong. The table and decorations are wonderfully festive, but the food and relations between my staff and the Ashleys' are definitely not. Henderson looks as if he's about to lunge at Mrs Butters every time she serves anyone, while poor Lizzie is trying not to cry into the already soggy vegetables. And no one else at the table would be able to spot it, but I've never seen you upset like this.'

His lips pursed. 'I am not upset, my lady. I am—'

'A butler. I know. And the finest there is, which means you would never countenance appearing as anything other than the epitome of composure. But I'm still holding on to the belief that there might also be a man hiding underneath your impeccable coat-tails and, to my eyes only, I think he is quietly struggling. Can I deduce that below stairs is resembling Hell just a little?'

He shook his head. 'Indeed not, my lady. Hell hath nothing on the staff wars which have broken out.'

'Oh gracious! But over what?'

'Perhaps it would be a swifter conversation were I to tell you what the two factions have not fallen out over.'

'But our ladies know how to behave. Surely they're...' She tailed off as he shook his head again.

'Your staff do indeed know how to behave. I cannot, however, say the same for Lord Ashley's. It has become an "us" and "them" standoff, particularly regarding the Ranburgh cook who seems determined to terrorise everyone into a state of paralysis.'

'You mean Mrs McKenzie?'

'One and the same. Regrettably my arrival was significantly too late. Mrs McKenzie and Mrs Trotman were already locked in a fierce battle of wills over the correct way to prepare anything. From how to crimp pastry on a partridge pie to how to scoop tea leaves from the caddy into the pot.'

'But Mrs Trotman's signature additions to that' – she tilted her head towards the dining room –'disastrous meal are the only thing making it edible.'

He nodded. 'Mrs McKenzie is clearly a competent cook. She is merely trying to spoil the dinner as a silent protest. She believes she has been usurped in her own kitchen and also that celebrating Christmas is sinful. Distressingly, the food had all been prepared before I arrived, with no time left for Mrs Trotman to prepare any replacements.'

'I see. And Henderson, what's his problem?'

A muscle along Clifford's jaw twitched. 'Perhaps he is simply unused to fulfilling all of his duties. Or indeed, any of them.'

Eleanor shook her head. 'I'm sincerely sorry for all this. It's my fault. I realise now I should never have asked you all to come up. And I never would have if I'd known the other staff were here.'

His uncharacteristically terse expression softened. 'You really did not know, my lady?'

'Absolutely not! Clarence said they'd all stomped off in a mutinous huff. I promise.'

The corner of his lips quirked. 'Perhaps you might recall from your telephone conversation with Lord Ashley the words "Crook?", "Woodman?" and "One spade?" It is evident now that he was referring to his "cook", "footman", and "one maid" who remained.'

Eleanor slapped her forehead. 'Oh, dash it, Clifford! My humble and unreserved apologies.'

'Are not needed, my lady. However, I am.' He adjusted his gloves and winked at her. 'Round three, I believe.'

She leaned against the wall and sighed as he strode away. *Oh, Ellie, what a mess!*

7

As Eleanor resumed her seat at the dinner table, Mrs Butters approached bearing a dubious pink dessert garnished with suspect green and yellow sprinkles. Eleanor discreetly waved it away.

'I've kept everyone waiting too long already, I'll just skip this one, thank you.'

Her return coincided with Gordon Cameron holding court on the woeful state of the Scottish economy. Sensing more conflict bubbling up between the guests, Eleanor tried to come to her hostess' aid and restore the festive cheer by chipping in. Sadly, with limited knowledge of Scotland's national affairs, she was soon forced to wave her napkin in metaphorical surrender. Gordon Cameron, however, continued to hold forth, slapping his bear paw of a hand on the table to emphasise each point.

'Ninety per cent! Ninety per cent of shipyard workers cut loose just like that. Even the jute trade was whisked away on a whisper to India. Our men were considered good enough to make munitions for the war, but then counted for naught the day it ended. Where are they to find a wage now?'

Baron Ashley leaped in. 'New investment in the area is clearly needed, wouldn't you agree? New jobs, what? Get everyone working again.'

Gordon Cameron eyed him sceptically. 'Aye, but only by those we can trust. Too many tracts of land have been underhandedly taken under the guise of legitimate enterprises. Often by those who should have known better!'

'We've been over this, son,' the Laird said smoothly. 'Times are changing. We need to move with them. It's called progress.'

'Aye, I've heard what you and others have to say, Father, and it's fair ruining my appetite.' He looked scathingly at Randall.

'Eugene, old man,' Baron Ashley called across. 'Why don't you tell us what Christmas is like down your neck of the woods?'

'I'd like to hear that,' Eleanor said. 'Where exactly do you live, Mr Randall?'

The American leaned heavily on the table and stared at Gordon Cameron. 'In the real world, Lady Swift. Not in a badly written history book.' Amused by his reply, he lapsed into nodding to himself with a sporadic chuckle.

While serving a deliciously sweet, plummy Madeira to the guests, Clifford quietly selected a glass of lighter coloured liquid for the tipsy American.

Baroness Ashley looked around the table with an air of dismay. 'Well, I confess to not being a history buff at all.'

Eleanor remembered a conversation from the last time they'd met. 'I seem to recall you are more of an art aficionado, Wilhelmina?'

Baroness Ashley smiled with relief at the change of conversation. 'Yes. Obsessively so, I'm afraid.'

Lady Fortesque shared a look with her husband. 'That reminds me, Wilhelmina. Edward and I were mystified by some of the paintings hanging on the grand staircase. Have you perhaps decided the Ashley Collection needed the unorthodox injection of modern works? I only ask because Clarence's uncle went to great pains to establish the family name in classical collector circles. What would he say, I wonder?'

'How delightful that they caught your eye, Lady Fortesque,'

Baroness Ashley replied sweetly. 'They are, if you hadn't noted by the signature, works of mine.'

'A dabbler, I see,' Sir Edward muttered.

Baron Ashley jumped in. 'Actually, Edward, Wilhelmina is a great artist. You must make time to view her paintings properly.'

But to Eleanor's dismay, his words seemed too little, too late to appease his wife, who was clearly upset at the conversation.

Dash it, Ellie! We need Clifford's infallible knack for knowing exactly what to say to smooth a room's worth of ruffled feathers. She looked hopefully across at Doctor Connell, who had said little the entire meal.

'Doctor Connell, you intrigued me earlier. How many of the area's beautiful Munros have you conquered?'

'All of them, Lady Swift. Many twice over.'

'And your favourite?' It must have been obvious to everyone she was floundering.

He smiled at her. 'I climb for health, nay to honour the mountains with my judgement of their distinctions and merits.' As if to make his point, he waved away the Madeira Clifford offered him. 'Nay for me, thank you. Sobriety, on the other hand, has many distinctions and merits.' He shot Eugene Randall a sharp look.

'Abstinence should be a choice, pal,' the American shot back. 'Don't be pointing your pious finger at me. I've been living dry thanks to prohibition back home.'

'No pointing intended, Mr Randall. Only a free word of medical advice that working through Lord Ashley's cellar now will leave you in dire need of head and stomach relievers tomorrow. And I fear my dispensary might have run dry as my supplies have nay made it up this week.'

Clifford stepped in with a sulky Henderson in tow, both carrying silver trays bearing coffee pots.

'After the coffee, I think it will be time for the gentlemen to retire with the port,' Baron Ashley said. 'And let the more delicate sensibilities among us have a little peace.'

Lady Fortesque sniffed. 'And the Randall man?' she said under her breath. 'Neither a gentleman, nor a delicate sensibility!'

'No!' Baroness Ashley jumped up. 'Actually, Clarence, no! Perhaps instead, our guests would like to advance the spirit of Christmas goodwill that brought us all together by remaining as a group for something diverting?' She looked to be on the point of tears. 'A harmonious group of friends and family, like Christmas is intended to be.'

The room swallowed hard. Even Lady Fortesque shared a look with Eleanor. The gentlemen all stared down at their laps, except Baron Ashley who was staring at the glassy-eyed Eugene Randall. He went to open his mouth.

'A perfectly charming suggestion, my dear,' the Laird interrupted him, gesturing discreetly for Clifford to top up the American's water glass.

Baron Ashley smiled contritely at his wife. 'I think that's a wonderful idea, Wilhelmina, my love. Genuinely. After all, it is Christmas Eve.'

Her cheeks flushed. 'Thank you, Clarence.'

'An unusual occurrence for a formal dinner,' Lady Fortesque said, 'but not unwelcome.' Her tone softened. 'Edward and I haven't spent an entire Christmas Eve together for years, have we, dear?'

'Not since Lord M's bash in' – Sir Edward leaned back in his seat, hooking his thumbs into his buttonholes – 'eighteen eighty-seven. No, eighty-six. Good times,' he muttered to himself.

'Eighteen eighty-six,' his wife said dreamily. They shared a wistful glance, which made Eleanor look at them with fresh eyes. Could it be that this uptight, upright couple had actually enjoyed the follies of youth in their day? Partying? Laughing? Maybe even falling in love? It would have felt a stretch of the imagination from their pious demeanour throughout dinner, but not now with the way they were still holding each other's gaze. Lady Fortesque turned the wedding band on her finger back and forth with a smile.

Never judge a Christmas gift by the wrapper, it seems, Ellie.

The Laird chuckled. 'Gordon? Can you temper your billiards passion until tomorrow eve?'

His son nodded. 'As the majority wishes, Father.'

Doctor Connell nodded at Baroness Ashley. 'A marvellous idea, Lady Ashley. Stimulating activity is so adept at bringing out the best in us all.' He pushed his glasses further up his nose. 'Do you have something particular in mind to start the proceedings?'

A look of panic crossed Baroness Ashley's face. 'Oh goodness, not exactly. Clarence, any thoughts?'

Her husband looked back, wide-eyed. 'Give me just a moment, dear heart.'

Eleanor racked her brain. There had to be something to keep the long-awaited festive atmosphere burning as brightly as the main fire should have been. She noticed earlier Clifford had been discreetly remonstrating with Henderson over having let it die too low. She peeped up at her butler as he set a coffee down in front of her from the silver tray he held. It was accompanied by a brandy, two exquisite miniature chocolate yule logs and a muttered suggestion that reached her ears only. She turned to the other guests.

'How about an engaging table game?'

Surely nothing could go wrong with that, Ellie?

8

'Splendid idea!' the Laird said, consulting Baroness Ashley with a questioning smile. 'It's probably warmer in here than any of the drawing rooms, so if we're going to play, let's do it here.'

Their hostess sighed with evident relief. 'Perfect. Thank you, Eleanor.'

As the staff cleared away the remains of dinner, Sir Edward called up the table, 'But what game? I'm too full for leaping about playing festive charades.'

'A series of memory tests?' Doctor Connell said.

This brought a chuckle from the Laird. 'Suggests the significant advantage of youth!'

'Alright, an observation game, then.'

Baron Ashley laughed. 'Which calls for the sharp eye of a doctor!'

Eleanor laughed, not caring what they played as long as Baroness Ashley was happy. As more suggestions were called out over her head, she bent to retrieve her lap rug that had slipped to the floor. As she sat back up, Baroness Ashley clapped her hands.

'Oh, brilliant. I haven't played that for years! It's such fun. And fiendishly tricky.'

The consensus seemed in favour. Even Gordon Cameron

nodded, albeit reluctantly. However, Eleanor had missed what the
room had chosen.

'It's wonderful, I'm sure, but what are we playing?'

'Wink murder,' Sir Edward said. 'Quite the hoot.'

Eleanor smiled back blankly. 'Wink... murder? That doesn't
sound very festive. Perhaps someone could tell me the rules?'

'You've never played wink murder?' Lady Fortesque said.

Clearly the only one in the dark, Eleanor shrugged. 'Too many
years abroad and travelling alone, perhaps.'

The Laird beamed at her. 'It is quite the Great British institution, dear lady. And actually very festive.' He turned to Randall.
'Eugene, you're in for an insight into both our countries' shared
love of the ridiculous.'

Randall waved an unsteady hand. 'Then let the game begin.
I'll teach you how we do competition back home.'

Baroness Ashley clapped her hands in delight.

'Now, let's see. We need some paper and a—' She stopped in
surprise as Clifford materialised at her elbow with a smart silver
box. He held the lid open for her to look inside. 'Goodness, how
very efficient.' She closed the lid and shook the box hard. 'So,
Eleanor, on one of these neatly folded pieces of paper that your
butler has magically conjured up, will be the word "murderer". All
the others will say "victim". Whoever ends up with the first one has
to very cleverly murder everyone else round the table by subtly
winking at them. But the tricky thing is, if anyone who isn't being
winked at sees them do it, they shout "murderer" and point out the
miscreant and the game has to begin again. The only way to win is
to be the only one left alive at the end of the game. Do you see?'

Eleanor laughed. 'I do. And, as you said, Robert, that must be
one of the most ridiculous games I've ever heard of. It's absolutely
perfect for a Christmas Eve among friends.'

Lady Fortesque shuffled from side to side in her seat.

'But with the candelabras, I can't see most of you properly. We
need them cleared out of the way.'

'Good idea,' Doctor Connell said. 'Faint lighting makes it so much harder to work out if someone is winking or not. Much more fun.'

'Good point.' The Laird beckoned to Clifford. 'Let the fires stay damped right down to add to the atmosphere.' He turned back to the table. 'If the ladies are warm enough?'

They all nodded. Eleanor rather felt that Baron Ashley was being usurped in his own home, but he didn't seem to mind. *I suppose the Laird naturally takes control, Ellie.* Dismissing the thought, Eleanor clasped the hand warmer between her palms. The rest of her wasn't too bad, the lap rug and the generous brandies having done a remarkable job of warming her up, despite the draught wafting around her legs.

At Clifford's discreetly lifted finger, Henderson looked back at him blankly. Mrs Butters tutted quietly and beckoned to Lizzie. They hurried forward, and each removed the nearest of the candelabras, both struggling under the weight. Clifford moved two at once. Grudgingly Henderson collected the remaining one. With the candles now gone, an eerie gloom filled the room, shading the faces of everyone around the table. Eugene Randall had been quietly encouraged by the Laird to drink his coffee, in the absence of any more brandy being offered. But as he swigged the last of the cup, he broke into another round of spluttered coughing. Doctor Connell rose and patted the man between the shoulder blades.

'Coffee can be a marvellous restorative if you can keep it down, Mr Randall. Credit for moving on to it. Good man.' He tugged the red velvet cushion out from behind the American and pressed him upright in the carver chair. 'Oxygen can be the greatest medicine of all. Sit straight. Deep breaths.'

Whilst this was going on, the silver box had been passed from guest to guest. Eleanor unfolded her paper close against her chest so no one else could see. Glancing at it, she smiled to herself at Clifford's familiar meticulous handwriting.

Victim – Beware the wink, for you're out in a blink!

She tried to guess what message the murderer's paper held. *Murderer – Prepare to wink, for you're... what, Ellie?* She couldn't think of anything relevant to rhyme with 'wink' except 'blink' again, which didn't work. Peering around, she was amazed that despite the general excitement, everyone had adopted something close to a poker face. Whoever the murderer was, they were certainly not giving the game away.

She leaned to Lord Fortesque on her right. 'How does one start the game?'

Just then, Clifford appeared at the head of the table and gave an impressive drum roll on the dinner gong.

'Ah! That's how.'

'Bravo!' Baron Ashley said. 'We're off.'

Almost immediately, the Laird gave a remarkably authentic death rattle and fell back in his seat, accompanied by much laughing around the table.

'Straight in, I see,' Sir Edward said.

Immediately, everyone's expressions became neutral again. Heads swept back and forth, suspicious glances a-plenty cast on both sides.

Doctor Connell slumped forward with a lingering gurgle, which made Eleanor laugh.

'Sorry. You probably know better than any of us how it sounds, after all.' She blushed as she caught Clifford pinching the bridge of his nose at her words.

Lady Fortesque collapsed next with much dramatic arm flailing and clutching of her throat.

'Good show, dear,' her husband called out.

'Thank you, dear,' she said, sitting back up.

Baron Ashley tutted in mock disapproval. 'Really! You're supposed to be dead, Fanny. You can't converse from the other side in wink murder, you know.'

'No ghosts allowed,' the Laird whispered loudly enough for everyone to hear.

'Oh, Robert, really,' Lady Fortesque tittered.

Baroness Ashley giggled and clapped her hands in delight. 'I don't mean to interrupt the game, but can I say how perfect this is. It's just the right time to play—'

The lights snapped off. In the dark, the whole room gasped.

'Henderson!' Eleanor heard Clifford mutter behind her. 'Matches.'

'Finished 'em, lighting the fires.'

'Then follow me,' came the terse reply.

For a moment, everyone round the table seemed to sit motionless, trying to take stock.

Baron Ashley's voice cut through the darkness. 'Don't panic. It's just the storm having knocked the generator out.'

There was the sound of several heavy carver chairs being scraped back. *Three or four of the men standing to reach into their pockets for cigarette lighters, Ellie?* But no flames appeared.

'Oof!'

The table jerked as someone bumped into it.

'Stay calm. On my way.' That had sounded like Sir Edward.

'Haud yer weesht!' The Laird, Gordon or Doctor Connell, Eleanor guessed, seeing as the words meant nothing to her.

'Back in your seats, all,' Baron Ashley's voice called. 'We're just banging heads and treading on each other's feet. I'll get a... ah, that's better!'

Clifford had returned bearing two of the candelabras, both filled with flickering candles. Then, with a series of flashes, the lights came back on.

'Thank goodness!' Baroness Ashley said. 'Sometimes the electricity can be off for ages.'

Clifford placed a candelabra near Eleanor and she saw him looking at the American oddly.

'Mr Randall?' she called. 'You can't have been wink-murdered while the lights were off, that would be cheating on the murderer's part.'

Half the table chuckled but quickly tailed off at the lack of reply. Doctor Connell leaped up and bent over the silent man.

'Wretched alcohol,' Eleanor heard him mutter. He straightened up and stared hard at the slumped American. 'Ah!'

'Ah, what?' Baron Ashley said.

Lady Fortesque leaned round past the Laird and let out a piercing scream.

'You can't be wink-murdered twice in one game, can you?' Sir Edward said in confusion.

Eleanor half rose. 'Doctor Connell, what is it?'

He turned to the table. 'Well, Lady Swift, it seems Mr Randall has been murdered for real!'

9

In the stunned silence, the only sound was the sputtering of the dying embers of the fire. Clifford appeared beside Eleanor, a discreet, yet protective distance away.

Baroness Ashley was the first to speak. 'Doctor, please, can't you do something to save him?'

Doctor Connell looked up, his hand still on Randall's slumped shoulder. 'There's naught that can be done for this man, Lady Ashley. There's nay any medication for death that I know.'

The finality of his statement drew a collective gasp, immediately followed by a piercing wail. All heads turned as Baroness Ashley clutched her stomach and pointed a shaking finger.

'D-d-dead! Mr Randall is dead! At our Christmas Eve dinner!'

'Wilhelmina, calm yourself,' Baron Ashley called up the table. 'There must be some mistake, surely?'

Doctor Connell shook his head. 'There's a knife sticking out of his back and nay heartbeat. I dunnay think I'm mistaken.'

He looked around the stunned ring of faces, his gaze stopping at the Laird. The Laird nodded and addressed everyone.

'We all need to stay clear-headed whilst appropriate steps are taken.'

'And just what are the appropriate steps when a man has been bloody murdered?' Sir Edward barked. Eleanor noted in surprise that he'd already moved around the table to hold his wife. She was swaying from side to side, her face pale. Eleanor's wartime training as a nurse cut in. *Shock, Ellie. She's about to faint.* Sir Fortesque buried his wife's face in his chest.

'It's alright, Fanny. I've got you. Hush, hush, Edward's here, dear.'

Baron Ashley opened and closed his mouth several times. The Laird gently helped the baroness back into her chair before walking over to him, where his imposing presence seemed to dwarf his trembling host.

'Clarence, we'll clear the room, save for Mr Randall, of course.'

Doctor Connell removed his hand from the dead man. 'Someone should keep a watchful eye on the ladies too.' He glanced at Lady Fortesque. 'Shock can get a tenacious grip if it is nay dealt with properly.' He looked pointedly at Eleanor. 'Though some ladies can handle a great deal more than others.'

Clifford cleared his throat and, catching the Laird's attention, pointed to the door.

'And,' the Laird said to Baron Ashley, 'this room should also be securely locked until the police arrive.' He gestured around the table. 'Everyone, please remove yourselves. Mr Randall should be left in peace for now.'

Eleanor jumped as Gordon Cameron growled next to her. 'Eternity is peace, Father. He's in God's hands now, nay, yours.'

The Laird steeled his gaze. 'I merely ask that we clear the room. This is not the time for theological discussion.'

'Of course it is nay,' Gordon spat. 'This whole episode at Ranburgh has been a sin from the very start. See what you've done!'

'Haud yer weest!' the Laird snapped back. His calm demeanour instantly returned as he swept up the other guests, as if he was rounding sheep. His impressive stature added an authoritative gravity to his words. 'Good folks, out we all go with no more ado, if you will.'

Eleanor moved to help, but Clifford discreetly tapped her wrist. 'Please do not leave my sight, my lady,' he whispered.

'Nor you mine,' she said quietly.

Offering the sobbing Baroness Ashley an arm around her shoulders, Eleanor helped her from the room. In the corridor, she paused and pressed the baroness into one of the velvet-upholstered chairs flanking the doors to the great hall. Sir Edward hurried past with his wife, murmuring to her. Gordon stomped after them, his stout-heeled boots resonating long after he could no longer be seen.

Eleanor patted Wilhelmina on the arm. 'Just take a moment, I'll get you some water.'

She tiptoed back into the room and took one last look at the dead man. However, the Laird motioned her out again before she could do any more than wince at the sight of Mr Randall's motionless form, a pool of crimson blood forming behind his chair.

'Lady Swift, my dear. Stay with our hostess if you will.'

From the doorway she watched as Clarence, Doctor Connell, Clifford and a very sullen Henderson paired up to retrieve two enormous planks from the end of the hall. Back in the corridor, Clifford took the handles of the double doors and, with a reverent nod at Randall, pulled them closed.

'Lift the first plank into place,' the Laird said.

Finally, the locking bars were wrestled into the solid U-shaped iron brackets with many shouts of, 'Watch your fingers!'

Baron Ashley looked at Henderson. 'Where is the key?'

All he got in reply was a shrug. Clifford stepped forward with a huge medieval-looking item in his hand.

'I believe this might be the one, my lord.'

Eleanor wasn't sure what she expected to unfold back in the drawing room, but her prediction that they were in for a drawn-out night proved true as Clifford approached Baron Ashley.

'A Constable Magoon will be arriving in due course, my lord.

Once he has managed to source a rowing boat and negotiated the loch.'

'And just how long is that going to take?' Sir Edward demanded.

'As long as it does!' Baron Ashley swept up a brandy decanter from the drinks table and poured himself a large measure.

In a corner Eleanor sat deep in thought. She was troubled by a lot of things. Randall's death to start with. But also that Baron Ashley still hadn't attended to his wife. He seemed to have retreated into his own world, taking gulps of brandy and constantly glancing towards the door as if expecting Randall's ghost to make an appearance.

Clifford had somehow arranged for a tray of tea to be brought by Mrs Butters without, it seemed, leaving the room. He poured Baroness Ashley a cup and added several sugars. Lady Fortesque declined hers with a sniff and rapped the table.

'Clarence, do you really expect us to just sit here like good little children until we are told we may go to bed? After what has happened? Because I for one, see no point—'

Baron Ashley swung around, his face suffused with anger. 'In making things harder!' With an effort, he contained himself. 'For once, Fanny, please be amenable.'

Sir Edward rose from his wife's side. 'Now, look here, Clarence. You're the wretch who invited a murderer to stay!'

'I did no such thing.'

'Then just how do you explain the dead man' – Sir Edward raised his voice – '*slumped at your dining table?*'

'Gentlemen,' the Laird said. 'We all need to stay calm and ride this calamity out as best we can for now.'

'A calamity, is it?' Gordon grunted. 'For whom really though, Father?'

'Gordon! Even patience as long as mine has an end to its tether.'

'Like Mr Randall's life!' Baroness Ashley blurted out. 'Ended. Done. Finished.'

Eleanor looked imploringly at Baron Ashley, but he'd gone back to gulping his brandy, his eyes still flitting to the door.

An hour and a half later, despite Eleanor and the Laird's collective efforts, the conversation in the drawing room had worn as thin as the ragged tempers of the guests.

Not a moment too soon, Clifford appeared and announced, 'I believe Constable Magoon is with us, my lord.'

Baron Ashley pushed himself off the wall and swallowed hard. 'I'd best see to him, I suppose.'

'We'll both go,' the Laird said quickly, slapping an arm around the baron's shoulders. 'And you, Doctor. I'm sure they'll want to speak to you.'

Clifford caught Eleanor's eye as he went to follow the three men. She ducked out after him.

In the hallway, Constable Magoon looked as though he had already seen a ghost, if the pallor of the short, weathered policeman swathed in voluminous folds of a dripping yellow sou'wester was anything to go by. On seeing the Laird, however, his expression changed to something closer to panic.

'The body is this way, Constable.' Baron Ashley pointed down the corridor.

'Body, sir?' Magoon shuddered, causing a rivulet of water to pour from his hat. 'I'm nay too used to bodies.'

'None of us are. Not since the war anyway.' The Laird clapped a firm hand on the policeman's shoulder. 'But this one needs dealing with. And quickly.'

'And there was a suggestion that it wasn't... natural causes?' Magoon's eyes looked everywhere but at the Laird.

Doctor Connell stepped forward. 'Constable Magoon, I did nay need all my years of medical training to diagnose that the dirk sticking out of the man's back was the cause of his demise.'

'Dirk?' Magoon whispered.

The Laird took the wide-eyed constable by the shoulders and propelled him off down the corridor.

Clifford had somehow scooted ahead and rounded up Henderson. Together they were midway through removing the heavy locking bars from the door as the four men arrived at the grand hall.

'Said it were a waste o' time lugging these stupid beasts into place before police got here,' Henderson grumbled to Clifford.

'No precaution is a waste of time when a man has been murdered, Mr Henderson,' Eleanor's sharp ears heard him reply.

Baron Ashley pulled the key from his pocket and turned it in the lock. He opened one half of the double doors and stepped back. 'It happened in there, Constable.'

'Ah! And he's... um... still there, is he?' Magoon stuttered, peering into the room.

'Oh, get in there, man!' The Laird pushed the policeman forward. 'There's no need for this to take all night.'

'No, m'lord. Best make it quick, as you say.'

As Eleanor went to step in after the men, the Laird turned around and placed his hand on her arm. 'My dear, this really is not a sight for a lady, however strong her constitution. May I suggest you return to sit with the others? Immediately.' His expression told her it wasn't a suggestion.

She smiled coolly. 'Thank you for your solicitude, Robert, but I shall remain close to our reassuring police presence, while we have one. Safety first has always been my motto.'

For a moment she thought she saw anger burning in his eyes, but in a blink his ever-ready smile slid back into place.

'Of course, my dear.'

Magoon was standing a good six feet from Randall's body, looking decidedly green over everything Doctor Connell was showing him. When the doctor had finished, Magoon made a cursory examination of the body. *If you can call walking around it once without actually touching it or noting anything down an examination, Ellie.* Despite the cold, the constable was sweating.

'He's... he's dead alright.'

'And?' the Laird said.

'Looks like there might have been an element of foul play, m'lord.'

Might have been! This man is hopeless, Ellie!

Magoon swallowed hard and fumbled under his sou'wester. 'I'll just take a wee set of notes, but I'm afraid this is a job for far shinier brass than a mere constable.'

Baron Ashley sighed wearily. 'Just do what you need to do, Constable.'

Magoon made some hasty scribbles in the soggy-looking notebook he wrenched from a pocket. 'Dirk. Dinner table.' He waved his pen over the row of glasses around Randall's place setting. 'Alcohol. Body. Bl-blood.' He closed his notebook shut.

'Is that all from you, then?' Baron Ashley said in disbelief.

Magoon nodded. 'It is, m'lord. I don't wish to detain you all any further.'

'The room will be kept locked like it was when you arrived,' the Laird said.

Magoon nodded again. 'Thank you, m'lord. I shall file a full report at the station once I've' – he swallowed hard – 'made it back across the loch.'

The news that the police had been and gone was met with relief and a general rush to the bedrooms. Arguments still reigned all the way up the stairs as the Fortesques sniped at Baron Ashley. The baroness shook her husband's arm from hers and stumbled on ahead, a handkerchief clutched to her face. Even the Laird had thrown his genial patience to one side and castigated Gordon up the first three landings.

'It's not me who let the clan down, son. Ashamed, that's where you need to lay your head tonight, not on your pillow!'

Doctor Connell took a deep breath as the last of the raised

voices died away and looked at Eleanor. 'I hope sleep manages to creep under yer door before the dawn, Lady Swift.'

Knowing it wouldn't, she simply bid him good night.

Once alone with Clifford in the hallway, she smiled at the hip flask he put in her hand.

'Despite everything I drank at dinner, I'm not feeling in the least squiffy.'

'There is nothing as sobering as a murder, my lady.' He scanned her face in concern. 'I will escort you to your room and check there is a chair of suitably robust construction for you to jam under the door handle. With your permission, of course.'

'Thank you. But then, promise me you won't spend the night perched on some stiff-backed instrument of torture watching my corridor for an intruder.'

He bowed. 'A Clifford never breaks his promises, my lady.' He gestured up the staircase. 'Which is why I promise nothing.'

10

The next morning, Eleanor shivered as she prepared to leave her bedroom in search of breakfast. It wasn't that it was particularly cold – a fire burned dimly in the grate – but the image of Randall slumped at the table with a dagger sticking out of his back kept swimming in front of her eyes. She took another look in the mirror. Her nose wrinkled at her reflection. No doubt Clifford would give a disapproving sniff at her wardrobe choice, for it could not be considered elegant in any regard. But she'd resolved that refined style could bow down to the warding off of frostbite. Therefore she sported her favourite sage-green tweed trousers and several layers of close-fitting cashmere jumpers topped off with the snug cardigan that matched the bottom half of her outfit.

Outside the room, the miles of dimly lit stone corridors felt claustrophobic this morning with their closely woven bricks forming low-arched ceilings. More dark and sombre paintings peppered the many alcoves where a brightly burning lamp would have been so much more welcome. Narrow staircases and wide oak doors seemed to lead off at every turn, all further scrambling her sense of direction.

She remembered that whilst escorting her to her bedroom door the night before, Clifford had suggested a clever mnemonic to help her find her way back down in the morning. It had involved the particular paintings, suits of armour and battle shields they had passed along the way. But the murder of the night before had muddied her recollection of the finer details, along with making the shadowy alcoves and corridors appear rather menacing. However, compared to her bedroom and the endless stone-cold corridors she lost herself in, the morning room she eventually came across felt almost snug in comparison. Apparently, her ever-resourceful butler had managed to conjure up a roaring fire in there at least.

She sensed a presence behind her.

'What ho, Clifford.' She glanced around. It seemed she had beaten everyone else down and they were alone. 'Happy Christmas!'

'And to you, my lady, most heartily.' He looked her face over. 'Father Christmas was not benevolent enough to bestow a restorative sleep as your stocking present, perchance?'

She groaned and slid into the chair he held out. 'Absolutely not. Hence me being the first to breakfast.'

He gave a quiet cough and busied himself at the row of lidded silver salvers sitting on miniature braziers.

'Ah! I'm not the first then?'

'Indeed not, my lady. But since breakfast is not a race, there can be no shame in coming last.'

She laughed, but then felt bad, realising she might have unintentionally ruined the remains of whatever schedule he had been able to cling to.

'I couldn't sleep at all until I finally dropped off about three this morning. And then only because a flask of warmed milk with a dash of brandy appeared mysteriously outside my door. Thank you for your thoughtfulness. Just like the hand warmer at dinner.'

'My sincere pleasure,' he said without turning around.

'But you can't have got a wink either.' She gave an involuntary shudder. 'Oh gracious, Clifford, remind me not to use that word for a while, after the awful way that game ended. Anyway, let's try and forget that for a moment. I spent far too much of the night thinking about it. As Constable Magoon told us, the police from the nearest town will be here soon enough, no doubt. In fact, don't let me keep you. It's Christmas Day. And much as I earnestly wish you could be sitting feet up in blissful peace and quiet, with a second glass of your favourite tawny port, enjoying Voltaire's wisdom, I know sadly that isn't an option. Randall's murder notwithstanding, I'm sure you've got beyond plenty on your plate.'

'More to the point, hopefully so on yours, my lady.' He returned to her side with an unladylike-sized serving. She clapped her hands.

'Wonderful, I'm famished.'

She surveyed her plate. Kippers with a generous knob of melting butter, nestled against smoked salmon curls, black pudding rings, potato scones and two silver-topped egg cups. All were neatly arranged around a central ceramic dish of something welcomingly familiar.

'Mrs Trotman's famous paprika relish!'

'Indeed, my lady. But with a local twist.'

She spread a liberal helping of the relish onto a scone he had placed on a separate plate, savouring the warming, sweet addition she couldn't quite place.

'Whisky,' he said in reply to her questioning look.

That made her smile. 'I know it's Christmas, Clifford, but if Mrs Trotman keeps adding spirits to everything she cooks, I shall be literally swimming in good cheer. It's heavenly.' She peered at his face. 'Speaking of heavenly, how are things in your less than harmonious domain?'

'Fine enough, my lady.' His hand strayed to one of his perfectly aligned cufflinks.

'So, things are still tricky downstairs then?' She waved her fork over her plate in confusion. 'But hang on, this breakfast is sublime. Nothing like last night's dinner at all.'

'Reassuring news.'

'You've managed to negotiate a truce then?'

He took a deep breath. 'Only a temporary compromise. And that, only out of deference to the shock of Mr Randall's passing. I fear, after the more senior police officers have attended and gone, hostilities will resume with renewed gusto.'

Eleanor gratefully took the rich-roasted cup of coffee Clifford held out to her and sighed. 'I hope not for your sake and, if I'm honest, mine and the rest of the guests. But either way, here we are again, unwittingly in the midst of a murder! And at the risk of repeating myself, the local constabulary didn't fill me with much confidence last night. Constable Magoon seemed more preoccupied with having rowed out across the loch in the dark than focussed on Randall's murder. Disgruntled would be an understatement!'

'Perhaps disgruntlement was intended to disguise his fear at also having to make the return journey, alone in a tiny rowing boat, on an inky-black lake inhabited by a monster.'

She threw her hands out in disbelief. 'Come on! You don't really believe there's a monster, do you?'

He cleared his throat. 'I apologise for offering a contrary opinion, my lady, but I am not vain enough to suppose I know better than generations native to an area I have never previously visited.'

She gave a mock bow of contrition. 'Fair point. But Constable Magoon basically took one look at Randall's lifeless form and closed his notebook.'

'Indeed. The gentleman did not examine the body at all. Were it not for Doctor Connell's description of how he found Mr Randall slumped over the table—'

'With a knife sticking out of his back!'

'With, as you say, a knife sticking out of his back, I am not certain the constable would have known Mr Randall *had* been murdered. However, I saw, as you did, his reaction at finding the Laird present and, therefore, that he might be one of the suspects.'

She nodded. 'I know what you mean. I get the feeling no one around these parts would dare point a finger at the Laird. Even if they *saw* him sticking a knife in someone's back!'

'I agree, my lady. Although, I also feel Mrs McKenzie falls into that category. I think it would take a braver man than Constable Magoon to interview that woman, let alone accuse her of anything untoward.'

Eleanor laughed and shook her head. 'Anyway, we can at least be sure that nothing will be moved or touched at the crime scene until the proper police arrive. You and Henderson secured the dining room again most thoroughly.'

'Quite.'

'In truth, the awful scene being preserved for the more senior police to investigate was the reason I couldn't sleep.' She bit her lip. 'Knowing that poor Randall was lying in his chair alone all night in that enormous great hall. The tragic Christmas guest left behind after the party has long broken up.'

'If you will forgive my observation, I do not think, in his condition as it were, that would have bothered the gentleman, my lady.'

She nodded. 'I know. Even with all your wily efforts to keep his alcohol intake down, the poor chap was like a starved dog released into a butcher's shop. Prohibition itself had obviously nearly finished him off.'

'I was referring to Mr Randall being dead, not drunk, my lady.'

She nodded distractedly. 'Dead *and* drunk, in fact.' She took a long sip of coffee. 'Who do you think it could have been, though?'

'I wish I could answer with any certainty.' His jaw clenched. 'Especially as you were in the room at the time and the chances are that the culprit is amongst us. You must take extra care, my lady, as we discussed last night.'

She tried to lighten the mood. 'Don't worry, I will. But in one way, I'm glad you don't know who the murderer is, actually.'

'My lady?'

'You going after the murderer to ensure my safety would be noble and sincerely appreciated, but would only add to the stress of all this very un-Christmassy mess. And it would throw your busy schedule out even further.' She winked, but then shuddered again. 'No more parlour games this year, I say. Whose idea was wink murder, anyway?'

'I missed who suggested it.' He held his hand out for the napkin in her lap and sniffed at her choice of attire.

She wagged a finger at him.

'Don't start! Despite your best efforts, it's freezing in most of the castle. And I thought it would be in here, but I can see I under-estimated you as usual. I bet you've got six extra layers of woolly underthings on below your impeccable coat-tails, haven't you?' At his horrified look, she shrugged. 'Sorry. I just meant that even the world's best butlers must feel the cold on occasion.'

'In my experience, only on being seconded to a Scottish castle in December, my lady.'

'Touché.' She leaned back in her chair. 'Well, I shall be amazed at whoever the police reveal the murderer to be. Assuming that is, the town police put more effort into investigating than Constable Magoon. Either way, we know it wasn't you or I. Nor any of my staff, obviously. Aside from the fact they are entirely above reproach, the ladies only arrived the day before yesterday. They could never have fallen foul of Randall sufficiently to want him dead in that time. Although we did see a horribly belligerent side to him once he'd consumed a fair few glasses, didn't we?'

'If I might refrain from speaking ill of the deceased, my lady. Let us simply take comfort that none of our ladies were even in the dining room when the terrible event occurred.'

'Ah, and neither were you or Henderson for that matter. That should make the police questioning nice and quick for you. You'd dragged Henderson out by his ear to sort some lighting out, hadn't you?' He nodded. 'And as Mrs McKenzie was in the kitchen and Lizzie seems an unlikely candidate for murdering anyone, we're resigned to the murderer being one of the guests then.'

'Or your hosts, my lady.'

She opened her mouth to argue, but then sighed. 'I suppose you're right. In which case we have six... no, seven candidates for Randall's murder.' She looked up at him, thinking she needed...

He magically produced her notebook and pen from a hidden inner pocket.

She took it gratefully and counted off their suspects on her fingers. 'The Laird and his son, Gordon, the Fortesques, Doctor Connell...' She caught his eye. 'Oh, alright, and the Ashleys.' She caught his eye again. 'What is it?'

'I am sure now I come to think of it, my lady, that Henderson *did* leave me for a few moments when the lights were out. He said to collect the key to the room housing the generator.'

The hairs on the back of her neck bristled. 'To collect it by fumbling in the dark rather than grabbing some matches from the kitchen to light candles and then see to the generator? Then he's definitely on the suspect list... which makes eight. Well, as all of them had pretty much equal opportunity and probably means, I think the key to solving this murder is going to come down to motive – *why* someone would want Randall dead.'

She stared at the open page of her notebook for a moment and then wrote:

The Laird

Motive?

Gordon Cameron (Laird's son)

Motive?

Fortesques

Motive?

Doctor Connell

Motive?

Clarence

Motive?

Wilhelmina

Motive?

Henderson (footman)

Motive?

She looked up. 'On reflection, I've lumped the Fortesques together for ease until we find out more about them individually.' A thought struck her. 'How long have the guests been here?'

'Lord Dunburgh and Master—'

She flapped a hand. 'I know, particularly as a butler, Clifford, you try to address everyone correctly, but between you and me could we just say "The Laird and his son", or "The Laird and Mr Cameron", just to save time?'

'Very good, my lady. The Laird and Mr Cameron have been here on and off since Mr Randall arrived, which was several days ago according to the grumblings I was forced to endure from Henderson. The Fortesques, however, have barely unpacked, so must have come the night before us, I think. Doctor Connell has visited several times in the last week, but never stayed until last night. Lord and Lady Ashley obviously arrived before Mr Randall, but exactly how long before, I am not sure.'

She waved a hand. 'I don't think it's important. The doctor's comings and goings might be though. Mind you, unless the doctor had been subjected to Randall's sharp tongue when administering advice to cut back on his drinks, say, I can't imagine how they might have argued in the short space of time the doctor seems to have been here. Certainly not enough for the good doctor to stick a knife in Randall's back. Mind you, the same stands for the Fortesques and the Laird.' She frowned. 'I got the definite impression that the Laird is helping Clarence with whatever project he has on the go. And that it's the same project Clarence was working so hard to get Randall involved in.'

'Indeed. To Mr Cameron's chagrin.'

'I definitely detected that too. So that only really leaves...' She glanced at the door and lowered her voice. 'Clarence and Wilhelmina. And I know what you're thinking, but objectivity be damned. It simply couldn't have been either of them. Clarence's father is a friend of a friend after all, and Wilhelmina is simply too sweet.'

'If I might decline to comment, my lady.'

'No, you may not, because your insights are invariably illuminating, and, if I'm totally honest, equally infuriating, at the same time.'

'Thank you. I merely meant to point out that your friends may have been friends with Lord Ashley's *father* for a great many years, but likely his son for a briefer time and less personally.'

'Eloquently put. But Wilhelmina...' She tailed off, remembering the Laird's description of their hostess and the black looks she had thrown Randall's way. 'I admit she was pretty furious with Randall, but—'

A knock on the door interrupted them. It was a sullen-looking Henderson.

'Police is here. Everyone's been ordered to go to the western-end drawing room.'

As Eleanor stepped out into the hallway she was bowled back against the wall by her bulldog charging past, with a large cat spitting menace hot on his lumbering heels.

Clifford watched them round a corner. 'Ah, my lady, I believe I forgot to mention that whilst Polly has made a firm friend in Lizzie, Master Gladstone has made an equally firm enemy in Macduff, the castle cat.'

11

'The castle has been searched and we can be sure that the perpetrator is nay hiding anywhere 'cos it was conducted by my men.'

The short, heavily bearded man standing astride the fireside
rug rolled his eyes, muttering something even Eleanor's keen ears
couldn't catch. That the inspector had a battered brown leather
satchel slung sideways across his body was unusual, she thought.
That it hung at an awkward angle over his considerable paunch
however struck her as too droll. Prone to wild gesticulations to
emphasise his words, with every wave of his right arm, the bag rode
up his chest. His habit of jerking it back down became quite
hypnotising. Eleanor found herself trying to predict how many
seconds would elapse before he did it again.

*Surely, he'll have sawn himself in half in a moment, Ellie! And
what does he keep in there?*

From his position towards the back of the room, Clifford
caught her eye and shook his head, letting her know he'd read her
impish thoughts.

Lady Fortesque sniffed. 'Inspector Lockhart, you say that the
perpetrator is not hiding in the castle. Is that supposed to reassure
us that one of us won't get stabbed in the back next time we take a
cup of tea! Or retire to bed!'

Lockhart scowled. 'The best ye can do is to be on yer guard and cooperate with my men. There's nay reason to imagine the killer will act again, mind.' He gave Lady Fortesque and the others in the room a hard stare.

Eleanor noted, however, he didn't include the Laird and his son. They received a courteous nod, which the Laird acknowledged with a slight raise of one finger from where his arm laid along the padded side of the settee.

The inspector tugged his bag down again. 'Interviews will begin shortly in the library. Dunnay go anywhere far from there. The days are shortest already.'

'Inspector?' Baron Ashley called with an air of authority.

'Aye? What is it?'

'I would like a word with you.' Baron Ashley pulled himself up to his full, impressive height. 'About certain expectations this end of things. I am sure you are anxious to execute your duties expeditiously since it is Christmas Day.'

Inspector Lockhart snorted. 'December twenty-fifth is a working one for me as it is for all good folk round here. Especially when evil's taken a walk.' His substantial chest puffed, threatening his overcoat's already straining buttons. 'And fear not. I am known for efficiency, not expeditiousness. The murderer will be caught. And soon! Now, I shall begin the interviews. Someone within the walls of this once proud castle knows about the dirk.'

'For those of us not from this area, Inspector,' Lady Fortesque said. 'What exactly is a jirk?'

'A *dirk*, Lady Fortesque, is a Highlander's dagger of a long and illustrious tradition.'

'Although today it is seen more as a ceremonial piece,' the Laird said. 'Carried by members of our regiments. I have several myself at home.'

Interesting, Ellie!

'Aye.' Gordon Cameron suddenly seemed roused by the discussion. 'And an army of our good men who could nay read nor write were forced to swear oaths against their heritage on theirs. Sacrilege!'

Eleanor was about to ask forced by whom, but Clifford's quiet cough reached her ears.

The Laird nudged his son's side. 'Raking over bygones will ne'er make amends. Let them lie, son.'

Doctor Connell tilted his chin in Eleanor's direction but seemed to address the room in general. 'The notable characteristic of the dirk is that its blade is normally twelve inches long. Long enough to kill a man when plunged into his back.'

Lady Fortesque shivered. 'Thank you. Now, we're all on the same page, pray continue, Inspector.'

Lockhart beckoned Clifford over and thrust a list written in a spidery hand at him. 'See that these people come to the library in this order. Ten minutes apart.'

'Ten minutes,' Sir Edward muttered. 'One would barely have got names and addresses in that time.'

The policeman drew himself up. 'After thirty years of being an instrument of justice, I will nay need any longer. Nothing will divert me from finding the truth!'

Clifford gave a respectful bow. 'However, perhaps you might require coffee and sandwiches first, Inspector?'

'Oh aye, that I will.'

As he turned to leave, the Laird raised another finger and rose gracefully. After making his excuses, he joined the policeman who was waiting respectfully by the door.

Once they'd gone, Sir Edward laughed drily. 'I rather thought you were lord of the manor here, Clarence, old man. You seem to be playing second fiddle to our Scottish friend. Again.'

Baron Ashley rounded on him. 'At least I own this place, Edward! Have you managed to pay off the debtors who were circling you last time we met?'

Lady Fortesque jumped to her feet. 'How dare you speak to Edward like that! And such lies!'

Baroness Ashley also jumped to her feet. 'I... I know emotions are running high. After all, a man was... murdered just last night and the culprit is still at large. But let us at least *try* to remain civil to each other.'

Eleanor caught Clifford's eye. His face remained impassive, but he consulted the list Inspector Lockhart had given him and discreetly spread out four fingers of his left hand. *Great, Ellie, you're fourth in line for the dirk that is Inspector Lockhart's sharp tongue!* That meant she had at least half an hour to kill. *Oops! Bad choice of words.*

At a loss as to how to fill her free minutes, she looked at Clifford, but he was occupied orchestrating the policeman's bidding while directing a decidedly reluctant Henderson. She'd just decided to see if she could comfort Baroness Ashley when their hostess rose and hurried from the room. Then she overheard Baron Ashley instructing Clifford to ensure lunch would be ready for twelve noon. She sighed. That meant sneaking down to wish the Henley Hall ladies happy Christmas was also out. They would be too busy. And likely, despite it being Christmas Day, engaged in a full-scale battle with Mrs McKenzie.

She thought of sitting quietly and observing her fellow guests, but the highly charged atmosphere made her restless to be elsewhere. A little castle exploration would be just the thing, so long as she stayed on her guard and didn't go anywhere too far from the main hall. Besides, as Inspector Lockhart had said, there was no evidence that the murderer had any reason to kill again. And even if the inspector was wrong, it seemed highly improbable that the murderer would risk doing so while the castle was swarming with police.

As she passed Clifford pouring the Laird a glass of whisky, she motioned discreetly with two fingers that she was taking a quick walk. His brows flinched. Sweeping up a bottle of Tanqueray gin and another of Angostura bitters, he intercepted her.

'Perhaps, a Christmas Day cocktail, my lady? A delightful concoction I believe you are entirely unfamiliar with' – he lowered his voice – 'called patience and prudence.'

'Sounds unnecessarily racy for what I've got in mind, actually, which is just a stretch of the legs.'

As she went down the impressive central hallway, her Oxford heels clicked against the acres of flagstones and bounced off the curved ceiling. Various fearsome black-oak doors punctuated the walls, which looked to be hewn from boulders. Several of the doors were open, mostly displaying rooms with their sparse furniture covered in thick dust sheets. However, the billiard room had been used recently as the full ashtray and filled drinks trolley attested.

Pushing on one partly opened door, she found herself on the threshold of a gentleman's study. She frowned. This couldn't be Clarence's main office when at Ranburgh. Surely he would have kept that locked? She tiptoed forward to peer at the papers on top of the wide mahogany desk. Some general letters, a tailor's bill and what looked like a swathe of other unpaid bills. She retreated, embarrassed that she'd let her curiosity get the better of her.

A few doors down on the opposite side, another door stood ajar. Peeking in, Eleanor was entranced by the artist's studio spread out before her. With floor-to-ceiling windows, much wider than any others she'd seen in the castle, it was easy to see why Baroness Ashley painted here. On the central easel, a large canvas was covered with a cornflower-blue silk throw, hiding a master-piece in progress.

When Eleanor was almost at the enormous arched entrance to the great hall, she was pulled up short, something catching the corner of her eye. She walked back to the deep inset alcove. In the dim lighting it appeared to be nothing more than a decorative architectural recess. An unremarkable porcelain statue of a woman in a traditional pose stood on a tall plinth, half filling the centre of the narrow space. But the rear wall, draped in a faded tapestry, had a peculiar soft glow. Stepping around the statue, she ran her hand along the wall and gasped. An ingenious trick of the eye, it was in fact two separate walls, the shorter section set back, leaving a concealed gap just wide enough to admit a person turned side-ways. Despite her conviction that there was no evidence the killer would strike again, especially today with the police there, she hesitated. Her natural curiosity, however, got the better of her again, and she ducked behind the tapestry.

On the other side, she stood rooted to the spot, jaw slack as she stared around. Before her was an oval room with a galleried landing, the walls filled with armour, bayonets and halberds, a kind of long-handled medieval axe and pike combined. Interspersing them were tiers of chainmail vests and menacing-looking helmets.

The glow she'd spotted came from the bright winter sun streaming through the single, round, yellow stained-glass window. As the Laird had promised, the rain and sleet had subsided in the night. As she surveyed the chamber, a thick black cloud moved across the sun, throwing the room into gloom. The change of light made the weapons of war seem even more menacing. And deadly.

Drawn to the three long, glass-covered display tables dominating the room, she wasn't surprised to see that they were occupied by rows of knives, daggers – *or are they dirks, Ellie?* – and rather ghoulish-looking axes lying on rivers of blood-red velvet. Halfway along the second table, she paused and hunched over the glass. Between two long knife-type swords, the correct name of which she had no clue, there was a flattened section of velvet where another weapon had obviously lain. But whatever it was, it was clearly no longer there.

'Strange place for a lady to take a walk,' a rough voice hissed in her ear.

Instinctively she spun around in Bartitsu mode, for she was a disciple of that school of self-defence, which the Suffragettes had made famous.

'Clifford! You frightened the wits out of me.'

Her butler pursed his lips. 'My lady, I fear that must already have happened, if you will forgive my forthright observation.' He shook his head. 'A man has been murdered and yet you are wandering around the castle alone?'

About to offer a firm retort, she saw the concern in his eyes. 'Sorry. I didn't mean to worry you. I shall genuinely try and pally up with prudence a little more in future.' She wrinkled her nose. 'Though she is terribly dull.'

Her attempt at humour went unappreciated as Clifford sighed. 'My lady, the inspector is waiting for you.'

'Oh great, more farcical perfunctions.'

He gave her a quizzical look.

'Isn't that a word?'

'Not that I have encountered in my humble experience with the English language, my lady.' He glanced through the glass where she had been staring. 'Hmm.'

'I know. It looks like whatever was there—'

'Has been removed recently.' He frowned. 'And whatever was there has made a small cut in the velvet. Most irregular.'

She laughed. 'Clifford, only you would notice something like that.'

He turned away from the display cabinet, his brow furrowed. 'The inspector awaits, my lady.'

Ha! He's just as intrigued as you are, Ellie.

12

'How did you find me in the weapons room, by the way?' Eleanor said as they made their way back down the corridor to the library.

He gave her a withering look. 'Sobering experience again.' He opened the door and announced, 'Lady Swift for you, Inspector.'

Lockhart consulted the mantelpiece clock and waved impatiently.

'Please sit, Lady Swift.' He returned to writing in a small leather-bound notebook.

She did as he bid and perched on the chair on the other side of the wide desk his portly frame presided over. She glanced around. The shelves of musty-smelling books and dark oak furniture did nothing to lighten the heavy atmosphere in the room.

He finally looked up and stared at her. Up close, she couldn't help thinking that he must never have seen the sun. The pale face she'd noted in the drawing room now seemed whiter than paper. She sat back in her seat, noticing for the first time that he still wore his satchel.

'What would you like to know, Inspector?'

'What did you see the night of the murder?'

Keen though she was to get this over with, she paused in confusion. 'A great many things. I mean, it was a whole evening.'

His eyes narrowed. 'Comedians have their place on the stage, but this is nay a theatre, Lady Swift. To be specific then, who was seated near enough Eugene Randall to have stabbed him, would you say?'

She frowned. *After the lights went off, Ellie, anyone could have got up, moved around the table, stabbed him and sat back down before they came back on. Or, in the case of Henderson, returned to join Clifford in sorting the lights.* She looked at the inspector's face. *That's not the answer he's looking for, Ellie.*

She thought for a moment longer. 'Doctor Connell and the Laird, I suppose, since they were either side of Mr Randall. Clarence, I mean Lord Ashley, was just to Doctor Connell's left. But Mr Randall could have been—'

Lockhart held up a hand impatiently and then pulled on his bag strap to tuck it back against his side.

'What did you know of Mr Randall?'

'Very little. I only met him a few hours before dinner. I arrived late yesterday as my butler and I drove up from Buckinghamshire. In the south of England.'

'I asked,' he said wearily, 'what you knew about Mr Randall. Not a minute-by-minute account of your travel itinerary.'

Fighting the urge to reach across and throttle him, she bit her tongue. 'Mr Randall? Well, he seemed charming enough to start with. Gentlemanly and respectable, but alcohol was far from a friend to him. He became quite vocal as the evening wore on.'

'Why was he here?'

She shrugged. 'I don't really know. He was a guest of Lord and Lady Ashley, like all of us. Hasn't Lord Ashley already answered that for you, though?'

'What did you see when the lights went out?'

Hmm, Ellie. Maybe this inspector isn't quite as amateur as he seems. Perhaps he's deliberately trying to throw you off balance.

'Um, darkness. Not wishing to be facetious. What I *heard* was the scraping back of chairs, two people seeming to collide and then... the table lurching as if one of them had fallen against it.'

'Or a dead man had fallen on to it?'

'I suppose.' She thought it through. 'Actually no, it was more like someone banged into it while they were hurrying past.'

He flicked open a fingerprint ink pad and gestured for her to hold out her hand. Recoiling at his icy touch, she watched him roll each of her fingers in the ink and then press them onto a sheet of paper, smudging them slightly. He held out a pen for her to sign her name underneath the prints and then swept the lot to one side.

'How much champagne had you drunk?'

'Inspector, really. I'm not a giddy debutante attending her first ball!'

'How much champagne?'

'Two, maybe three glasses. Plus a sherry. Oh and a brandy or two.'

With a disinterested scrawl of his pen, he looked up at the clock. 'You can go, Lady Swift.'

'Excuse me? But you haven't—'

He waved a dismissive hand and pulled his satchel back down beside him.

As she reached the door, he called over, 'Lady Swift, you seem very observant.' *He means nosey, Ellie!* 'What word would you use to describe Lord Ashley and Mr Randall's relationship?'

She thought to herself. *Cordial? Reserved? Distant?*

'Terse, Inspector.'

'He is too infuriating for words!' Eleanor said to Clifford some-time later as she set off around the outside of the castle to calm her temper. With Gladstone scampering on ahead, they descended the long run of stone steps down to the wall encir-cling the main buildings. 'But I'm sorry. I didn't mean to chew your ear off.' She pulled her thick shawl closer against the bitter breeze.

'Eminently understandable, however, my lady.'

'Ah! You too, then?'

'Inspector Lockhart has, as I believe the local expression might run, "an uncanny knack for bristling even the hairs on a bald cow."'

That made her chuckle. But then she frowned.

'I take back what I said about Constable Magoon. At least he was upfront about not investigating. I have a distinct and decidedly uncomfortable feeling about Lockhart merely going through the motions because—'

'Because the gentleman has already decided on the guilty party?'

'Yes!'

He nodded. 'At the risk of speaking out of place, my interview with the inspector was, as you shrewdly predicted earlier, extreme in the level of *farcical perfunctions*.'

'Whatever they are.' She smiled, relieved he was no longer annoyed by her wandering off somewhere he considered unsafe. 'Did he ask you anything sensible?'

'Not, to my mind, beyond enquiring after my name.' He frowned. 'And perhaps, asking what word I would use to describe—'

'Clarence and Mr Randall's relationship?'

Clifford raised an eyebrow. 'He asked you exactly the same question?'

'I imagine he asked everyone the same question. But maybe Lockhart is not entirely the blunt brick he appears.' She lowered her voice. 'However, I wonder if we should begin our informal... I hate to call it "investigation".'

'Assessment?'

She nodded. 'Much better. I wonder if we should begin our informal assessment of Mr Randall's death? After all, as Lady Fortesque so eloquently put it, a murderer is running around the castle and the police have filled neither of us with confidence in their abilities, or commitment, to finding him.' She glanced at Clifford. 'Or *her*, to be objective.'

'Indeed. Two of our suspects are women – Lady Fortesque and Lady Ashley.'

'Exactly. And there's another reason for our... assessment.'

'My lady?'

Her eyes darkened. 'Even though my acquaintance with Mr Randall was brief, and perhaps I did not see the best side of him, his death was a little too much like my parents' disappearance.'

Clifford's brow arched. 'In what way?'

She swallowed. 'I know it's silly, Clifford, but last night took me back to... that night. One moment they were there in the light putting me to sleep, and then in the dark some unknown hand took them from me.' She paused and took the handkerchief he held out to her. 'As I said, I know it's silly, but one moment Randall was sitting there, and then... in the dark someone took his life. It was all just so sudden.' She dabbed at her eyes and looked up at him. 'No one deserves that, Clifford. Everyone has someone near and dear who they leave behind. Maybe Randall had a wife? That person deserves to know what happened. And why. And, most importantly, to know *who* was responsible, and to know they have been brought to justice.' She handed him back the now soggy handkerchief. He took it between finger and thumb, and waited for her to continue. After a moment, she sighed. 'I may never find out what happened to my parents. Or who was responsible. But I *can* help find out who was responsible for stealing Randall away from his loved ones in the dark.'

Clifford pocketed the handkerchief and bowed. 'Your sense of justice does you proud, my lady. I am, as always, happy to assist. And, to quote the ancient Chinese military strategist, Sun Tzu, a favourite of his late lordship's, "Attack is the secret of defence."'

She smiled at him. 'Exactly!'

At the bottom of the steps, she paused to accept the half-chewed stick Gladstone dropped at her feet with an expectant woof. In the distance the long, jagged line of mountains seemed almost indigo blue, save for the generous cloak of snow shrouding their tops. Below them Loch Vale stretched out like an endless grey-green slab. The day was bright and crisp, the blue sky dotted with white clouds, but the wind was biting cold with a chill that would turn arctic when the sun set. She shivered. *You wouldn't want to be caught out tonight, Ellie.* She turned to Clifford.

'Not the best Christmas Day I've ever experienced so far. But not the worst, either.'

'"Damn with faint praise, assent with civil leer", my lady.'

'Wilde?'

'Pope. Alexander.'

She laughed. 'In truth, I've definitely known worse Christmases.'

'And I, my lady.'

At his faraway tone, she glanced at his face. But it was as impassive as ever. A movement below them caught her eye. She gasped, which made Gladstone paw at her leg.

'Clifford, look! Lockhart is leaving already. But surely that is Clarence's boat following, with the other policemen in it?'

He nodded. 'Indeed. I was in the room when the inspector told Lord Ashley he was confiscating the vessel until his return, and that his lordship and his guests were to remain on the island as they were suspects. He anticipates being back within a day or two.'

'I bet Clarence was fuming.'

'Resignedly so, but, yes.'

She looked back to where the boats were cutting smartly across the loch. 'But hang on, there's a third boat. Constable Magoon is rowing. And he's got' – she strained her eye – 'Mrs McKenzie in there with him!'

He cleared his throat. 'Mrs McKenzie demanded that she be allowed to leave with the inspector and return on Boxing Day evening. She stated that as she was not in the hall at the time of the murder, she therefore was not a suspect and they had no right to hold her. I have observed before, my lady, that Mrs McKenzie is held in fear by all who know her.'

Something tugged at Eleanor's thoughts. 'Hang on, Clifford. Please tell me there's another boat and we aren't trapped here?'

'There is another boat and we aren't trapped here, my lady.'

She sighed in relief, but then saw his expression and groaned.

'That was two big fat lies, wasn't it?'

'Most assuredly, my lady. But I aim to please.'

His mischievous humour eased her irritation at their situation.

'Well, that settles it, Clifford. If we are stuck on this rock with a murderer and no way off until Lockhart's return, then attack is definitely the best means of defence. Nevertheless, I still feel I should report Lockhart for incompetence.'

'Perhaps. Although cowardice might be more appropriate.'

'Dash it! Now I can't even go for that tramp in the snow I was so looking forward to. Sorry Gladstone, old chum. On reflection, this is the worst Christmas Day ever!'

'Uncharacteristically near-sighted, if I might be so bold, my lady.'

He produced a green-and-white-striped paper bag from his pocket and held it open for her. She gratefully popped a mint humbug into her mouth and then felt something land on her nose and immediately dissolve. She looked up as the first swirling snowflakes of the day fell from the leaden sky.

She looked back at him with a puzzled frown. 'Alright, clever clogs, enlighten me. Why am I uncharacteristically near-sighted'?

'Well, my lady, duties aside, if Mrs McKenzie is away this evening—'

'Of course!' Her eyes lit up. 'Oh, Clifford, would it be an unforgivable misdemeanour of propriety to ask if I might possibly be counted in?'

'Indeed, it would.'

Her face fell.

He winked. 'But only because, my lady, you have been unanimously counted in already.'

13

Eleanor tiptoed along the moonlit-flecked corridor at eleven o'clock that evening, her arms full.

If Castle Ranburgh had seemed gloomy before, it was positively creepy now. Even with the small torch Clifford had given her, each suit of armour silently guarding its inky-black recess seemed to reach out a macabre hand as she passed. The uneven stone floors echoed her hesitant footsteps, while the creaking of the wooden boards on the unlit back stairs had her holding her breath.

As she elbowed open the double doors into the castle's kitchen with a sigh of relief, Gladstone hauled himself out of his quilted bed by the range and lumbered up to her. On seeing the packages, he woofed and jumped up, giving the nearest one several exploratory scrabbles with his paws.

Remonstrating with the excited bulldog proved fruitless. She and the presents were saved, however, by Clifford appearing on the cellar steps.

'Master Gladstone. Down!'

The bulldog sat blocking Eleanor's path, his stumpy tail wagging furiously. She handed the packages over to Clifford before the dog could do them any more damage. As she was feeding him one of his favourite liver treats as compensation, Mrs Butters popped through the low, wide arch on the left.

'Oh, m'lady, happy Christmas! 'Tis such a treat to see you.' She bustled forward. 'I hope you're ready for some proper Christmas celebrations. Polly's been beside herself since we heard. Me and Trotters have been over the moon and back too.'

At that moment the lady in question appeared. Eleanor beamed at them both. 'A happy Christmas to you both!'

'Happy Christmas, m'lady.' Mrs Trotman set down a long plate of golden-brown pastries, wafting tantalising aromas of cheese, sausage meat and rosemary.

The two women bumped hips. Clifford shook his head.

'I fear, my lady, your staff has disgracefully already partaken in festive spirits of the bottled variety.'

Mrs Trotman's face broke into a cheeky grin. 'Just how do you plan to manage a kitchen's worth of tiddly women come the small hours, then, Mr Clifford?'

'With weary resignation, Mrs Trotman. However, Christmas comes but once a year.'

Delighted that he intended to let the ladies truly enjoy themselves, Eleanor looked around the kitchen.

'But where is Polly?'

The two women shared a fond smile.

'Soppy thing, she's worried about leaving Lizzie,' Mrs Butters said.

Mrs Trotman nodded. 'Bless her. Said it wasn't right that she had all the fun and Lizzie none at all, so we invited her along as well.'

Eleanor clasped her hand over her mouth. 'Oh, gracious! How terrible of me. I'd forgotten about her. Oh! *And* Henderson. Supposing he appears and witnesses us all partying together?'

'I sincerely doubt that he will,' Clifford said. 'Although we need to remember to keep the noise down for everyone else. As for Henderson, I relieved him of his final duty this evening and dispatched him with two bottles of beer, a round of sandwiches and a plate of mince pies. I pointed out that a decent fellow might choose to remember the spirit of Christmas cheer in which they were given when he awoke tomorrow. I do not think he will give us any trouble. The moment Mrs McKenzie departed, he lost his bravado and became more amenable, if no more efficient.'

The tap of tentative footsteps made them both look up.

'Polly!'

The young maid led in her new friend and closed the door quietly behind them.

'And Lizzie too. How wonderful. Happy Christmas to both of you.'

'Merry Christmas, your ladyship,' Polly mumbled.

'Merry Christmas, m'lady,' Lizzie said.

The two maids curtsied, but stood rooted to the spot. Clifford beckoned them forward and then gestured for Lizzie to step to one side with him.

'In a remarkably short space of time, you have shown me that you have the right attitude and conscientious desire to fulfil your duties well, Lizzie.'

'Thank you, Mr Clifford.' The girl beamed. Eleanor couldn't miss the respectful but quiet confidence the girl's extra two years on Polly had given her.

'However,' Clifford continued, 'this evening's invitation is a very special privilege. Whatever goes on amongst those in this room tonight, stays entirely amongst those present. Is that clear?'

'Perfectly, Mr Clifford. I would ne'er say nothing. So very kind of you to allow me to stay.'

Eleanor smiled at the gentlemanly way he waved them towards two seats with a flourish.

'In that case, ladies, welcome to Christmas, Lady Swift-style.'

The maids bobbed respectfully but failed to hold back their giggles as they scurried round to the other side of the table and held on to the backs of the chairs.

Mrs Butters and Mrs Trotman reappeared, both carrying more plates of cheese, sausage meat and rosemary pastries. They looked over to Clifford, who removed his white butler's gloves. The women's shoulders relaxed as they nudged each other, unable to control their grins.

Ah, Ellie! Another of those secret signals they all understand that you don't.

'Now, at the risk of regretting my question in the morning' – Clifford's hand hovered over a crate on the floor – 'where, amongst your home-made distillations, do you suggest we start, Mrs Trotman?'

With glasses of bubbly rosehip perry for the adults and diluted versions for the maids, plates were loaded with golden pastries as the easy chatter flowed back and forth across the table. Even the two young girls occasionally joined in. Mrs Trotman's cheeky humour soon had them all in stitches, including Clifford, who uncharacteristically could not hide his amusement.

Eleanor listened more than talked, captivated by the warm friendship among her staff. Polly and Lizzie were nudging each other and clearly itching to speak. Mrs Butters cupped Polly's chin.

'What is it, my girl?'

Wide-eyed, Polly whispered, 'We made something.' Then her courage seemed to fail her. 'But 'tis nothing really, 'pologies.'

'Something cannot be nothing, if it was made with the kind thought of it being a gift,' Clifford said, refilling her glass. He leaned down. 'After all, 'tis Christmas, don't you know.' He glanced at Eleanor. 'My lady?'

'Well, we'd normally do presents on Boxing Day but we might all be caught up tomorrow in... other business. So, what do you say we do it now, ladies?'

Her staff rose and scattered in different directions, Lizzie scurrying after Polly, chattering excitedly.

When everyone returned to the table, the laughter continued as Mrs Butters fitted Gladstone out in a bright-red Christmas jumper she had knitted for him the year before. With a happy woof, he spun in lopsided circles, as if they might better admire him in it. A change of glasses for pretty fluted affairs with handles and a pyramid of hot buttery mince pies then heralded the giving of presents.

Eleanor ran her finger over the intricately beaded make-up bag Mrs Butters had given her, tracing her initials. Her housekeeper's sewing skills were way beyond anything Eleanor could ever hope to achieve. As were Mrs Trotman's cooking skills, attested to by the two jars of her famous home-made boiled sweets she gave Eleanor.

The next present Eleanor picked up was from her young maid.

'And Lizzie too, your ladyship,' Polly said with a deep blush.

'Oh gracious, these are beautiful.' Eleanor held up four lovingly homespun bookmarks, each decorated with different patterns of pressed flower petals and finished with a plaited tassel of emerald-green embroidery threads.

Polly jiggled in her seat. 'Lizzie did the writing for me.'

Eleanor looked up from reading the words on each of the bookmarks.

'Girls, I'm truly overwhelmed. Thank you so much. And, yes, Polly' – she held one up, which had a wobbly drawing of a house on four button wheels with five stick people inside – 'I absolutely remember our wheels and buttons conversation from when I first came to Henley Hall. And I always will.'

That finished both her and her maid off as Eleanor dabbed at her eyes with her handkerchief and Polly dabbed at hers with her sleeve.

Mrs Butters pulled Polly into a hug. 'Goodness, we're a sentimental bunch, aren't we? But Christmas is a special time for friends, particularly without family, and no mistake.'

The next sampling of her cook's home brew, a rhubarb and ginger gin, came with side plates of Eleanor's favourite savoury snack, her cook's signature Stilton straws. Polly and Lizzie stared in delight as Clifford set down a jug of rhubarb cordial with lemon slices and mint, as if it were the ultimate in sophisticated aperitifs. He then arranged a bowl of ice cubes, tongs and a cocktail glass for each of them.

'Thank you, Mr Clifford,' they whispered in awe.

'A sincere pleasure, ladies.' He held up a finger. 'Go steady, though. No carriage in the world would make it up the backstairs of this castle to ferry a lady who has overindulged.'

He then busied himself over at the long counter. After a moment he returned with his hands full of beautifully wrapped gifts, one of which he placed in front of Eleanor. There was no mistaking his hand, the waxed paper having been meticulously folded and the green ribbon tied just so. She read the copperplate writing on the card:

'To expect the unexpected shows a thoroughly modern intellect' –
Oscar Wilde.

Clifford cleared his throat. 'Since coming to Henley Hall, my lady, you have taught me to expect the unexpected.' His eyes twinkled. 'And on balance it has been an honour and a delight.'

She laughed. 'On balance? Are you sure?'

He pretended to think. 'You are right. Would it be agreeable if I took the next few years to fully come to a decision?'

For the second time in as many days she wished it were acceptable to hug him as if he really was her uncle, a role he adeptly stepped into on more and more occasions.

A moment later, after carefully unwrapping the package, she stared at him in choked wonder. 'Clifford, that is not only exquisite, it means the world.' She ran her finger over the foothigh carved wooden sculpture that bore a remarkable resemblance to herself with her soppy bulldog leaning against her legs. That they were both cradled in a hand made her voice croak. 'The hand is to represent Uncle Byron, watching over us, isn't it?'

He gave only his customary half bow from the shoulders in reply.

Mrs Butters placed a plate of iced fruit cake and cream-filled brandy snaps in front of Eleanor.

'I don't think there's much of anything Mr Clifford can't do, m'lady. 'Tis beautiful, and it's from the silver birch tree that fell in early spring. His lordship used to love sitting beneath it.'

Clifford eyed his drink. 'Let us hope for Christmas' sake we survive the next round, Mrs Butters, for,' he said, shaking his head, 'I fear it is the dreaded chestnut liqueur. But first I believe a toast is in order.' He dinged his glass with a spoon to gain everyone's attention, and then nodded at Eleanor.

She held up her glass and looked around the table.

'I'm not the best at speeches, as you know, but I want to thank you all from the bottom of my heart for giving up your usual Christmas to come to Ranburgh. And for everything you do for me every day, always so willingly and so diligently. Even though I'm sure plenty of days I must have you tearing your hair out over missed meal schedules. To say nothing of all the other routines, which are still a bit of a mystery, if I'm honest. But, sincerely, thank you again and merry Christmas!'

Everyone clinked glasses, then Eleanor walked around the table, placing an envelope in front of each of the ladies. It was then she realised with embarrassment that she didn't have a present for the young Castle Ranburgh kitchen help. Clifford, however, came to her rescue.

'I believe your gift for Lizzie became separated, my lady.' He held out a tissue-wrapped parcel.

'Ah, there it is,' she said gratefully. 'Lizzie, thank you for everything you have done and will do for me. And for being a wonderful friend for Polly while we are here,' she whispered in the girl's ear.

Clearly overawed, the young maid managed a quiet, 'Thank you very kindly, your ladyship. I didn't expect nothing at all though. Not being part of your staff.'

As the ladies opened their envelopes with excited clucking, Lizzie unwrapped two pretty hexagonal tins, one of patterned shortbread biscuits, the other of tiny chocolate Florentines. She traced her finger over the pictures of fine ladies in beautiful dresses on the first, then those of the dapper gentlemen in carriages on the second. She stood and looked to Clifford, who indicated it was fine for her to speak up.

'Your ladyship, these are too special. Thank you.'

As she sat back down, Polly whispered to her, 'One for your hair things.'

'And one for flowers I shall start pressing like you do,' Lizzie whispered back.

'My lady!' Mrs Butters exclaimed, holding up the gold-embossed card she had pulled from her envelope, which Eleanor had had printed to look like a formal invitation. 'My stars, 'tis too much!'

'A trip to Boswells Department Store in Oxford!' Mrs Trotman cried. She clapped her hand over her mouth as Clifford suggested they needed to be quieter or they might wake the rest of the castle.

Mrs Butters helped Polly read hers, which was the same as the women's.

'For a new coat, hat, gloves and boots of—'

'Of your choosing,' Mrs Butters finished for her. 'Polly, my girl, we're going to be fitted out like proper ladies!'

The young maid trembled with excitement. 'Can we get matching ones?'

Eleanor laughed as Mrs Trotman shook her head in horror.

'The only rule,' Eleanor said, 'is that you each come away with exactly what you want. And then we'll all go for lunch by the river and explore the rest of Oxford before Clifford drives us back to Henley Hall. If that isn't against the rules?'

He pretended to consider the matter for a moment.

'After turning the ladies' heads with such overt, but richly deserved gratitudes, I think we can let it go just this once.'

Waiting until the others were all busy chattering together, she slid his envelope across to him.

'You're almost impossible to buy for, you know. You already have the full set of Voltaire's works and you mentioned a while back that you want for nothing in the way of fishing equipment. So, I took another route. Please say if I've got it wrong.'

'I sincerely doubt that is possible.' With his usual care, he slit the envelope open with a small knife he produced from his waist-coat pocket. 'My lady, that is beyond thoughtful.' He was clearly moved. 'A subscription to The Royal Society's revered journal *Philosophical Transactions*.'

'Which despite its name, is devoted entirely to science and engineering advances, I understand.' She pulled a face. 'Sounds deathly, if I'm honest.'

He shook his head, smiling. 'No, my lady, it sounds like endless hours of fascination. Thank you.'

'Time for games!' Mrs Butters said a while later, once most of the food had been eaten and the plates cleared.

'I vote for cards, seeing as winning at Christmas is extra lucky,' Mrs Trotman said. Eleanor's cook loved to gamble, if only a few shillings on cards and on the local pig derby.

As the rounds of pontoon rolled on, so did the cheerful chatter, until Mrs Trotman frowned while dealing the next hand.

'Not looking forward to that inspector chap coming back, are you, Butters?'

'Not a bit. He fair wasted time I could ill afford. Didn't take a blind bit of notice of anything I said, mind. He was so... what's the word?'

'Pompous?'

'And brusque.'

'And snappy,' Polly said, emboldened by the relaxed atmosphere. 'Didn't let me answer properly nothing he asked.'

'And sneaky,' Lizzie muttered.

Eleanor and Clifford shared a look.

'What was it about Inspector Lockhart that seemed sneaky?' Eleanor said gently.

The girl's face fell. 'Didn't mean to be rude, your ladyship. Nor to speak out of turn. Just, it was odd, him and Laird Dunburgh like that.' She stared down at her lap.

'Like what, Lizzie?' Clifford topped up the young girl's cordial.

'Huddled in a corner, whispering.' She paused and looked at Eleanor, who nodded encouragingly. 'Only the inspector had already told us downstairs he would talk to everyone in the library, in turn, so it just seemed odd them... them whispering, like I said, and Laird Dunburgh giving the inspector an envelope.'

Eleanor exchanged a look with Clifford. 'Did you see what was in the envelope by any chance, Lizzie?'

The girl nodded. 'Yes, m'lady. The inspector opened it and had a look but Laird Dunburgh seemed cross at him, so he put it away.'

'And what was it?'

'Money, m'lady. More than I've ever seen ever.'

Eleanor and Clifford shared another look.

'Have you told anyone else about this, Lizzie?'

'No, m'lady. Promise.'

'Then let's keep it as our secret, shall we?'

Before Lizzie could reply, Macduff the castle cat skittered past, hissing menace over his shoulder, followed by Gladstone, barking furiously, dripping with blood from a long scratch on his nose.

She stared after the two animals and then turned to her staff. 'Well, ladies, there doesn't seem much point in keeping quiet now, does there? Let's party!'

14

Eleanor's face was always the telltale barometer of her mental, and physical, state. Having partied until the early hours with her staff, it seemed bent on betraying her completely this particular morning. *Thankfully, Ellie, that is precisely why some ingenious soul invented kohl and rouge.*

She finished giving her cheeks a final extra pinch of colour in the gold-rimmed mirror as her stomach let out a loud gurgle. She groaned. *Finishing last night with several rounds of Mrs Trotman's walnut whisky might have been an error, Ellie!*

Before leaving her bedroom, she looked out once more at the fairy-tale Boxing Day scene. The snow had fallen silently all night and the peaks of the surrounding hills were coated in the pristine white blanket she'd dreamed about. The perfect Christmas chocolate-box scene.

Outside the breakfast room, she greeted Clifford with forced jollity.

'Morning. How's your head?'

'Still attached is perhaps the only surety, my lady.'

She grimaced. 'Same here. I have a head like a sore Scotsman.'

Gliding around her, he slipped a glass filled with a hideous-looking green concoction into her hand.

She peered at it. 'Penance or cure?'

'I believe the jury is yet out, my lady.'

'Good-oh!' She pinched her nose and swigged the contents down, recoiling with a violent shudder. 'Gah! Positively revolting! Definitely penance.'

'Heartening news.'

She shook her head and immediately regretted it. 'Honestly, when this is all over, I shall dispatch you back to butler school for a reminder of the appropriate protocol in dealing with your employer. Assuming, of course, such an establishment exists?'

'I am unaware of any establishment that can reconcile maintaining propriety with being coerced into drinking and wagering with the lady of the house and the rest of the staff. And until the most unseemly of hours at that.'

'Coerced? Ha! You and Mrs Trotman were fiendish when it was a case of winner-takes-all in the final hand of pontoon. And we were only playing for pennies. It was dashed good fun though, wasn't it?'

'I really couldn't say, my lady.' His coat-tails swished behind him as he turned to open the door for her. As she drew level, he added sotto voce, 'But, perhaps.'

As she stepped into the breakfast room, she scanned the long oak table hoping, as it was Boxing Day, the festive spirit would be uppermost. Unfortunately, it wasn't. Sir Edward Fortesque appeared to have irritated the mild-mannered Doctor Connell sufficiently for them to have angled their chairs away from each other. Opposite them, Gordon Cameron was engaged in taking the Laird to task, while further along the table Lady Fortesque was remonstrating in taut tones with Baron Ashley. The one person Eleanor had been hoping to see, Baroness Ashley, was the only one not present. She sighed to herself. *So much for everyone rallying around, Ellie.* She helped herself to sausages from the first of the silver salvers, overhearing Lady Fortesque as she did so.

'Disgracing the family name again, Clarence. As if the *other* matter wasn't enough!'

Baron Ashley threw his napkin onto the unbuttered toast on his side plate. 'Fanny, if family are not going to stick together, then what the deuce is the point of them coming together?'

'Because it is Christmas, cousin. Although you couldn't even manage to do the decent thing and stay in London. Dragging us all the way up here. Ridiculous!'

Eleanor caught Baron Ashley's eyes narrowing.

'At the risk of sounding churlish, *cousin*, I believe the invitation was of your *own* making.'

'Well, really!'

Baron Ashley sighed and ran a hand over his forehead. 'Look, Fanny, I'm not saying you and Edward aren't welcome. It's fine that you invited yourselves. You know I didn't invite you because I thought you wouldn't countenance Christmas here, given the family's general disapproval of my matrimonial match.'

'And how right you were! And how wrong we were to come! Not only have we found ourselves having to collude in a secret celebration of Christmas like naughty children, but we also had the indignity of being interviewed by the police over a *murder!*' She leaned forward. 'That we are now stuck on this ugly, icy, pile of rocks is unforgivable, Clarence. But why am I surprised? You surpassed even your previous idiocy when you became involved with that... *American.*' She rose and beckoned her husband with a crooked finger. 'Edward!'

As her husband hurried after her, Eleanor's brows knitted for a moment. At least the identity of the mystery guest she'd seen the night she'd arrived was solved. The man she'd seen look up and down the corridor on the second-floor landing and then hurry off had had a slight limp. And she saw the same limp now as Sir Edward passed her. Obviously, it only showed itself when he hurried. As if by an unspoken signal, Doctor Connell and Gordon Cameron followed the Fortesques out, neither of them showing any sign of a limp. The room fell silent, making Eleanor's clattering serving tongs sound horribly loud.

The Laird turned to her, his face momentarily betraying

annoyance – *maybe even anger, Ellie?* – rather than his usual geniality. However, on seeing who it was, his ready smile slipped back into place like a mask.

'Morning.' She added a third sausage and an equal number of eggs to her plate. In truth, she wanted to sit next to him as the most genial of the company remaining, but Clifford appeared at the Laird's elbow with a silver tray before she had the chance.

'A message for you, my lord.'

The Laird opened the note and eased himself out of his seat. With a nod to Eleanor, he strode to the door, clapping his host on the shoulder as he passed.

'I'll catch up with you later, old chap.'

Eleanor turned to Baron Ashley.

'Well, it seems like it's just you and me for breakfast. How are you holding up, Clarence?' She slid into the chair opposite, which Clifford's gloved hand held out for her.

'Oh, you know,' he said with a wan smile. 'Fine enough. As one must.' He shuffled the barely touched food around his plate, then seemed to catch himself. 'But, apologies, I'm being a dreadful host. How are you doing?' He looked up, focussing on her for the first time. 'Not too well, I see. So sorry.'

'Me?' Eleanor caught the almost imperceptible upward quirk of Clifford's lips as he stepped over to the salvers. *Dash it, Ellie! Not enough kohl and rouge.* 'Oh, it's just the excitement of Christmas. And' – she faltered, scrabbling for something positive to say – 'of course, being at Castle Ranburgh. It's quite the magical setting.'

Baron Ashley sighed. 'Not much of the Christmas you expected so far, I'm sure. For which, I can only apologise once more. Wilhelmina's dream of spending it up here has certainly nosedived into the depths of the loch, never to be seen again. Like her perhaps.'

Oh, Ellie!

'It can't be easy for either of you. How is she doing?'

'Honestly, I don't know.' His face fell. 'We haven't exchanged anything more than polite formalities since—'

Instinctively, she reached out and put her hand on his arm. He nodded with a weak smile, but his stiff upper lip quickly returned and he cleared his throat. 'She'll come round in time.'

In the awkward silence, Eleanor buttered her toast. She was stirring an absent-minded amount of sugar into her coffee when Baron Ashley jerked upright. He stared at her, his gaze so intense she felt prickles on her skin.

'I find it a total mystery, you know, Eleanor. Unfathomable, in fact.'

'Er, what? Randall's murder?'

He shook his head. 'No. Women! No offence, obviously. But I mean, how the devil is one supposed to fulfil their expectations without... without...' He waved an arm stiffly around the room. 'All this doesn't support itself. God knows it costs enough to keep up!'

Eleanor set down her cup. 'Clarence, I don't want to pry, but I hate to see you and Wilhelmina struggling together. Even temporarily, which I'm sure that's all this is. Is... *was*... Mr Randall the cause of your... difficulties?'

He opened his mouth as if to refute her suggestion, but instead nodded wearily.

'I guessed as much. But tell me, was Mr Randall actually here, not for Christmas, but because you shared a business interest?'

He closed his eyes momentarily and sighed. 'I had hoped so. But these things rarely run smoothly.' Again, he jerked into life. 'He should have seen it. The possibilities!' He waved his hand in the air. 'They're... practically limitless.'

Her mind ran back over the raised voices she had heard before she was introduced to Randall. What was it he had said so vehemently? That was it. 'Underhand tactics are for desperadoes.' *And Clarence had naturally seemed incensed by that, Ellie. Maybe Clifford was right to insist you included your host in the line-up of suspects.*

She took a sip of her coffee. 'So, Randall obviously didn't agree?'

'No, he didn't! Short-sighted fool.' He rubbed his hands over his drawn cheeks. 'Or he was a shrewder negotiator than I gave him credit for. He might have simply been pretending he wasn't interested to try and drag a better deal out of me at the last minute!'

Keen though she was to find out what that entailed, Eleanor bit her tongue and let him continue.

'Either way, I'm the real fool.' He took a deep breath. 'Wilhelmina, poor girl, I should never have ruined her life with all my faults. She's so young. So bright. It's no wonder she acted that way.'

'Clarence,' Eleanor said firmly. 'It's not my place, I know, but whatever problems have cropped up, Wilhelmina married you for love. Just as you did her.' She smiled wistfully. 'That was evident the first moment I met you both. Long before we'd even been introduced, actually. And why I agreed to come up here for Christmas. To spend the festive season with a couple who married for love, not duty or necessity. And, since we're unexpectedly sharing, I confess it restored my faith that matters of the heart might finally work out even for me one day.'

He stared at her in surprise. She nodded and stabbed a fork into her sausage.

'So, no more thoughts about business matters spilling over and spoiling the ultimate idyllic romance that you two embody. Anyway, if Randall couldn't see the merits of your proposal, someone else surely will. Like the Laird, perhaps? He seems very keen to bring regeneration to the area.'

Baron Ashley nodded slowly. 'Yes, he's a man for the local people. And something of a good egg too. But,' he said, looking over his shoulder, 'he's already on board. We really needed Randall too to make up the shortfall.'

'Ah!'

Well, Ellie, that seems to knock Clarence – and the Laird – off our suspect list, despite Clarence's row with Randall.

Baron Ashley picked up his refilled cup and drained its contents in one go. 'Best get on, if you'll excuse me.' He half rose, but then sank back down. 'Eleanor, I'm sorry for rabbiting on like that. I'm supposed to be your host. Whatever must you think.'

She flapped a gently dismissive hand. 'Don't be daft, I was just as much the confessional rabbit.'

But her words only seemed to increase his anxiety.

'Confessional?' He ran a finger around his collar.

'Clarence, I didn't mean to say anything out of turn.'

'None of us ever do. Like we never mean to do anything hurtful, either.' This time, he stood. 'As I've made a fool of myself in the eyes of my guests, my beloved wife and, now horrendously, you, I might as well finish the job.' His tone turned pleading. 'Eleanor, if it comes to it, I shall need a favour which is a frightful cheek as we aren't actually that well acquainted.'

'Anything, Clarence. Although' – she hesitated – 'honestly, I think we are considerably better acquainted after this breakfast conversation, which I greatly appreciate.'

'Thank you. Me too, in a way. Then if, no probably *when* it comes to it, please tell Wilhelmina it was all for her. Everything was for her. And I am desperately sorry.'

He pushed his chair back and hurried through the door Clifford held open for him.

'Whisky is an institution in Scotland, dear lady,' the Laird said with a fierce pride that was echoed in the way his son's chest swelled at the words.

Eleanor laughed. 'Ah, a veritable gentleman's paradise, then.'

He chuckled and slapped his son on the back. She found his easy laughter infectious, his ginger whiskers dancing with each chuckle as he took her on a tour of the castle's tiny island. There was something reassuring about his presence. Perhaps it was because his relaxed demeanour provided a welcome buffer to his son's far more brusque manner. Physically, no one could have confused that they were father and son, but their personalities! Mind, the Laird had told her that his father had sent him to England to be educated at Eton, something the Laird had decided against for Gordon. *Which explains a lot about each man's outlook,* Eleanor mused. *And even the way they speak. Take away the Laird's Highland accent and it would be hard to distinguish him from any Eton-educated English lord.*

The three of them stared out over Loch Vale to the ribbon of water cascading down the slope of the snow-capped, slate-grey mountainside. From this distance, even the tall pine trees looked like cake decorations. They had stopped far from the main buildings, in the lee of a narrow free-standing stone fort. It rose four storeys but was only the width of three men. The Laird nodded to Clifford, who placed a fold-out table and three chairs on the only patch of even ground not covered in an inch or two of snow. From somewhere he produced a miniature sandbag and draped it over the table's cross-members to make sure no drink was spilled. The sun was shining, but there was a cold wind whipping over the hills and water, made even colder by the snow. *Nevertheless*, Eleanor thought, *it is one of the most spectacularly beautiful places to be on Boxing Day.*

'Our whisky is so superior because our water is so pure,' the Laird continued. 'And our barley is of the finest quality. They are, as they have been since the fifteenth century, a marriage wedded in heaven.' He cleared his throat and stood straighter. '"Fortune! if thou'll but gie me still. Hale breeks, a scone, an' whisky gill."'

'Sorry?'

He gestured to the table and waited until she sat before taking his chair. 'Not a poetry fan, I see.'

She wrinkled her nose. 'I have tried.'

He smiled. 'Well, forgive me for silently tutting, for you are missing out to my mind. If you ever fancy a dabble, I suggest starting with the author of those lines, for he was a master of his art.'

'I'll think about it. Although I have no idea who it was.'

Clifford placed a silver tray, set with four small whisky measures in crystal-cut tumblers on the table. 'But my butler will know.'

The two other men looked confused until Clifford spoke. 'I believe, my lady, his lordship was quoting the eminent national bard, Robert Burns. From his poem "Scotch Drink", first published in the Kilmarnock Volume in 1785.'

The Laird nodded appreciatively. 'Your man is surprisingly knowledgeable about our culture for a servant. And an English one at that.'

'Aye, but that were nay appropriate,' Gordon muttered.

Clifford placed two silver-handled dishes partitioned into three in the centre of the table and stepped back. Eleanor peered at the offerings and frowned.

What on earth? He's finally flipped, Ellie! Oysters, cheese and chocolate for a Boxing Day picnic?

The Laird's face lit up as he nudged the nearest dish closer to her. 'Whisky tasting is another of our fair nation's arts. And your man knows what goes well with it, as well as he knows our national poet!'

She mentally admonished herself for doubting her infallible butler.

'I'm up for the challenge, although' – she peered at the accompaniments again – 'I am beginning to wonder why I ever bothered to travel abroad to experience unusual customs. I could simply have come up here to Scotland. Which, I must admit, I've never visited before.'

Gordon swirled the amber liquid in his glass thoughtfully. 'And why is that, Lady Swift?' He knocked back two oysters with practiced skill.

'Well, I spent most of my life abroad as a child. And, in fact, my early adulthood, with the exception of a gap in between when I was not in charge of such decisions. I've been back in England less than two years, so I haven't really had the opportunity.'

'Dear lady' – the Laird gestured at the view – 'tell us, what is your impression so far?'

'In a word, breathtaking. I only wish I had more time and perhaps the weather was more conducive, so I could take a proper tour of the area. And, of course, if I had access to a boat. But that will have to wait until Inspector Lockhart sees fit to return Clarence's, it seems.' She paused, considering her next words carefully. 'But then, I'd love to see where Clarence's new business venture would be based.'

Gordon's fork hesitated in hovering over the slender wedges of various cheeses. He looked up at his father, who ignored him.

'That, dear lady, would be a tour Clarence and I would both be delighted to take you on. In more clement weather, that is. You would need the stoutest of snow boots today. Nobody wants a resort at the bottom of a mountain.'

'Aye, Father, and some dunnay want it at all,' Gordon said.

Aha! So, it's a resort Clarence has in mind, Ellie.

She cocked her head at Gordon. 'Holidaymakers would generate a great deal of income and employment, wouldn't they? Or is that an ignorant assumption?'

The Laird smiled. 'No, dear lady, it isn't at all. Hence why I am right behind Clarence on this. His idea of a ski resort is inspired. The Scottish ski club has been running successfully for well over ten years now. And the popularity among our class for travelling to the European slopes has been increasing steadily. What better luxury than being able to indulge only a hop and skip from one's home. It will provide opportunity and employment in the area for years to come.'

Ellie tried a sip of whisky followed by an oyster chaser. It was surprisingly good. 'My old employer and friend, Thomas Walker, would love to hear your plans.' The Laird's smile faltered. 'Rest assured,' she hurried on, 'he wouldn't muscle in on your idea since he is firmly of the mind that holidays should be taken abroad.' She shivered. 'And preferably in warmer climes.'

'Your old employer?' The Laird's smile had swiftly returned. 'The founder of the world-famous travel company of the same name? Forgive me, I'm intrigued.'

'Yes, that's him. I happened to bump into him when I was travelling through Siam. We got on famously and he asked if I would scout out new routes for him. When I was done reshaping unmentionable parts of my anatomy with a bicycle saddle, of course.'

This brought a loud guffaw from the Laird and even a half smile to Gordon's face. It also drew a quiet sniff from Clifford, who had materialised to refill their whiskies.

'And where did you do the majority of your intrepid scouting?' the Laird asked.

'Oh, all over, but South Africa mainly. I scouted out new safari routes for his more adventurous clients. I think Mr Walker made an error on not sending me here though. Despite the, er, variable weather. It is truly beautiful.'

'But nay for long if some have their way,' Gordon said, back to his brooding self.

She turned and smiled at him. 'Mr Cameron, are you not a fan of skiing, then?'

'Aye, I am. But as a means of getting about in the deeper winter months. Nay' – he raised a finger – 'as a sport, and certainly nay one worthy of decimating our lands for.'

'Progress cannot always falter in the face of tradition, son. Nor heritage.'

'Perhaps, Father.' Gordon scraped the feet of his chair over the stones as he stood up abruptly. 'But what *you two* have planned is more like dumping the two at the bottom of the loch, to my mind. Lady Swift, if you'll excuse me.' He strode away, his thick-heeled boots kicking up pieces of slate from the path.

The Laird's amiable demeanour momentarily faltered. Then there it was again, that genial smile back in place as if by the flick of a switch.

'Please excuse my son. He is a staunch supporter of our people, as am I, but he is fearful of progress on their behalf.'

'A noble stance.'

'But not one he manages to articulate without breathing the fire of fierceness that burns in his breast.'

The image made her smile. 'I can handle a metaphorical roasting, don't worry.'

The Laird chuckled again and then looked her over like a grandfather seeing his grandchild for the first time. 'I knew you would be a remarkable young woman, of course, but it seems the passing of time has merely nourished your family's spirit like' – he held up his glass – 'a fine whisky.'

Eleanor's heart skipped. 'You knew my uncle?'

He shook his head. 'Sadly no. Although I heard a great deal about him. A gentleman of the most exceptional talents.'

'Then who—?'

She glanced over at Clifford, who quirked a brow indicating he had no idea either.

The Laird offered his hand. 'Dear lady, will you permit me to conclude our tour at the fort there? There is something I think you would love to see.'

Her natural impetuousness made her leap up. 'Of course.' However, in her peripheral vision, Clifford's suited form shifted a step closer and she hesitated.

The Laird glanced over his shoulder. 'Does your man fear I may be the murderer in our midst?' He grunted. 'Then bring him along.'

She saw Clifford relax.

'Thank you,' she said. 'I think we are all naturally a little... cautious at the moment.'

'Naturally.' He turned and led the way.

The fort had the forlorn air deserted buildings always take on. As Clifford shouldered open the massive oak door, which screeched on rusty hinges, the unmistakable smell of old birds' nests and damp hit them. The only light came from a few narrow slits cut high up in the rough-hewn stones, allowing shards of light to pierce the walls like the slashes of a dagger.

Clifford produced a long, slim torch and offered it to the Laird.

'Perfect, man. Ever prepared, I see.'

On the fan-shaped stone steps, she had to keep to the wider part to avoid tripping off the tapered edge. Spirals of dust and tiny white feathers rose in the shafts of daylight and the torch's beam as the Laird led the way. Glad of her thick coat, she couldn't resist running her hand over the walls as she climbed behind him. Even with Clifford's presence, she wondered now about her foolhardy acceptance of this invitation. Her mind briefly flitted back to the envelope of money Lizzie had seen the Laird hand Lockhart. Randall had been stabbed only a short while before and here she was in a deserted tower with a potential murderer.

It seemed Clifford, as usual, had read her mind, for he held up another, longer, heavier-looking torch. That he grasped it by the wrong end told her it had to be one of her late uncle's wonderful inventions. Likely it doubled as a cosh.

As they emerged at the top of the tower, she was distracted by the even more spectacular view offered by their elevated position. The piercing cry of an eagle echoed around the snow-capped hills.

The Laird pointed to the far right where a rift in the snowy mountains running down to the edge of the loch suggested there was another world beyond. With her hand over her eyes as she squinted, she could just make out a channel of water flowing out of sight.

'I wanted to show you the Straits of An-Dòchas,' the Laird said. 'Notoriously dangerous and well-nigh unnavigable. There is still only one person who has ever managed to sail through at high tide when the waters run fastest and most deadly.' The Laird's tone held a hint of awe.

'One of your relatives?'

'No, dear lady. One of yours.'

16

Had there been a chair behind her, Eleanor would have fallen back into it.

'You knew my parents?'

Since their disappearance, she had yearned to find out anything she could about them, as if she could somehow make up for all those missing years. And here, unexpectedly, was another chance, however small.

The Laird scanned her face before replying. 'Not as well as I wished, sadly. I met them through the previous owner of Castle Ranburgh. They were quite an extraordinary couple. That your mother readily accepted the challenge from a local sailor who told her it was impossible to navigate those straits at high tide is evidence enough. But it was also evident in the other times our paths crossed during the short time that they honeymooned up here.'

Formality could have leaped from the top of the fort for all she cared as she spun round to Clifford. 'Did you know this?'

'Indeed not, my lady. I would have said in advance. His lord-ship merely mentioned that Scotland had been a destination his sister and his new brother-in-law enjoyed on their honeymoon, but he did not state where in Scotland.'

'Oh, gracious!' She breathed. 'They honeymooned *here*.'

The Laird was watching the exchange carefully. 'I know that you lost your parents at an early age. My sincere apologies if I've caused you upset. They had the deep-seated love and ease of a longer married couple. I had no idea they were honeymooning when I first met them.' He shook his head. 'How could I? What titled lady would choose to go mountaineering and sailing in Scotland over elegant dancing and dinners on the Riviera coast?'

'Only my mother, perhaps.' Eleanor smiled fondly, remembering.

'And her daughter too, I have a strong suspicion. It was many years ago now, but I still remember her. And looking at you, it's as if she were here again.' He shrugged. 'I wish there was more to tell you, but our encounters were brief. They did dine with my wife and I one evening at Castle Dunburgh where they told me of their educational work abroad. Suffice to say, they left an endearing memory and an enduring legacy in your mother's incredible sailing accomplishment.'

Taking the field glasses Clifford held out, Eleanor focussed on the distant straits again. Memories of her parents swam back and forth: waves washing over the boat, her mother calm at the helm, her father up the wildly swaying mast grappling with the sail.

Ellie, the minute we can get off this island, we have to go to those straits. Maybe, just maybe, we'll feel a connection. Something. Anything.

'Clifford?' she said, without lowering the field glasses.

'Yes, of course, my lady,' he said softly. 'I will make all the arrangements at the first opportunity. With the inclusion of an exquisite velvet bag for the many stones you will collect from the shoreline, no doubt.'

She turned and gave him a warm smile. Not just for having read her thoughts, but because she knew he would somehow engineer to be free to accompany her.

Again, the Laird watched their exchange with interest. He put a gentlemanly hand on her arm. 'I should leave you with your memories, dear lady. May the news lay a few ghosts to rest, perhaps?'

'More than you could know. Thank you so much.' She turned back to examining the straits, listening to his footsteps recede down the staircase.

It was almost half an hour later that she tore herself away from the tower. And then only because Clifford pointed out that it had started snowing again and she could return later with a pair of her uncle's hand warmers and a small flask of brandy revivers. As he jerked the door closed on its screeching hinges, she ran her hand through her curls, brushing out the newly falling snowflakes.

'Are you alright, my lady?'

'Better than ever, if a little bowled over, Clifford, thank you. It's incredible. And marvellously comforting that my parents were here.'

She shoved her hands into her coat pockets as they set off along the winding path. After a few moments of silence, she glanced at him.

'What do you make of the Laird, Clifford? He seems so genial and generous-spirited but yet—'

'Yet, there is the odd hint of a rather different gentleman residing underneath?'

'Precisely. You too then?'

'Since you have asked my opinion, especially after Lizzie's information, I confess, my judgement has one leg dangling on the side of doubt.'

A snorted laugh erupted from her. 'You have no idea how much I wish I could ask Wilhelmina to paint that as a portrait of you for me to hang in Henley Hall. Mr Ever-Impeccably-Suited teetering inelegantly on the edge of the fence. Too fabulous for words!'

He sniffed. 'Fortunately, during the Christmas Eve preprandial drinks, I overheard Lady Ashley telling Mr Randall in quite firm tones that she does not take commissions.'

'Dashed shame, that.'

'The truth is, my lady, the Laird comes from a lengthy line of leaders of the Highland clans. Even today, such a man needs to have grit in his constitution if he is to be respected. I believe he merely disguises his iron fist in a velvet glove, as is the modern way.'

She nodded. 'Perhaps that iron fist plunged a dagger into Randall, velvet glove or not. We must find out if he had any direct dealings with Randall, or if everything went through Clarence. And what that money he gave Lockhart was for.'

'Indeed. Although one might employ considerably more caution. No more scampering up isolated forts alone with any of the other guests, for example. Certainly not until Inspector Lockhart has hauled the murderer from the island.'

'Those steps were too steep and uneven for scampering. I'd twist an ankle.'

He gave her a steely look. 'Promise?'

'Why do I feel like Henderson when he's irked you beyond all reason?'

'I really couldn't say, my lady. Although short of locking you in the castle's dungeon, deeply concerned is the only card I can play.'

She sighed. 'Alright, I promise.'

'Thank you.'

'And in case it makes you less anxious, rest assured, you would never find me alone at all, ever, with Gordon Cameron. I don't trust him an inch.'

'Might I enquire why not, my lady?'

'Seriously? How about because he is permanently brooding and angry, and ungentlemanly enough to show it? He was unspeakably rude to you after you'd noted the Laird had quoted Robert Burns' poem. Formality aside, he denounced you having spoken up even though I'd asked you to.'

Clifford gave a quiet cough.

'What now? Don't tell me that you can find a redeeming feature in that man.'

'In regard to the gentleman's comment of it being "Nay appropriate"? Yes, my lady, since I believe he was, in fact, reprimanding his father, not me.'

'For what exactly?'

'Quoting that particular poem.'

'But I thought Burns was the literary hero of the Scots? Why would he mind his father quoting that poem?'

'From Mr Cameron's stance on Christmas I deduce he is devout in his religious beliefs. And Mr Burns' opening epigraph quotes Solomon's Proverbs, Chapter thirty-one, verses six and seven from the Bible. Some have suggested his biblical reference was a pointed censure of the Calvinist beliefs, they being at the foundation of the Presbyterian doctrine which Mr Cameron seems to hold dear.'

'Ah!'

'And the other reason I believe he may have been censoring his father is' – Clifford's hand strayed to his tie – 'the opening line of the poem. "Gie him strong drink until he... wink.", my lady.'

'Oh, gracious! We're back to the dashed wink murder game where it all went so wrong for Randall. Well, Gordon is obviously set against this resort idea that Clarence and the Laird had hoped Randall would invest in.' She stopped abruptly. 'Set against it enough to kill Randall, do you suppose?'

'Perhaps, my lady.'

'Hmm. It seems we suspect both father and son equally.' She frowned. 'But laying that aside for the moment, I'm worried about Clarence, you know. He was like a man possessed at breakfast. So up and down, filled with despair one minute, then suddenly animated the next. I'm not sure he said anything of sense. Although the strain of this is clearly driving a wedge between him and Wilhelmina. You must have seen it too.'

He replied with only his best impassive butler expression.

She sighed, a corner of her heart aching. 'They're newlyweds,

Clifford. Well, they've only been married a year or so at most. Imagine if this awful business did the unthinkable and finished their marriage off before it ever had a chance? They both took an enormous gamble in marrying, given their age and class difference.'

He adjusted the seams of his gloves. 'Unthinkable indeed. In which case, to ease your mind, it might be worth noting that Lord Ashley ate nothing last night, nor this morning. But he did devour several cups of very strong coffee at breakfast. A possible explanation for the irregularity of his mood.'

'Possibly, but I think it may be more than that. Between us, I got the impression that he is in a mire of trouble over something.'

Clifford nodded. 'As to the nature of which, Lady Ashley it seems is entirely unaware.'

'And added to that, his only hope of an investor is murdered at his own table. Poor man. At least that seems to put him in the clear for Randall's murder. And the Laird too, since he supports the project.' She pulled out her notebook and wrote next to each name.

The Laird

Motive? No motive. Supported Clarence's scheme, so needed Randall alive!

Evidence? Lizzie saw the Laird give Lockhart an envelope full of money. For what?

Gordon Cameron (Laird's son)

Motive? Wanted to stop Clarence's scheme that Randall was financing.

Evidence? Openly outspoken against it, but nothing else so far.

Clarence

Motive? No motive – needed Randall alive to finance his scheme!

Evidence? None so far.

She tapped her chin with the pen and then frowned.

'You know, Lady Fortesque was very vocal about Randall to Clarence at breakfast. She had no time for him at all. Nor for "the other matter" that she was tearing him off a strip about.'

'The resort, do you think, my lady?'

'I guess. But why would she care? She clearly never comes up here.'

'Lady Fortesque is renowned for her unwavering determination in achieving recognition of her position, shall we say? Financial ruin in any part of the family would be seen as shameful to disastrous.'

'That's not really a reason to kill Randall though, is it?' She tutted. 'A social climber and the poor-ish cousin of a baron?' She mused, considering. 'That can't be easy if you let social standing define who you are, as I know all too well.'

He arched a brow. 'Do you, my lady? Then perhaps there is still some hope.'

17

The castle seemed eerily quiet later that morning as Eleanor descended the main stairs. She'd taken a bath to warm up after being chilled to the bone standing at the top of the tower.

The Ashleys' footman appeared at a door, the very same one through which she had overheard the raised voices on Christmas Eve.

'Ah, Henderson.'

The young man turned respectfully and stood, hands behind his back. But he seemed on edge. *Not surprising, Ellie, there has been a murder. And he is one of our suspects!*

'My lady?'

'Where might I find Lady Ashley?'

'In her suite. However, her ladyship requested she nay be further disturbed.'

There was something in those two final words that struck a discordant note.

'Hmm. Did she tell you that herself?'

'Nay, my lady. The message came via his lordship.'

Just as we thought, Ellie. She told Clarence to leave her alone, and he has relayed that as a general instruction to spare both their blushes.

'Henderson, please return with a tray of whatever Lady Ashley favours as a tipple and a large selection of chocolate.'

'As you wish, my lady.'

She hid a smile. Henderson had unwittingly adopted one of Clifford's signature phrases in less than two days. Her butler's firm but fair hand and Mrs McKenzie's absence were clearly wearing down his mutinous tendencies. Although, if he had stabbed Randall then, along with those mutinous tendencies, he obviously had murderous ones. But why?

On his return, she took the tray from him and dispatched him back to whatever duties she'd dragged him from. She knocked with her foot on the carved set of double doors he had led her to.

'I said my piece this morning,' came the taut reply. 'Just let me be.'

'Wilhelmina, it's Eleanor. I wondered—' She reeled backwards as the door was flung open.

'Oh, Eleanor, thank you so much!' The young baroness' normally rosy cheeks were alabaster pale, her eyes rimmed red. 'Do come in.'

Eleanor looked the distraught woman over, noting the thick blanket around her shoulders and the belted mustard cardigan she wore over a mismatched pink jumper. 'Are you sure? I only want to check you are alright. However, I did bring the ultimate make-everything-bearable-if-only-for-a-few-delicious-moments medicine.' She tipped the tray, making the plate bearing an impressive display of chocolates nestled on an ivory napkin clink against the bottle of sherry and the two crystal glasses.

Baroness Ashley let out something between a laugh and a sob and threw her slender arms around Eleanor. 'Thank you. That's so sweet. But, oh goodness, I'm sorry.' She pulled back. 'Whatever must you think. I've been a terrible hostess since you arrived and here I am now making you stand in the corridor. Come in! Please do.'

Eleanor carefully entered Baroness Ashley's bedroom, tentatively balancing the tray and wondering how Clifford managed it with much larger trays filled with all manner of spillables. *Perhaps, he glues the tray to his hand, Ellie?* She set it down and turned back to the baroness.

'Well, I haven't even been a hostess. I should have invited you and Clarence to Henley Hall months ago, as I've intended to ever since we met at Lady Langham's but—'

'But you aren't one for formal entertaining. I gathered that. And' – she closed the door – 'after all of this, I'm not sure I shall ever be again either.'

Eleanor tutted. 'Don't be silly, Wilhelmina, it's hardly likely anything like this is going to happen again if you entertain.'

Baroness Ashley sighed. 'I suppose not. Do excuse me a moment.' She attended to her streaked make-up while Eleanor took in the room's exquisite decor. Two cornflower-blue velvet settees faced each other across a thick silk rug of vibrant sunshine orange. Matching cushions and floor-length curtains echoed the two colours in the upholstered window seat. But it was the artwork that entranced her.

'Wilhelmina, is this all by your hand?' She pointed to the many twirling branches of a fruit-laden orange tree, covering the room's inset ceiling panel, all inhabited by a raft of exotic birds and animals.

'It is. But it's not to everyone's tastes. That's why I stopped in this suite.'

Eleanor kneeled to stare at two darling velvet grey mice, gazing back at her from their mouse hole, their tiny pink front feet together as if holding hands. 'I've never seen anything so perfectly beautiful. Nor so lifelike. If I were small enough, I would scamper through there and snuggle up with this loving couple.'

'Goodness, thank you. But it's just a technique. Trompe l'oeil or "trick of the eye" to roughly translate. I'm sure you've heard of it.'

'Yes, but I'm not sure I've ever seen such a wonderful example. If you had time and took commissions, I would ask you to paint something, anything, of this exquisite make-believe reality at Henley Hall.'

Baroness Ashley smiled wanly. 'If you start entertaining and invite me, I'll paint whatever you want.'

'Deal, if only to appease my staff. They are forever complaining that I rattle around Henley Hall on my own. Seriously though, these two mice remind me of how you and Clarence... usually are.'

Baroness Ashley hung her head. 'You're very perceptive, Eleanor. I... I didn't mean to push him away, but this whole episode has got the better of me. And he's been acting quite unlike the man I married. And with the other matter as well, I've got a bit muddled, if I'm honest.'

What is this other matter, Ellie? Has Clarence's change of character been caused purely by stress over his money worries or was there some darker cause? Had he been planning Randall's murder for some weeks?

Eleanor went over and put her arm around the baroness' shoulder. 'If you hadn't got a little confused, I would think you are a most peculiar specimen, you know.' She steered her to the nearest settee. She poured them both a sherry and placed the plate of chocolates in the young woman's lap. 'Now, what's it to be? Nuts, liqueur or fondant filling?'

'All of the above,' Baroness Ashley said with more animation. 'But I'm still being a terrible hostess.'

'No. You're being human. And soon enough you'll be sufficiently restored to go back to being the wonderful wife Clarence adores.'

'Adored. That was before...' Thrusting her glass at Eleanor, she fumbled for a handkerchief but came up empty. Tears tipped over her lashes and ran down her cheeks. 'Before it all went wrong.'

'Oh gracious, we need Clifford.' Eleanor whipped the napkin out from underneath the chocolates and handed it to the young woman. 'He's much better at this sort of thing. He has a seemingly limitless supply of pristine handkerchiefs in his pockets. That's probably why I never have one if he's ever not there. Instead, I end up being incredibly unladylike and start using my sleeves or the hostess' tablecloth. Anything to hand, in fact.'

Baroness Ashley laughed as she dabbed at her eyes. 'I can't tell you how refreshing you are to be with, Eleanor. Marrying Clarence'– she paused and stared over at the two mice – 'was so much more than I could have ever dreamed of. But I wished on our wedding day he wasn't a baron. I'm not sure I don't still.' She shrugged. 'Isn't that ridiculous? Most women of my... my standing would bite a baron's arm off if offered his hand. But I love Clarence for who he is.... or *was*. But his title. And family. It's... it's all so daunting.'

Eleanor patted her arm. 'I know how you feel. Between you and me, I still don't really understand what I'm supposed to do or say half the time as a lady of the manor. But it's getting easier and more familiar every day.'

'Really?'

'Really.' She took the young woman's hands in hers. 'Wilhelmina, can I be frank? I think Clarence would give up his baronetcy in a moment if he could and that was what you wanted.'

Baroness Ashley pulled away. 'I'm not at all sure about that. Not after... everything.'

Eleanor thought back to the broken man she'd breakfasted with. 'Well, I am.'

Baroness Ashley pointed to the window seat, her tears still trickling down. 'That's where Clarence would fold me into his lap and sit and read or sing to me for hours on our previous visits to Ranburgh. But now...'

Eelanor's own lone evenings with only her faithful bulldog to cuddle up to made her chest constrict for a moment. 'And he will again. Trust me, Wilhelmina. Clarence is still the man you fell in love with.' *You hope he is, Ellie!*

'Thank you. And' – Baroness Ashley sniffed back her tears and clinked glasses with her – 'if you'll forgive me being so frank, I hope to be sitting in Henley Hall one day, saying the same to you.'

Eleanor raised her glass. 'Here's to that. Before I'm a totally hopeless cause.'

They both laughed and then munched in silent companionship for a moment, Eleanor dreaming of being ensconced in the window seat with a certain impossibly handsome, if gruff, detective chief inspector.

Baroness Ashley turned her glass in her hand. 'What did you think of Mr Randall?'

'Oh, well, I didn't really speak to him that much. I didn't get the chance before he—' Eleanor cursed her runaway tongue.

Baroness Ashley nodded. 'Was murdered? I know. I still can't believe it.' She drew her legs up under her. 'He didn't deserve that. Whatever kind of man he was.'

Eleanor glanced at her sharply. 'No, he didn't. But what kind of man do you think he was?'

'The worst kind!' Baroness Ashley blurted out. She paled and bit her lip. 'How... how terrible of me. He died in our house and here I am saying awful things about him. It... it must be the stress.'

It doesn't sound like stress to me, Ellie. It sounds like the truth. Perhaps, just perhaps, Clifford was right to make you include your hostess as well as your host in the suspect list!

Baroness Ashley leaped to her feet and paced the room, her cheeks flushed. 'And Clarence, he... he left me to face it all. I tried to do the right thing, but I had no idea what I was doing.' She shook her head violently. 'Oh, what a mess!' She spun around, her eyes wide at Eleanor's nodding. 'But... but how did you know?'

'Because I felt for you every time Clarence was caught up with Mr Randall on Christmas Eve, leaving you to shoulder the responsibility for the guests. I could see you needed his support, not, you know, really knowing all the formalities and what to say. Not to mention the problem with the staff.'

'Oh, you mean that. Yes, yes, that was it.' Baroness Ashley flopped back down, suddenly listless. She pushed the chocolates around on the plate between them. 'The walnut ones are nice.'

So that wasn't it, Ellie.

She surreptitiously scanned the young woman's face. Popping another chocolate in her mouth, she let the salty sweetness of the caramel dissolve on her tongue as she chose her next words carefully. 'Were you worried about Clarence... before the awful business at the Christmas Eve dinner, then?'

'In... in what way?'

'I just thought you seemed so upset. So upset that maybe it was something... more long-standing?'

Baroness Ashley smiled, but it didn't quite reach her beautiful blue eyes. 'I can see you're going to be the shrewdest friend I'll ever have.' She let out a long sigh. 'I can confide in you that Clarence isn't in the best place... financially. Although I shouldn't say. Especially as he thinks I don't know. He's played this whole resort scheme as something he's doing for prestige. A feather in the cap of the Ashley family name. Not as a last-ditch attempt to solve his money worries, which is what it is.' She put down her glass and rose. 'It was sweet of you to come. And, yes, Clarence was a good man. When I married him.' As she closed the door behind Eleanor, Eleanor's sharp ears heard her mutter. 'But I never believed he would put his wife's honour second to business!'

18

Dressing for Boxing Day lunch had turned into something of a major dilemma for Eleanor. Christmas Eve had been a washout in terms of celebrating, even the dinner being close to inedible. And, to cap it all off, one of the guests had been murdered at the table! With the arrival of Inspector Lockhart and the police, Christmas Day had virtually been cancelled. For her hosts' sanity and the guests', she hoped this meal would pass off without a hitch. And certainly without another dead body!

But what to wear? She let out a long sigh. *Do you think anyone has some seasonal good cheer left, Ellie?* She nodded to herself. *Yes. Me! And somehow I'm going to help Wilhelmina make this a Boxing Day she'll remember for all the right reasons.*

Opening the heavy ebony wardrobe, she stared at the row of fine gowns with matching shawls, afternoon tea dresses and in-between ensembles that Mrs Butters had packed for her.

What on earth is appropriate, Ellie? How do you dress for seasonal gaiety and yet at the same time show some respect that a man died less than forty-eight hours ago?

A folded note skimmed under the door, coming to a stop at her feet. She picked it up and read:

*The snowdrop and primrose our woodlands adorn, and violets
bathe in the wet o' the morn.*

She smiled and reached out for the dress she had yet to wear
outside of twirling in front of her bedroom mirror at Henley Hall.
One of her mother's she'd discovered her late uncle had preserved
in honour of his beloved sister. In the softest of blackberry-violet
velvet, the delicate scoop of the neckline nestled demurely against
her collarbones while the full-length sleeves, ending in matching
silk-ribboned cuffs, sat perfectly at her wrists. The fitted bodice
hugged her, as it had her mother. The lightly pleated skirt swished
a few inches above her ankles, cutting just the right tone. What
made it even more perfect was the delicately embroidered spray of
ivory and vanilla yellow buds swirling up from the hemline and
running around the waist sash. It was respectful, elegant, yet
quietly cheerful. But above all, it was warm! *If only a certain, handsome, detective inspector could be here to see how it makes you
glow, Ellie.*

In the drawing room, Clifford glided around, serving glasses of hot
spiced punch. The delicious scents of red wine, whisky, cinnamon,
citrus and cloves infused the air. Even Henderson seemed to have a
spring in his step as he followed behind, proffering oven-warmed
canapés. Like the other guests, Eleanor was in raptures over the
tiny pastry cups filled with salmon mousse, smoked cheese and
peppered mackerel flakes. The slender toast fingers with duck paté
and orange slices were sublime, the watercress and bacon
pinwheels too heavenly. Then there were the herb-dressed olives,
and mushroom and Stilton palmiers.

*And there's still lunch to come, Ellie. Hurrah for Mrs Trotman
making the most of having free rein in the kitchen while Mrs
McKenzie is absent!*

With the room chattering more readily than at any time since
she had arrived at Ranburgh, she rose and stood beside the tall

Christmas tree. Hung with red and gold baubles that matched the room's decor, its myriad miniature candle lanterns offered the soft halo of positive tidings. Looking around the room, she delighted in drinking in the long-awaited genial atmosphere.

The Laird, smartly attired in a velvet plum jacket, was regaling the more conservatively suited Doctor Connell with an amusing anecdote, Gordon Cameron resplendent in his kilt, occasionally adding to his father's story. Even the Fortesques had been bitten by the festive spirit and were listening attentively.

Thus, when the door opened and the baron led his wife into the room, it was a very different atmosphere from the one that had greeted Eleanor on Christmas Eve. Even the worry, anger and remorse she had witnessed in her hosts' faces earlier had dissipated like the gossamer curl of white smoke which wafted up the chimney from the crackling fire.

The baroness patted her husband's arm as she left him to see to the other guests, while she came over to join Eleanor.

'You look absolutely stunning.' She glanced around the room and lowered her voice. 'I'm so sorry about earlier.'

Eleanor smiled. 'You look stunning too, Wilhelmina. And there's nothing to be sorry for. It was just two friends sharing over way too much irresistible chocolate.'

They both laughed.

'And your cook!' Baroness Ashley waved at the array of platters. 'Those appetisers are simply divine. I'm—' She looked over to her where her husband stood, looking dapper in his holly-green jacket. He smiled lovingly back at her. '*We* are so delighted you're here and very grateful for your support. And for your friendship.'

Eleanor slid her arm through the young woman's, relieved to see she had recovered some of her sparkle. 'Likewise, Wilhelmina, truly. But if you think the appetisers are good, just wait for luncheon!'

As if on cue, Clifford appeared with the gong, waiting for the baroness' signal.

After a few seconds, Eleanor gave her a gentle nudge. 'This is the only bit I'm really sure of. You nod so we can all start munching.'

'Goodness, our butler just gives it a wallop out in the corridor!'

Baroness Ashley nodded to Clifford, who sounded the gong.

The second dining room had been prepared with such care and exquisite decoration, even the men paused to take it in. Instead of the expected long formal table, a magnificent round expanse of green and ivory linen held the promise of a relaxed and welcoming meal. At each place setting sat a palm-sized iced gingerbread cottage, its snowy roof glistening in the soft light of the gold candles. Baroness Ashley pointed in delight to the artfully displayed three-dimensional napkins. Eleanor caught Clifford's eye, recognising that only his meticulous hand could have instructed the ladies to create the wondrous tiered Christmas trees from starched linen alone. Atop each one, a delicate silver star twinkled. As he held her chair, she mouthed a 'Thank you' for the note under her door.

Ringing the centre of the table, a red-holly-berry garland was decorated with ice-frosted grapes, dried orange slices and tiny silver fir cones, all dusted with icing sugar. Matching ribbons and baubles adorned the base of the eight brandy glasses arranged in the centre. Each was filled with softly bubbling soda water that made the floating silver and gold sequins sparkle as they bobbed up and down below the tiny star-shaped candle flickering above. It seems her resourceful staff had managed to somehow bring a season's worth of festive supplies with them from Henley Hall.

'Have you seen the lanterns too?' Baron Ashley asked his wife. 'Perhaps you could fill the castle with some of your own beautiful hand.' On each side table and corner of the room where an electric lamp would normally be, the tall ornate lanterns drew everyone's gaze. The delicate white and silver snowflakes that had been painted on each panel softened the light to a cosy festive glow.

'I feel as though Father Christmas himself has been quietly working away in here all night just for us,' Baroness Ashley breathed.

Baron Ashley gestured to Clifford. 'I believe this wonderful effort calls for our collective appreciation.'

Clifford returned a few moments later, leading the staff to stand in a pristine black-and-white uniformed line just inside the door. They all looked a little tired, but Mrs Trotman and Mrs Butters beamed at each other while Polly and Lizzie looked awestruck. Henderson's chest swelled as he stood to attention, only the tiniest of tugs on his waistcoat giving away he was unused to being recognised. A spirited round of applause followed. The Henley Hall staff failed to hold back their grins except Clifford, but she could see he was delighted that the team's exceptional hard work and thoughtful creativity was being acknowledged. At the barest twitch of his finger, the line curtsied and bowed in perfect unison before filing out.

With the women seated, the men took their places. Baron Ashley remained standing, champagne glass aloft. He looked around the ring of faces.

'Dear friends and family.' He swallowed hard. 'Most regrettably, you were all witnesses to a terrible tragedy from which I know we are all still reeling. And at Christmas of all times, when we had come together in festive spirit and good faith. All I can offer is my sincerest of apologies and immense gratitude that you are all maintaining a cool head.' He paused again. When he found his voice, it was choked. 'However, Christmas comes but once a year and I made a promise to my beloved wife that this would be the one she has always dreamed of—' He broke off, having lost the battle with his composure.

'Oh, Clarence,' his wife breathed, sliding her hand into his.

The Laird rose and went round to clap the baron on his shoulders, dwarfing the man's slender build with his broad frame. 'And so it shall be from here on in, old man. Friends,' he said, addressing the table, 'are we agreed, no mention of the previous incident will be uttered over luncheon?'

Collective head nodding followed without exception.

'As if that would ever be countenanced as appropriate!' Lady Fortesque said tartly.

'Good men, and dear ladies,' the Laird said. 'Since I believe we are the only folk celebrating Yuletide for nigh on a hundred miles, let today's luncheon bring us together in faithful companionship, for today we gather as one.'

The cries of 'Hear, hear!' made the baron's shoulders relax, but Eleanor felt hers tighten.

Except the 'one' amongst us who put paid to Randall celebrating this or any other Christmas, Ellie!

19

Once the starters were dealt with, Eleanor's unseasonal thoughts were distracted by the arrival of the first course – devilled quails' eggs presented in individual miniature cheese-and-rosemary baked lattice baskets. True to their word, not a mention was made about Randall's murder as the table tucked in.

'Well,' said Doctor Connell in answer to a question from Baroness Ashley, 'traditionally Hogmanay is the biggest celebration for us, being on New Year's Eve, of course.'

Gordon Cameron nodded. 'First footing is a special custom, and nay mistake.'

Eleanor was not the only of the non-Scots to be confused.

'What is that, then?' Sir Edward said. 'Sounds like staking a claim on a mine or something.'

The Laird laughed, but Gordon rounded on the Englishman, although he was clearly attempting to temper his words.

'We're not all about grabbing everything that isn't ours up here.'

'Relax, son,' his father said calmly. To the others, he explained. 'First footing is the tradition of being the first to cross the threshold of a friend's or neighbour's house after midnight. The "First

Footer" must bear with him an item symbolic of good luck such as a piece of coal, salt or, of course, whisky.'

'Can you imagine the chaos that would cause on the streets of London?' Baron Ashley said.

His wife sighed. 'But it's a lovely idea.'

Doctor Connell tutted. 'Aye, but like me, doctors work to the bone on January first on account of the injuries the whisky revellers sustain staggering home out of their skulls at lunchtime.'

Given that her hangover from partying with her staff had only just subsided, Eleanor sat quietly, but saw Clifford glancing at her mischievously.

Amid the genial chatter, the second course arrived. The Laird watched his son savour several mouthfuls of traditional cullen skink, a creamy yellow smoked haddock and potato soup, but unusually sprinkled with mini crab cake bites and drizzled with a rich red swirl of paprika oil.

'A wonderfully creative take on a local recipe, eh, my boy?' He pretended to cuff Gordon's chin. 'See, some progress is good.'

Testament to Mrs Trotman's amazing cooking, Ellie.

The geniality continued over the exquisitely braised lamb cutlets, dressed with steeped figs. Eleanor bit back a smile at Doctor Connell surreptitiously spooning up every last morsel of the delicious accompanying Madeira sauce. As a man who only indulged in spirits lightly, the rich plummy warmth had enlivened him to a point of being positively animated. The course was passed entirely with him entertaining the table with amusing tales of his experiences conquering the Munros.

It's all too perfect for words, Ellie! Fingers crossed the festive bonhomie lasts.

Baroness Ashley courageously took up the mantle as the table was cleared and Clifford topped up everyone's glasses.

'It's the colours of each season that are so special up here. Really, they are quite unique and so inspiring to paint.'

Eleanor nodded agreement while tucking into her beetroot, orange and celeriac salad, savouring the accompanying bowl of fresh local mussels in whisky and cream sauce with fingers of fresh toasted bread liberally spread with garlic butter. Relaxed conversation continued to flow around the table, moving easily from painting to Scotland's rugged beauty to interesting local winter diversions. As the next course arrived, the whole table was engaged in sharing their hopes for the following year.

'What a wonderfully abundant land Scotland is,' Eleanor said genuinely as she admired her local smoked trout, nestled on a bed of delicate scalloped potatoes with strips of buttered leeks.

Any secret fears that she would in fact be too full to enjoy the main course faded a while later as Clifford and Henderson arrived with a long silver trolley. Mrs Butters and Lizzie stepped up on either side of the two men. With perfect synchronisation, they lifted the six salver lids, Clifford holding that of the grand central dish.

Baron Ashley slid his hand over his wife's. 'Since we're relaxing some customs—' he said to Clifford.

'Certainly, my lord.' Clifford bowed and then gestured across each of the salvers. 'Roast goose with dainty Yorkshire puddings filled with slow-roasted beef twists and horseradish dressing. Redcurrant and peppercorn gammon. Rosemary roasted parsnips, local Yetholm Gypsy potatoes, lightly battered cauliflower florets in a honey glaze, and savoury crumble topped creamed leeks. Sage and shallot stuffing and bacon-wrapped chestnuts. And, of course, pigs in blankets accompanied by devils on horseback.'

A round of impromptu applause followed.

'Are you planning to stay much longer?' Lady Fortesque said to the Laird as they were served the delicious fayre.

'Well, that rather depends on our wonderful hosts.' He smiled at Baroness Ashley.

Sir Edward snorted. 'I think Inspector Lockhart will be the one to render an opinion on that.'

'Edward!' his wife hissed. 'We all agreed.'

'Ah yes, so we did.' He had the good grace to look abashed and attacked his roast goose with gusto.

'But...' Baroness Ashley glanced at her husband, hesitated, and then seemed to seize her courage. 'We'd love you to stay on Robert. Clarence particularly was hoping you might.'

Panic flitted across her husband's face. 'We don't need to abandon everything, old man. Not to my mind.'

As the Laird nodded, Baron Ashley relaxed.

'Nor to mine, Clarence,' the Laird said. 'A small setback, nothing more than that.'

Gordon Cameron thumped the table, making everyone jump. As his customary scowl settled on his face, Eleanor groaned inwardly.

'What is it going to take, Father, for you to stop supporting this pact with the English devil? Does another man need to die?'

'Gordon! Watch yer tongue, boy!' the Laird's tone brooked no argument.

So he has got iron beneath that velvet glove, Ellie.

The Laird looked around the table and laughed awkwardly. 'We all know your views. However, I believe Clarence has come up with a great idea that will bring much-needed regeneration and life to the area.'

'Well, I believe—'

The Laird's iron tone returned. 'We've heard what you believe, son. And it will not sway things. The ski resort is not going to decimate the entire Highlands like you seem to think. Nor will the money all go south!'

Gordon opened his mouth, but at the look in his father's eyes, closed it again and glowered instead at his goose.

'Ski resort?' Sir Edward sat up straighter. 'Have you lost your bearings, Clarence?'

His wife snorted. 'No one goes skiing. It's just a fad. Really!'

Baron Ashley eyed them coolly. 'I had no idea you were both such experts. Perhaps you and Edward might like to invest in the resort? I'm sure I could lower the minimum sum required seeing as you're family.'

Lady Fortesque's glare was as icy as the layered lime sorbet with sugar-frosted cranberries that arrived in front of her. Baroness Ashley tried to disguise her discomfort by busying herself with her napkin, but Eleanor couldn't miss how upset she was at the exchange.

'I've only been skiing a few times,' Eleanor blurted out. 'It's enormous fun. Well, once you've learned how not to crash into everything.'

Baron Ashley nodded gratefully. 'Indeed. You see, Mr Cameron, the hordes you worry about would be coming on holiday wielding nothing more threatening than a ski pole.' He sipped his brandy. 'But most of them will never make it any further than the resort hotel and its many diversions.'

Gordon stared at him darkly but said nothing.

Baron Ashley raised his glass and took a long swig. Putting it down, he smiled coldly at the Laird's son. 'Seriously, Mr Cameron, as you are so keen to inform us as to the parlous state of the local economy at every opportunity, have you a better scheme?'

Before he could reply, Doctor Connell pushed his untouched brandy away. Nevertheless, he seemed almost tipsy, not surprising given the amount of alcohol Mrs Trotman had introduced into the various courses. 'As someone mentioned mines earlier, perhaps we should all set to on gold-digging again, eh?' He stiffened at the Laird's sharp look and returned hastily to his dessert.

Lady Fortesque frowned. 'Gold? Here? In Scotland?'

The Laird cleared his throat. 'A joke, of course. There's been nothing but fool's gold and the odd flake found here since around fifteen hundred.'

Eleanor was about to join in the conversation when Clifford and Henderson wheeled in two silver trolleys. 'Wonderful! Dessert, my favourite part of the meal.'

By the time she had finished her dessert, her resolve to be the life of the party was wilting. She dreamed of curling up with Gladstone in an armchair by a blazing fire with nothing more troubling to think of than how she might finally beat her butler at chess.

She looked around for Clifford in time to see him return to the room and utter something into Baron Ashley's ear. The baron nodded and waved him away before turning to the table, lines of worry etched on his brow.

'Forgive our second attempt at a proper Christmas being cut short, but I need to insist we gentlemen forgo the customary after-luncheon arrangements and join the ladies in the library. Now.' He rose.

'No billiards again, Lord Ashley?' Gordon Cameron shook his head. 'Is nothing sacred at Castle Ranburgh?'

'A great many things, actually, Mr Cameron,' Baron Ashley said stiffly. He downed his brandy in one go. 'But it appears they cannot feature at this precise moment as Inspector Lockhart requires our presence.'

Lady Fortesque sat back and folded her arms. 'Well really! As if there hasn't been enough disruption during our stay up here already, Clarence.'

'I've apologised for that, Fanny,' Baron Ashley said. 'But I think we all want this matter dealt with as soon as possible.'

All except one, perhaps, Ellie.

As they all trooped out of the dining room, she caught Clifford's eye. Something in his look sent a frisson up her spine.

20

Perched on the end seat of the horseshoe of chairs, Eleanor looked around at the faces of the other guests. They were all trying, and failing, to look as if they had no interest in the proceedings.

Sir Edward sat staring at the wall, his hands clasped, his fingertips beating an unsteady rhythm. *Impatience? Or a guilty conscience?* Looking to the other end of the line, she noted sadly that the baron and his wife had each retreated into their own troubles again. The small gap between their seats acting as if it were a hundred-foot chasm. Beside her, Gordon Cameron was a changed man. Somewhere between the dining room and the library, the fire in his eyes had gone out. Slumped back in his seat, he looked smaller, weaker, his gaze constantly darting to his father, as if seeking reassurance. The Laird, on the other hand, appeared his usual relaxed self. Leaning back in a carver chair, one leg slung over the other, the signature amiable smile unaltered. *And rather out of place, Ellie.*

The staff filed in and stood in a line, fidgeting nervously. Only Clifford had any air of measured calm but even his eyes strayed repeatedly to Henderson, who seemed even more on edge, and the now returned Mrs McKenzie. Eleanor spotted the feisty Ranburgh cook poke Mrs Trotman in the ribs and mutter.

'Ne'er been trouble like this until you lot arrived!'

At this, Clifford gave a barely perceptible flick of a white-gloved finger. Combined with his terse look, it was enough for her to shuffle to the end of the line, albeit with a ferocious scowl. Doctor Connell cracked his knuckles, making everyone jump. He mouthed an apology. He too looked on edge. At that moment Inspector Lockhart strode through the door, his battered satchel bumping against his paunch. He stood facing his audience.

Showtime, Ellie!

The inspector cleared his throat. 'I'm nay a fan of having my time wasted.' He narrowed his already beady eyes and stared slowly round the assembled company. Again though, Eleanor noted, his glare stopped short of the Laird who received a respectful nod instead. 'So, nay interruptions if you please. And definitely nay theatricals.'

Since this last comment was directed at the women in the room, Eleanor fought the urge to wrap his satchel around his neck. Instead, she smiled sweetly.

'Rest assured, we'll leave that entirely to you, Inspector.'

Out of the corner of her eye, she caught Clifford's lips twitching with amusement. Inspector Lockhart ignored her.

'You're all here to witness justice being delivered. Justice which, I might add, will have been reached in a very short space o' time.' Pausing like a stage actor anticipating applause, he clucked his tongue at the silence. 'Magoon, Stanton!'

The stamp of heavy police boots heralded two blue-uniformed policemen who took up guard on either side of the door. Eleanor squirmed with anticipation.

Lockhart rested one arm on the top of his satchel. 'In case you've forgotten, I will remind you that the local police and then my men and I searched the castle and found not another living soul than those in this room.' His accusatory finger skipped over the Laird and Ranburgh cook. 'Which means that whoever murdered Eugene Randall was one o' those sitting round that dinner table with him. Or serving.' He glanced at Henderson and

Clifford. Henderson visibly paled. Eleanor thought he might faint.

'But,' Lady Fortesque burst out, 'by the time the local police got here, let alone you, the murderer could have rowed away across the loch a hundred times!'

Lockhart laughed caustically. 'In what? A butter churn?'

'In a rowing boat, you imbecile!'

'Or they could have absconded in a motorboat,' her husband said quickly.

Baron Ashley shook his head. 'Mine is the only powered craft anywhere near the castle and when I checked shortly after the murder, if you remember, it was still at its pontoon. And the inspector'– he smiled icily in Lockhart's direction – 'has now confiscated it.'

'Commandeered, Lord Ashley,' Lockhart said. 'All quite routine. And, anyway, it is returned now.'

Baroness Ashley found her voice, although it trembled. 'But there are other rowing boats about. Lady Fortesque could be correct.'

Lockhart rolled his eyes. 'Aye, there are boats. But there was no one with the skill, nor the local knowledge, to survive the waves out there that night except Drummond and Magoon. And since at the time o' the murder both men were with the rest of the village in church' – he scowled around the room – 'where any decent person would a' been at the time of the murder, the facts can nay be proved otherwise. Magoon here' – he jerked his thumb at the constable, who was clearly reliving in his mind the horror of his trip – 'only made it on account of knowing the loch like the back of his hand, same as Drummond. So dunnay be wasting my time starting in with fanciful notions that a mystery person rowed, or swam, their way across after committing murder. Besides, I have summat e'en more conclusive than that.'

The baroness sunk back into her seat, twisting her handkerchief. Her husband glanced at her and wiped his brow.

'Now, you might a' thought yer fingerprints were taken as a

matter of course,' Lockhart said with the sly smile of a cat about to pounce on a party of unsuspecting mice. 'But, oh nay. We found a print on the murder weapon!'

The whole room gasped.

So that's why he just seemed to be going through the motions of interviewing everyone, Ellie. He wasn't looking for any other evidence. He was merely looking for a match for the print.

The young policeman clicked his heels. He must be Stanton, she guessed.

'Yes alright, Stanton here found a print,' Lockhart said sulkily. 'A definitive print. Exactly where the murderer would a' had to be holding the dirk to plunge it in at the angle we found it sticking out of the back of Eugene Randall.'

'The third,' Eleanor muttered.

Gordon Cameron shot her an odd look.

She watched with a racing heart as Lockhart looked around the room. 'All of you except one are free to leave Castle Ranburgh but nay the area until I say so. But the one among you who murdered Eugene Randall shall come with me and pay the price!'

He clicked his fingers over his shoulder and the two policemen at the door stepped closer together, blocking the exit. Everyone held their breath.

Bringing his arm up over his head, he brought it down dramatically. 'I am arresting you for the murder of Eugene Randall!'

Everyone stared at the pointing finger, but no one seemed sure who it was pointing at.

'Inspector,' Baron Ashley said. 'Where, or rather, *who* are you pointing at?'

Lockhart scowled. 'You, Lord Ashley! I'm pointing at *you*!'

In the tumultuous confusion of raised voices, Baron Ashley stared at the inspector, his jaw slack, his Adam's apple bobbing as he fought for words. He rose unsteadily. 'This is preposterous! I did not kill Eugene Randall. I would never—'

His remonstrations were cut short as Constable Magoon slapped a pair of handcuffs on him.

'Oh, Clarence! How could you?' Lady Fortesque said, as if scolding a troublesome child.

'A very bad business, old man.' Her husband nodded disapprovingly, as if the baron had been caught with his hand in the biscuit jar.

Eleanor stared at them both in disbelief. The baron's only family, and they had denounced him on the spot. She looked to the Laird who shrugged. Doctor Connell had risen with the others and now hovered silently on the edge, adjusting his glasses as he tapped his chin thoughtfully.

Gordon Cameron was the only one still seated, his fire restored as he shouted, 'I knew it!'

'This is preposterous,' Baron Ashley said weakly, looking at his wife for the first time. 'Wilhelmina!'

She seemed to be in a state of shock. But at the sound of her name, she jumped up and ran in front of the two policemen who were trying to lead Baron Ashley out of the room.

'Unhand my husband this instant! He is not a murderer.'

'Oh aye?' Lockhart said. 'And how is it that you can be so sure when his are the only fingerprints on the knife that killed the man who died at yer very dining table?'

She spun around to face the inspector. 'Because... because he's my husband! He's completely incapable of such an act.'

'The devil's boots dunnay creak, Lady Ashley,' Lockhart said darkly. 'If they did, there'd be no need for the police, would there? Yer husband has fooled you, just like most of the others here.' He jerked a hand at the two policemen who were now on either side of the baron. 'Take him away.'

'Eleanor!' Baroness Ashley shouted frantically, still blocking the policemen's way. 'Help me! Help Clarence. You have to do something!'

'Well, really!' Lady Fortesque sniffed disdainfully while her husband shook his head and tutted.

Eleanor instinctively leaped to Baroness Ashley's aid, but realised as she faced Lockhart that she had no idea what to say.

'Inspector, you might have found Lord Ashley's fingerprints on the weapon but... but what... what motive have you uncovered? Why on earth would he kill Mr Randall?'

'Nay that it's any o' yer business but I have nay honed in on a precise motive yet,' Lockhart said with too much nonchalance for her liking. Holding his hand up, he counted off on his hairy-knuckled fingers. 'But, number one, he had the opportunity. Number two, his fist was grasped round the murder weapon just so, as we know from the fingerprints.' He gave a vivid performance of stabbing someone. 'And number three, we have an eyewitness who not only saw but heard him having a blazing row with Eugene Randall. And only a salmon's whisker before you all sat down to dinner! How's that?'

At her stunned silence, he pulled his satchel back down, spun on his heel, and marched Baron Ashley from the room.

21

'Perhaps a chamomile tea,' Eleanor said gently, holding up the cup Clifford had passed her. 'It might help you feel... calmer.'

Baroness Ashley stared blankly at her from the pale-pink settee, her eyes swimming. 'It's like I'm trapped in a nightmare. Tell me it isn't real. Please.'

'I wish I could,' Eleanor said softly. 'But it is real. However, only for now. The truth will prevail.'

Her heartfelt honesty didn't seem to offer Baroness Ashley any comfort as the young woman's tears spilled over her lashes. She stared into her tea and then her shoulders shook. Eleanor took the linen napkin, which appeared at her side, and dabbed at the woman's dress where the tea had slopped. Baroness Ashley looked up.

'How can the truth prevail when the inspector found Clarence's fingerprints on the...' she faltered, 'on the dagger that killed Mr Randall?'

Eleanor tried hard to think of some crumb of comfort or hope. 'Because the inspector would still need to prove other things like motive before there could be any kind of foregone conclusion in court.'

'Would he?' Baroness Ashley jerked upright. 'I don't see why.

Inspector Lockhart is right, isn't he? It had to be someone in that room, that night. And the only person who touched the murder weapon was—'

'Clarence.' Eleanor sighed. 'I know.'

'But it's even worse than it seems,' Baroness Ashley said through her hands. 'There's something you don't know. Something even Clarence doesn't know.'

As if pulled on an invisible string, Clifford melted into the furthest recess of the sitting room. Fearing she was about to hear a confession, Eleanor swallowed hard before replying.

'What doesn't Clarence know?'

Baroness Ashley lifted her head. 'I'm with child.'

'Oh, Wilhelmina!' Eleanor gasped, not expecting that at all. 'Gracious. That's quite the... news.'

But perhaps far from good news with Clarence under arrest for murder, Ellie!

Baroness Ashley looked up at her, her eyes pleading. 'You have to help, Eleanor. I've no one else to turn to. You saw the disgraceful way Sir Edward and Lady Fortesque reacted just now. They believe Clarence is guilty. His own family! And the Laird did nothing, even though I'm sure he could have Lockhart dismissed if he wanted. Eleanor, please, I know you have done this sort of thing before. It came to light at that luncheon months ago when we first met.'

Eleanor hesitated. It was true she and Clifford had already started their informal investigation, but this was different.

'Wilhelmina, I'm not an expert. I helped Lancelot when he was in... in a similar situation, but that was different.'

Lancelot was the son of Lord and Lady Langham, Eleanor and Baron Ashley's mutual friends, and her former boyfriend. She had proved his innocence when he was accused of murder. But how could she explain that back in Buckinghamshire, Clifford knew everyone and everything that went on, while her late uncle's reputation, combined with her title, opened doors that had helped her solve the murder? Here Clifford knew no one, and her uncle's reputation and her title counted for next to nothing. And there was another, even bigger problem. Except for a few bleak moments, she had always believed Lancelot innocent. But how could she confess to Baroness Ashley that, after Lockhart's revelation, she was having serious second thoughts about her husband's innocence.

'Wilhelmina—'

'Eleanor, please! What am I going to do otherwise?' She grasped Eleanor's hand and glanced down at her stomach. "What are *we* going to do?'

After a moment, Eleanor withdrew her hand. Baroness Ashley rose and went over to the window, where she stared at the snow gently falling against the pane.

Eleanor turned to Clifford.

'Clifford, I think we need a—'

But he had already materialised at her side with a silver tray bearing a fresh cup of chamomile tea and a brandy. He scanned her face, an unspoken conversation passing between them. Then her shoulders relaxed as he gave a resigned nod. She mouthed a heartfelt, 'Thank you,' and turned back to Baroness Ashley.

'Wilhelmina, come here and sit down. You need to be completely honest with me if you want to help Clarence.'

'What!' She ran over and grasped Eleanor's hands. 'You mean you will help? Really? Truly?'

Eleanor nodded. 'Yes.' She passed her the new cup of camomile tea. 'Now, Wilhelmina, tell me the full truth. How badly did Clarence row with Mr Randall before the dinner?'

She hesitated, staring into her cup. Eleanor waited. Finally, Baroness Ashley sighed and looked up.

'Badly. Oh goodness, terribly badly, Eleanor. But I didn't tell you before when we were chatting in my suite because I feared you'd think the worst.' She closed her eyes. 'And for exactly that reason I didn't tell the police either.' She snapped to attention and stared at Eleanor, a deep frown marring her delicate features. 'But someone did tell, because Inspector Lockhart just told us a witness had come forward who saw and heard everything.'

'But you don't know who that is, do you? Which means they must have been hiding, otherwise you would've seen them.'

'Oh no, I wouldn't have.' Wilhelmina shook her head, sadly.

It was Eleanor's turn to frown. 'Why?'

'Because I wasn't there when Clarence and Mr Randall rowed. Clarence finally owned up about it after I insisted he told me why he was so agitated.'

'Just before we all went in to dinner?' Eleanor's mind jumped back to the vehement disagreement she had heard the two men having.

Baroness Ashley shook her head. 'No, I didn't know he rowed with him again. This was earlier.'

'Wilhelmina, please forgive my forthright question, but if I have understood correctly, Mr Randall was here as a potential investor in Clarence's scheme? Then, as I said, it would seem odd that Clarence would argue with a gentleman on whom he felt reliant for funding?'

'You're right. On both counts. Clarence is usually very mild-mannered. Stubborn. Impossibly determined on one course of action sometimes, but there is no fire in his temper. But it wasn't an argument, it was an absolute blazing row. The only reason they didn't come to blows was that they were interrupted. Clarence admitted as much.'

'But what was the row about, exactly?'

'It's a little more complicated than it appears. These investment things always are, it seems. Mr Randall wasn't the actual investor. He represented a syndicate or some such thing. I don't really understand how these matters work. But he was booked to return to America. Today, actually. And he told Clarence, in unmistakably clear tones, that he would be telling them not to invest.'

'Because?'

'Because...' Her cheeks flushed. 'Because he accused Clarence of being a charlatan. He said his wonderful scheme was based on nothing but underhand dealings.'

Eleanor digested this information. 'Hmm... I hate to ask, but have you not told Clarence about your prospective new family member because he was so worried about getting his scheme through?'

'In part.' The young woman shuffled in her seat. 'But mostly because I was undecided on what to do.'

'Wilhelmina! You mean you've thought of—'

'I did. At first. Clarence is terrible at business. Or he's had a run of terrible bad luck. I'm ashamed to say I don't know which and haven't quite found the courage to ask him, because I'm fearful of the truth. Money was never a concern to me before I knew I was pregnant.' She reached for the damp napkin Eleanor had mopped the tea up with. 'But I do know that if his ski resort doesn't go through, we'll be lucky to have anything we can call home. And Mr Randall was absolutely set to make sure that Clarence would fail. He went so far as to say he would discredit the scheme publicly, to warn others off losing their money. But as always, he'd had a lot to drink.'

Eleanor exchanged a glance with Clifford. His look told her he was thinking the same as her. Things were looking blacker and blacker for Baron Ashley. Eleanor looked into Wilhelmina's eyes.

'You have to understand that there are no guarantees, Wilhelmina. You do realise that?'

Baroness Ashley nodded. 'Yes, of course. I know you can't work miracles, although I know that's what I'm asking of you.'

Eleanor kept her thoughts to herself.

'Listen, Wilhelmina. You must tell no one about this. Just as I will tell no one about' – she nodded at the young woman's stomach – 'this. If Mr Randall's killer knows that we are looking for him, it could be much harder for us. He might work to cover his tracks, even more so than he's done so far.'

She glanced at Clifford, who arched one brow. *But more so, because the killer might decide he needs to commit another murder at Castle Ranburgh, Ellie.*

22

The minute Eleanor had left the baroness, she had changed and gone in search of Clifford. She found him waiting unbidden at the kitchen door, already dressed in his thickest overcoat and wool scarf. His signature shining black shoes had been replaced with stout walking boots and a large leather binocular case hung around his neck. In one hand he held an enticing-looking picnic hamper and in the other her moss-green wool coat and scarf.

'It seems a touch inappropriate to be off exploring now, especially after what we've just learned from Wilhelmina,' Eleanor said. 'I feel awfully sorry at her predicament. I only hope we can help her.'

Clifford held up his hand. 'My lady, time spent out in nature is always good for clearing one's head. And I fear until you have visited the Straits of An-Dòchas which, according to the Laird, your mother navigated, you will not be able to focus on the investigation.'

In the rowing boat, the light wind drifting over the water ruffled Eleanor's curls as they glided across the loch's still surface. For once, it wasn't the sharp cold that made her frosted breath catch. It was the savage beauty of the nature that surrounded her.

As a child on her parents' yacht, she'd learned to stare at the horizon to avoid any motion sickness. In such calm waters she had no need, which was lucky because her view was blocked by Drummond's grizzled face as he heaved on the oars, a brace of lifeless, white-pelted mountain hares hanging over his shoulder. However, the best part of her first nine years of her life spent aboard her parents' boat had taught her that even in such unusually calm water, Drummond would need to choose a very careful course as they neared the section of Loch Vale that fed into the narrow Straits of An-Dòchas. They were only cutting across the mouth of the straits, but it would still need a steady hand. Nevertheless, for a man who looked to be nudging sixty he still had amazing strength in his arms. As he rowed, a muscle along his grim-set jaw pulsed with each stroke.

The rowing boat lurched suddenly.

'Is there anything we can do, Mr Drummond?' she shouted over the slap of the waves. He seemed not to have heard. She opened her mouth again as a wave splashed over her that was so cold, the generous amount she swallowed made her teeth ache. With an unladylike lunge over the side of the boat, she spat out the rest of the gritty water with an involuntary gagging noise.

When she'd regained her composure, Clifford caught her attention and raised his eyes to the top of her head. Reaching up, she pulled a handful of pale-yellow leathery fronds punctuated with tiny bulbous bladders from her red curls.

'Egg wrack seaweed, my lady. In season, it is considered quite the local delicacy.'

'And a fabulous fashion accessory, I'm sure.'

'I'm sure not.'

Leaning over the side, even with the now constant waves and spray, she could see the difference in the colour of the water as it ran faster beneath and choppier on top at the mouth of the straits. As they reached halfway, Drummond nodded to a boulder-strewn strip of a beach. Before Eleanor could ask if that was their destination, the boat was snatched by some unseen force and swung wildly the other way.

'We're yawing badly,' she called to Clifford.

Running a leather-gloved finger along the thick wool scarf at his neck, he nodded ruefully and shouted back, 'I did notice, my lady.'

She glanced at their oarsman and could see that even with his decades-honed strength and experience, he was struggling to keep them on anything close to their planned course.

'There's no danger, but she'll ne'er make it wi'out her tail fin!' he yelled to Clifford.

'Once again, please. Mr Drummond?' he called back.

'On it!' Eleanor cried. Gripping the side with both hands, she slid over the back of the bench seat and scrambled the few feet to the end of the boat. There a removable rudder was tied fast, the telltale curve highlighting it had once belonged to a small sailing craft. Grateful that her thick leather gloves were keeping her fingers warm enough to work, she slipped the knots free. Then, leaning over, she yanked out the metal bar that pierced each side of the U-shaped bracket. With a grunt, she lifted the rudder and dropped it, spine edge on, into the bracket. A reassuring tug on the belt of her coat let her know Clifford was ensuring she didn't topple overboard. She squared the rudder with its mounting, then attached another, longer iron bar which acted as a tiller.

'Good teamwork, Clifford!'

Ten minutes later she jumped onto the shore with the boat's mooring rope firmly in hand. A flicker of respect suffused Drummond's face.

'Nay a bad run, m'lady. Nay a poor course you managed to steer either. Thank ye.'

'A genuine pleasure. I hadn't realised how much I've missed the sea and boats. The loch's waters – including the straits – are as fine and challenging a sailing ground as one could ever wish for.'

Brushing his wind-blown hair from his eyes, which she realised were the same colour as the waters they had just navigated, grey-green with flecks of almost white, he nodded.

'Aye. If ye wants to take on the wrath of the monster.'

About to ask what convinced him there was a creature lurking in the swirling body of water, she stalled. There was a mixture of genuine fear and reverence in his hard-set expression.

He shifted the dead mountain hares further up his torso. 'Long as you were happy it'd be the last battle you ever fought.'

'But you row across Loch Vale regularly.'

'Aye, I do, but I've got help.' Having seen no one else with Drummond since they'd arrived, she wondered who exactly this help was and how they were keeping themselves so hidden. Before she could voice her thoughts, he continued. 'And I dunnay ever stray near where his tail thrashes the waters fiercest.' He pointed to the beginning of the straits. 'It's nay only the rocks below that make An-Dòchas the most dangerous channel in Scotland. It's' – he tapped his nose with a calloused finger – '*him*.'

She frowned. 'I meant to ask the Laird what "an-dòchas" means?'

'Hope.'

'Ah! Now I know. Well, Mr Drummond, we're going to take the land route up and over to the straits from here.'

'That may be, but yer'll be hoping my boat'll still be waiting when ye returns, perhaps? It'll take you the best part of the night to make it back on foot to the castle jetty on the shore without. And then you'd best sleep in your lorry of a vehicle parked in the stone barn where you left it, 'cos there'll nay be a boat to take you across. I'm a busy man.'

Clifford stepped forward. 'Indeed, you are, Mr Drummond. However, her ladyship rather thought you might find just enough time for' – he opened the picnic basket, holding it out so their oarsman could see the full feast inside – 'a hearty lunch, with hot coffee and a dram or two of the finest whisky? And, of course,' – he produced a note from his wallet and added it to the hamper – 'a little recompense for your wait?'

Drummond licked his lips. 'Mebee I can.' He slapped the animals hanging against his chest. 'These rascals are nay haring off anywhere, after all.' Clearly tickled by his joke, he took the picnic basket with a nod. 'An hour and three-quarters. Light'll have left until the morn after that and me with her.'

Once clear of the beach, Eleanor paused at the start of a near-vertical slate-strewn track threading its way among the columns of granite. It was so steep, little of the still gently falling snow had settled on it.

'Did you have to give away the *whole* picnic, Clifford?'

He rolled his eyes. 'Lunch was but a short time ago. And, besides, my lady, I had anticipated Mr Drummond needing an extra incentive to wait for us. Hence the picnic was always intended for him. However,' – he undid the buckle on the binocular case and revealed the contents – 'we are still stocked with a generous portion of Mrs Trotman's cheese straws, ham-and-egg pie slices, cinnamon muffins and a half of his lordship's favourite sherry.'

Much cheered, Eleanor set off up the scree-covered slope, grasping at the craggy rocks for balance. Within minutes of their nearing the top, the snow turned to hail. But not the kind of hail Eleanor was used to. Rather than hard and stinging, it was soft and gentle.

Clifford shook his collar. '"Graupels" or "snow hail", my lady. It's caused by water freezing onto snowflakes as they fall.'

She laughed and shook it out of her hair. 'Well, it's certainly better than normal hail.'

'I agree, but it is nonetheless a reminder that we should not be complacent while out here. The elements are capricious and, to the unwary, change so fast that they can prove deadly. Especially at this time of year.'

She nodded, put her hood up, and carefully continued up the slope.

However, the hail soon passed and the sun re-emerged. From the top, the view down to the loch was spectacular, the sun kissing the becalmed water in the centre of the snow-wrapped scene. She drank in her fill before moving on, because on the knife-edge ridge in front of her, it would be too dangerous to take one's eyes off the path for a moment.

'It is but a short stretch further, my lady,' Clifford said from behind her after they had been inching along for ten minutes or so. 'We shall soon be able to see—'

'The straits!' Staring down at the turbulent channel of foam, she gasped as a wall of water hurtled along the surface like a mini tidal wave.

The path down was so steep she was grateful Clifford had thought to bring a collapsible walking stick for each of them. Several times she found her feet running away from her as her weight caused the snow-covered slate to cascade down the slope. A particularly loose stretch had her tumbling, but with a well-executed forward roll, she propelled herself back upright.

'Clifford, look!' she called out over the rush of the water in the straits. 'There's a seal! On that rock.'

Only twenty or so feet away, two berry-black eyes gazed at her from a mottled grey-whiskered face.

'Indeed, my lady. I suspect it is as surprised to see you, as you are it. This is hardly a route anyone will take as a matter of course.'

She felt under her scarf for the small set of powerful field glasses Clifford had given her at the top of the pass.

'Oh no!'

He hurried up to her. 'My, lady?'

'I must have dropped the glasses on one of my tumbles. I am sorry, Clifford. They were a special pair of Uncle Byron's, weren't they?'

'Perhaps their specialness is merely clouded by inappropriate sentimentality on my part.'

'Nonsense. Let's go find them now.'

He held up a hand. 'I will go and look for them. You only have a short time here before we need to return.'

As Clifford strode back to the path, she made her way to the water's edge, then dropped to her haunches. Never able to resist the grounding effect of stones, she ran her hands over the pebbles, feeling her heart rate calm a little more with each touch. One in particular attracted her. An ebony-streaked, pearly-grey quartz pebble, almost a perfect egg shape, bigger than her palm and with tiny flecks that shimmered when she turned it in her hand.

'Were you here when my parents sailed past?' she breathed, reaching for the velvet bag she'd brought along. After placing the stone in it, she looked up. 'Oh gracious!'

The seal was nowhere to be seen. But on the rock where it had been lying, a young woman now sat, facing out over the water, her long fair hair billowing around her. She turned to Eleanor and waved.

Where on earth did she come from, Ellie?

Eaten up with curiosity, Eleanor stumbled over the ridged rocks until she was within a few feet. The woman remained seated with her legs tucked sideways under her as she patted the rock beside her.

'You're built from the same mould as your mother, I can see.'

'I'm sorry?' Eleanor blinked, not sure she'd heard right. Lowering herself onto the rock, she tried not to stare at the woman's mink-grey dress next to her that hinted at being softer than a seal pup's pelt.

She must be freezing, Ellie. Not even a coat or hat. How's that possible? She glanced over at Clifford, now halfway up the slope, bent over as he searched for the glasses, and then turned back to her companion. She wondered if the poor woman was touched in the head. Who else would be out here dressed like that in this weather? And she'd never met her before, of that she was sure. So how could she have known her mother? To look at her she would have been a young child, if that, when her mother was here.

'How did you get here, if you don't mind my asking? It's so remote.'

'Not so remote you couldn't find your way, Ellie.'

Eleanor rocked backwards. 'How... how do you know my name?' *And your nickname at that, Ellie! No one's ever called you that, except... Mother!* Eleanor leaned forward. 'Who... who are you?'

'My lady?' Clifford's measured voice came from behind her.

She spun around.

'I found the field glasses.' He held them out, looking her face over in concern. 'Forgive my forthright observation, but you look as if you've seen a ghost.'

'Perhaps I have. But then she's a ghost that knows my name!'

'"She", my lady?' He pointed around the empty beach. 'There is no one here except us and the seal.'

Eleanor's mouth fell open as she stared into the seal's berry-black eyes. It blinked once and then slid silently into the loch and vanished under the waves.

23

Turning the enormous iron ring that served as the door handle, Eleanor heaved open the heavy oak doors to the great hall.

A discreet cough came from behind her.

'Are you sure you want to do this, my lady? So soon—'

She nodded. 'We need to act now. We're lucky that it's barely been touched.'

It had been several hours since they'd returned from the straits and Eleanor had warmed up enough – and eaten enough – to seriously start investigating Randall's murder. Before, the stakes had been high. Now, with Wilhelmina's cry for help, they felt even higher.

Another discreet cough came from behind her.

'Before we continue, my lady, I must apologise for not concluding our previous conversation over your experience on the beach. There may be a simple explanation.'

She spun around at this unexpected turn in the conversation.

'What... what explanation?'

'You had a visitation, my lady.'

'A what?'

'The young woman who spoke to you could have been as real as you and I.'

Her heart stilled. 'But she vanished into thin air, leaving just—'

'The seal.' Clifford nodded. 'Selkies, my lady. Scottish folklore has a strong legend of female creatures who appear as humans, able to converse and interact and then return to their natural form. That being of a seal.'

'A seal!' She felt the hot prick of tears. 'But, Clifford, that's... that's just legends and tall tales. You don't believe it really, do you?'

He cleared his throat. 'I may not have seen any of these creatures for myself, but that does not mean they don't exist. After all, I have never seen oxygen, yet I know it exists. I might be in considerable trouble if it did not.'

Eleanor digested this for a moment. 'Thank you, Clifford. I'll think on that. Although it doesn't explain how she knew the nickname that only my mother used.' She shook her head sharply. 'Anyway, let's get back to the matter in hand. That of catching a murderer.'

It felt eerie being back in Castle Ranburgh's great hall where the fateful Christmas Eve dinner had ended so tragically. She walked slowly up to the dining table and put her hand on the chair Randall had been sitting in when— She shuddered. Shaking the image out of her head, she counted off anti-clockwise where each of the guests had been seated.

'The Laird was sitting to Randall's right, and Lady Fortesque to the Laird's right. Then Wilhelmina and Gordon Cameron. Then there was me and to my right was Sir Edward, followed by Clarence at the head of the table. The last guest, Doctor Connell was to Clarence's right and Randall's left, which brings us full circle.'

Clifford held out her notebook and the fountain pen she had given him for Christmas last. 'Please continue.'

'Good idea. I'll take notes.' She quickly made a sketch of the seating arrangement.

Sir Fortesque   Me   Gordon Cameron
Baron Ashley   Baroness Ashley
Doctor Connell   Eugene Randall   The Laird   Lady Fortesque
Henderson?

'Well, if I remember correctly, we were on our initial round of wink murder.' She flipped to the list of suspects. Not wanting to lean on the table, she stood on one leg and leaned the notepad against her raised knee. 'Now, before the lights went off, the Laird and Lady Fortesque had been wink-murdered. Not real-murdered, obviously.'

'And Doctor Connell, my lady.'

'Are you certain?'

'Certain that I remember you having noted how accurate the doctor's, ahem, death rattle was.'

She grimaced. 'Ah, yes. Not my finest observation. So, the doctor was face down on the table, the Laird laid back in his chair and Lady Fortesque?'

'Still flailing dramatically, my lady, despite having been "murdered" long before the doctor. Perhaps Inspector Lockhart was right about ladies and theatricals?'

She took a swipe at him with the notebook, but he smoothly stepped back just out of range.

'Any more comments like that, Clifford, and someone else might be real-murdered!' She stared thoughtfully at the spot where Lady Fortesque had sat. 'I have to agree, though. She did get into the spirit of it rather enthusiastically, didn't she?'

Clifford frowned. 'Or was the exaggerated flailing purely to allow the lady to grab a certain something from somewhere around her person?'

'Like the dirk! Which she could have hidden under her seat? But how would she have known we were going to play the game? Unless she suggested it. I missed who it was as I was under the table.'

'So early in the proceedings?'

'I had hardly drunk anything, thank you very much!' Her smile faded as she stared again at Randall's seat. 'I remember he'd been choking on his drink and the Laird gave him a thump on the back.'

'A series of firm pats, I believe it was, my lady. But that was the first occasion. When Mr Randall was caught in the paroxysms of coughing a second time, it was Doctor Connell who attended to him.'

'Gracious, excellent memory. You're right. And so back to the point. After the three guests we've mentioned had been wink-murdered, the lights went out.'

Clifford gave a discreet cough.

'Alright, out with it.'

'If you will forgive my observation, they were extinguished a heartbeat after—'

She groaned. 'After Wilhelmina said... what was it exactly? You'll remember, you always do.'

He nodded. '"I don't mean to interrupt the game, but can I say, just how perfect this is. It's just the right time—"'

'And then the lights went out!' Eleanor walked over to where Baroness Ashley had been seated, at the opposite end to her husband. 'Are you suggesting she might have been giving someone a signal?'

'I am not suggesting anything, my lady. The coincidental timing merely struck me more readily than it did on the night in question.'

She looked down the length of the table, staring at the baron's place setting. 'Clarence was only one seat away from Randall, so if Wilhelmina gave the signal so he could—' She shivered again and shook her head. 'But that doesn't work, anyway. Someone else would still have had to turn out the lights. Which means three people would have been involved and that seems—'

'Unlikely? I agree, my lady. Although, if it were the case, Lady Ashley's coded message could have been for another member of the party.'

'Like Doctor Connell or the Laird who were either side of Randall?' She sighed. 'Wilhelmina *can't* be involved. She was so distraught when Inspector Lockhart hauled Clarence away.'

'Perhaps because the lady knew her husband was entirely innocent?'

'And at the same time, she knew who was guilty? And she was in cahoots with them?'

'Exactly. And she is now caught in the dilemma that to save Lord Ashley she must reveal not only the true murderer's identity but also her own hand in the act.'

Eleanor groaned. 'In which case, she probably only asked me to help as a smokescreen or out of desperation as she couldn't think of anything else.'

They both continued pacing around the table, silent in their thoughts. Eleanor knew, like her, Clifford was hopeful another scenario would present itself as being more plausible.

'Perhaps we should re-enact what occurred when the lights were extinguished, my lady?'

'Brilliant!' She stood behind Eugene Randall's final seating place. One by one, Clifford wound the handles on each of the long thin iron bars that moved the many folded oak shutters over the windows. With the snap of each one closing, the room darkened a little more. Then he extinguished the remaining lights, leaving it as dark as the inside of a coffin. Eleanor could see nothing, just like the night of the murder. A chill ran up her spine.

'What do you remember next, my lady?' Clifford's disembodied voice came to her from the opposite side of the table.

'Three or four of the men rose. At least I think it was four.'

'And why particularly did you believe they were all gentlemen?'

She shrugged in the dark. 'You're right, it could have been Wilhelmina. Or Lady Fortesque. But whoever they were, they scraped their chairs back noisily. If I'd stood up, I would have merely slipped around the end of the chair's arm.'

'As either of the other ladies would have been able to do as, ahem, you are all similarly slight of form.'

'Delicately put. I seem to remember being referred to as a boyish pencil not so long ago. But you've hit on something there, Clifford!'

'Writing accoutrements, my lady?'

'No, the fact that whilst the boys may well have jumped up, any of us women could have done the same without a sound.' She thought for a second, her eyes making up all manner of images in the inky blackness. 'Come to think of it, I heard Clarence tell everyone to get back in their seats. Someone – I think it was Sir Edward – also said that he was on his way over, or similar. Oh, and one of them said something very Scottish sounding.'

'"Haud yer weesht", my lady?'

'What does that mean?'

'It means to, ahem, "shut up".'

She jumped as a torch beam split the darkness.

'Clifford! How can you be only a few feet to my right and yet it sounded like you were still over there where I was sitting when Randall was murdered?'

'Forgive my startling you, but I needed to test my theory. With the general confusion and the lack of any light, it is eminently plausible that the murderer could have fooled everyone into thinking they were somewhere they were not.'

'Rather than behind Randall, plunging a knife into him!'

Clifford's torch beam swung over to the door, then the lights came back on. She blinked after the darkness while looking around the table once more.

'We're missing something major.'

'Although a minor something is often enough to unlock the puzzle, my lady, as we have found on previous occasions.' His brows knitted together. 'I fear, however, for desperate want of an answer, we are merely banging our heads—'

'Stop! Banging heads! That's what Clarence said when he told whoever else was stumbling about to sit back down.'

'I don't recall hearing that, my lady.'

'That's because you were out sorting the lighting. You weren't gone long.'

'And the first thing I noted on my return was Lord Ashley standing behind Mr Randall's chair. Not knowing the gentleman was dead, I assumed he had suffered another bout of coughing.'

Eleanor groaned. 'And that Clarence had been patting him on the back. But instead he may have been—'

'Stabbing him in the back.'

Her brow creased. 'Do you suppose someone slipped Randall something to keep him quiet when he was stabbed?'

'Possibly, my lady. But then why not just administer a strong enough poison to kill him? I am minded to think our murderer took the opportunity of Mr Randall definitely having overindulged.'

'He was quite gone by the end, alright. And the Laird had tried to make him so comfortable with that cushion.'

They snapped their fingers in unison, though Clifford's white butler gloves silenced his click.

'The cushion!' Eleanor said. 'It could have saved Randall. Or at least made it harder for the murderer to plunge the dirk in so far.'

'But, my lady, Doctor Connell went to great pains to remove it not long before Mr Randall died.'

'So he did. And who would know better than a doctor where to plunge a dagger and how far you'd need to plunge it in to kill a man!'

They stared at the back of the chair Randall had been seated on. Like the others, it was a large wooden carver. Eleanor gestured to the section where the ornate design left ample space for the thrusting of a dagger. Nodding to each other, they checked the floor on either side.

Eleanor pursed her lips. 'Not that I know what I expected to find. The dirk might have been concealed under any one of these seats, or in a gentleman's jacket pocket perhaps—'

'Or a lady's handbag.'

'True. But it left this room in poor Randall's back. And with Clarence's fingerprints clearly on it.'

'But most concerningly, my lady, fingerprints in the precise formation for administering the fatal blow, according to Inspector Lockhart.'

She straightened up and rubbed her face with her hands. 'And, as you said, when the lights came on, the first thing you saw was Clarence standing behind Randall's chair.' She groaned, updated her suspect list and stared at what she now had.

The Laird

Motive? No motive. Supported Clarence's scheme, so needed Randall alive!

Evidence? Lizzie saw the Laird give Lockhart an envelope full of money. For what?

Gordon Cameron (Laird's son)

Motive? Wanted to stop Clarence's scheme that Randall was financing.

Evidence? Openly outspoken against it, but nothing else so far.

Fortesques

Motive?

Doctor Connell

Motive?

Evidence? Just before Randall stabbed removed cushion that might have saved his life.

Clarence

Motive? No motive – needed Randall alive to finance his scheme!

Evidence? His fingerprints found on the dirk handle/rowed with Randall night of his death/standing behind Randall's chair when lights came back on.

Wilhelmina

Motive?

Henderson (footman)

Motive?

Evidence? None as actual murderer, but as accomplice in best position to cut lights.

Eleanor shook her head in frustration. 'Well, we've advanced to some extent, but not that much. The Laird, Gordon Cameron, Doctor Connell and Henderson have all got something against them in the way of motive or evidence against, but Clarence still has the most damning entry. But I really can't bring myself to believe— Ouch!'

'Are you hurt, my lady?' Clifford was immediately at her side.

She stared at the deep gash on the back of her hand and the trickle of blood already running along her wrist. 'It's just a scratch from a bit of splintered wood. It's fine. I was just re-enacting Randall being stabbed through the chair.'

Clifford tutted. 'Scratches do not leak so perceptively as to ruin the cuff of a lady's favourite wool coat.' He handed her a handkerchief and produced a pair of pince-nez. 'With your permission?' He held his hand out for hers and examined the cut and then the chair. 'There is a shard of metal caught in the wood.'

'Metal? But the chairs are wooden.'

'Indeed. Oak. And crafted entirely so.' From his inside pocket, he pulled out a folding magnifying glass. With a deft flick of his wrist, the glass circle slid out. After a moment, he nodded. 'Just as I suspected.' This time, he produced a pair of needle-nosed pliers.

Eleanor laughed. 'I swear you're actually only an inch wide, Clifford, and what is really filling your jacket is an Aladdin's cave of dubiously purposed tools.'

'Well, luckily on this occasion,' – he stood up – 'dubious or otherwise, they have allowed us to secure a suspect item from the scene of the crime. One overlooked by Inspector Lockhart's men.'

She peered at the squarish, dark piece of metal.

'Clifford, you clever bean!' But then her face clouded over. 'But if that's a bit of the dirk's blade that broke off, that won't help since Clarence's fingerprints are on the handle.'

'I took note of the dirk at the time of orchestrating the closing of this room, my lady. I suspect it is Jacobean, in which case the blade will be made of steel far too tough to snap off in wood. Even oak.' He stared at the piece of metal once more before wrapping it in a handkerchief and placing it in his side pocket. 'Now, we need to address your injury.'

'No.' She wrapped her hand more tightly in the handkerchief. 'We need to work out what that comes from.'

'You mean to hand it over to Inspector Lockhart?'

'Absolutely not! He is convinced of Clarence's guilt and would either dismiss it out of hand as irrelevant or find some convoluted way of using it as evidence against him. Whether we believe Clarence is guilty or not, we need to give him a fair chance. Now, as you're the font of all knowledge, you must have come across something like this before.'

'I fear not, my lady. This needs professional analysis.' He gave her that look she always dreaded. The one that said he was right, and she knew it.

She sighed.

'Alright. But playing the helpless maiden again is hardly my style.'

Clifford pinched the bridge of his nose and muttered. 'Would that it was, my lady.'

24

A long, frustrating hour later, Eleanor could bear it no longer. She snuck down the steps to the kitchen, leaning back out of sight until she could catch Clifford's eye and beckon him over.

'Have you been deliberately avoiding me?'

Clifford adjusted the perfectly aligned seams of his white gloves.

'Not at all, my lady.'

'Look, you know you'll have to tell me sometime. When I finished my phone call with a certain detective chief inspector, he demanded to speak to you but wouldn't say why.'

'Most unorthodox, my lady.'

'Clifford!'

Gladstone's head shot up from his quilted blanket by the range, ears twitching. Lizzie and Polly turned around from where they were polishing a raft of silver that filled the table in front of them. Polly put her hand on the top of Lizzie's head and turned her friend back to their work, but not without giving Eleanor a shy wave.

Eleanor folded her arms and fixed Clifford with her best stern look.

'Are you going to divulge the details of that dashed phone call or not?'

This time, he almost smiled. 'Forgive me, my lady, but I am merely following police orders. If Detective Chief Inspector Seldon makes a request, I am duty-bound to respect that request.'

'All I want to know is what Chief Inspector Seldon, I mean Hugh, said to you.' Sometimes she still found it hard to remember to call him by his first name.

'If you must pry, my lady.'

'I must.'

'The chief inspector was concerned for your safety. He instructed me to take every extra precaution in that regard.'

Her cheeks flushed. 'Really?' She shrugged. 'Perhaps I overdid the bit about my cut hand.' She held up the bandage Clifford had applied after dousing the gash with the most spitefully stringent antiseptic concoction she'd ever had to endure. 'We both know it's not that bad.'

He gave her a look that suggested she had the intelligence of a small child who had received a dull blow to the head. 'No, we do not. The chief inspector was more concerned, however, that a man had been murdered in the very castle in which you are staying.'

'Oh, that,' she said with a flap of her hand. 'Well, he might have mentioned that. As if I make a habit of being in the wrong place at the wrong time! He had the cheek to say I attract dead bodies like aged spinsters attract moth-eared cats! Well, it will be a good long while before I see him again, I can tell you!'

Her butler stood silently, with his hands clasped patiently behind his back. 'If you say so, my lady.'

She frowned, but let it go. 'Anyway, Hugh said he'll have that piece of metal you cleverly secured with the tweezer things analysed as soon as he can. I know we don't really know if it is part of the dagger that was used to kill Randall, or something completely unrelated, but as Randall died in that chair, it's worth pursuing. I guess Hugh asked you to make sure it got to him safely?'

'That he did, my lady. Chief Inspector Seldon also relayed to me the part of your conversation concerning his agreement to see if he could unearth any information on Mr Randall's background or any of our other suspects.'

'Yes, but he said it would be horribly slow. It is, after all, Christmas – in England, if not here – and things naturally run slower over the festive period. And for Wilhelmina's sake, he is also going to try to help us see Clarence by having words with Lockhart.'

Clifford winced. 'I can imagine just the kind of words, my lady.'

'And how badly they will be received, too. But we must speak to Clarence face to face. Lockhart has decided he's guilty as sin and, we both confess, in our minds we may think the same. However, I know there's something wrong somewhere. Sure, he had the means and opportunity—'

'And his prints were found on the dagger handle.'

'Yes, but his motive is all wrong. He had a row with Randall, true, but would he really kill the man who, we now know, held his financial salvation in the palm of his hand?' She shook her head. 'And maybe, just maybe, he'll be able to tell us something about that piece of metal. And we have a raft of other suspects still. The Laird and that mysterious money, Gordon and his open opposition to Clarence's scheme, Sir Edward sneaking out of someone else's bedroom the night of the murder, and Henderson slipping away from you in the dark just before the lights were cut.' She sighed. 'You know, I didn't really want to tell Hugh about any of this, let alone ask him a favour. I can't believe for once he's actually taking some days off. Even if it was on his superior's orders because he's so run down. Silly boy, I've told him before he should find someone to look after him.'

Clifford steepled his fingers. 'Hmm, someone forthright, impossible to sway, perhaps more stubborn than the gentleman himself and with an equal passion for fruit cake? I wonder where he might find such a person?'

Her nose wrinkled. 'Maybe, but forget that a moment, Clifford. More importantly, did you tell him?'

'Tell him what, precisely?'

'Oh, I so want to boil your head sometimes!'

'Too kind, I'm sure. If you mean, did I tell Chief Inspector Seldon that you are investigating the case, no I did not.'

'Good. Because I was just on my way to not-investigate the Fortesques!'

'Why the Fortesques, my lady?'

'Well, they are on our suspect list, but we haven't got anything on them yet. I want to know why they are here in the first place.'

He nodded. 'Agreed. They have made it plain that, like the rest of the family, they disagree with Lord Ashley's decision to marry below his station, as they perceive it. And yet, the rest of the family stayed away and they did not.'

'Precisely, Clifford. And I heard Clarence make it very clear that he and Wilhelmina *didn't* invite them. They invited themselves.'

'Which is even odder behaviour, my lady, I concur. I also observed that both Lord and Lady Fortesque seemed to dislike Mr Randall beyond even the normal, I hate to use the word "disdain"—'

'You just did, so go ahead anyway.'

'Very good, my lady. Beyond even the normal disdain certain stratas of English society hold our American cousins in, especially when they are, perhaps, wealthier than those doing the disdaining, as it were.'

She laughed. 'Which ties in very well with Clarence's barbed remark about the state of the Fortesques' finances. Which is another reason I am going to see the Fortesques. To find out if any of that has any bearing on Mr Randall's murder.'

A few minutes later in the drawing room, Eleanor seated herself on the faded blue flower-print settee at right angles to the caustic-faced Lady Fortesque. Sir Edward re-took his seat opposite his wife and made a show of picking up the hand of cards lying face down in front of him.

Undaunted that she obviously wasn't welcome, Eleanor nodded at the glass of white wine Lady Fortesque was holding.

'I'm more of a sherry girl. Or port. Although my cook makes a fabulous range of home brew concoctions.' She leaned forward conspiratorially. 'Though they're positively lethal.'

Lady Fortesque fanned herself with her hand of cards. 'Goodness, "lethal" indeed. What a choice of words given the boorish situation we were subjected to on Christmas Eve.'

'Oh gracious,' Eleanor said. 'How insensitive. Please forgive me. I fear we are all perhaps more shaken up by poor Mr Randall's passing than we realise. Especially, if one were long-standing acquaintances such as yourselves.'

Lady Fortesque spluttered into the drink she'd picked up.

'Us?' Sir Edward said. 'My wife and I were not acquainted with... *that* man.'

His wife sniffed. 'We do not mix with his type!'

Eleanor frowned. 'Sorry. It's just that you both seem to have such a... er, strong opinion about Mr Randall. It seems amazing that he had made such an impression on you in such a short time. And I'm sure someone told me you knew Mr Randall before coming to Castle Ranburgh.' *Well, it's only a small lie, Ellie, in a good cause.*

Lord Fortesque and his wife stiffened. They shared a look. Lord Fortesque shook his head almost imperceptibly.

'Well, whoever it was, was incorrect,' Lady Fortesque snapped.

Realising that was as far as she could go with that line of questioning, Eleanor switched tack. 'Your pearls. I was admiring them before the lights went out at the tragic dinner. And again at luncheon earlier today.'

Lady Fortesque stiffened again and shared a look with her husband. 'They were a wedding day gift from Edward. I wear them to every invitation luncheon and dinner.'

'And breakfast, too. They must be very special. I don't think I've seen you wear any other necklace. Perhaps you left for Castle Ranburgh in a hurry and didn't have time to pack your other jewellery?'

Lady Fortesque's eyes narrowed. 'Edward!' she said sharply. 'The bell.'

'What? Oh, yes, yes. Of course.' Sir Edward rose without taking his scrutinising gaze from Eleanor and went over to the sash by the fireplace and pulled it.

Eleanor tutted. 'Well, speaking of invitations, it was jolly sporting of you to come all the way up here without one. Or did I mishear the other day when you were talking to Clarence? I believe he said that you invited *yourselves* for Christmas?'

Lady Fortesque pursed her lips. 'One does not need an invitation. Edward and I are Clarence's family. His only relatives, I might add, who have put aside the disgrace he has brought the family name by marrying far below his station and come to support him this Christmas. And despite him being incarcerated and his wife having entirely abandoned her duties to her guests, Edward and I have stayed on rather than dashing back to the sanity of London.'

Eleanor's eyes strayed to Sir Edward, who was topping up his glass even though he was only halfway down it.

Perhaps stayed on more for the free hospitality, Ellie. And the fact that Inspector Lockhart has ordered us all to remain in the immediate area on pain of possible arrest.

She smiled sweetly. 'You really are an example of how family should be, Lady Fortesque. You must both be such a comfort to Wilhelmina and Clarence in their hour of need.'

Henderson appeared.

'Coffee,' Sir Edward said, without looking at him.

The door closed loudly and Lady Fortesque tutted. 'Clarence needs to engage a whole new staff up here.'

Staff, Ellie! That's what's wrong! She tried to think quickly. Blast it! If she could only ask Clifford, he'd know. She cursed her lack of observation. Or nosiness, whichever it was. She became aware the Fortesques were looking at her oddly.

'Er, you're quite right, Lady Fortesque. My bedroom, for instance, hasn't been properly attended to since I arrived.'

Lady Fortesque sniffed. 'Neither has ours. It's disgraceful.'

'I agree. And there's even less excuse for your room. Mine's on the third floor, but your room is only on the second floor, the first bedroom by the staff stairs. Hardly a long trek for a maid!'

Lady Fortesque sniffed even louder. 'Exactly! Although, our room is actually the second from the main stairs, not next to the' – she sniffed again – 'servants' stairs.'

'Oh, I'm sorry.' She quickly looked for another subject before they started to wonder why she was so interested in what room they were in. 'What line of business are you in, Sir Edward? I'm sure it's something frightfully exciting.'

'Edward is,' his wife said, 'extremely talented and sought after in certain rarefied circles that' – she flashed Eleanor a condescending smile – 'I don't suppose you move in.'

'Yes.' Sir Edward coughed again. 'That. What my wife said.' He marched to the drinks trolley and poured himself another generous measure of whisky.

Eleanor smiled sweetly again. *Time for another tiny lie, Ellie.* 'I'm sure you're right, Lady Fortesque. Being buried in the countryside as I am, I rarely get the chance to mix at all. Oddly, however, one of the circles I do mix in may be willing to back Clarence's scheme now poor Mr Randall can't. Isn't that glorious news?'

She jumped back as Sir Edward's glass fell to the floor and smashed.

He glared at her, then opened his mouth and closed it. Seeming to struggle with his emotions, he swallowed hard. 'An interest in business matters can be somewhat unbecoming for a lady.' Crunching his way over the glass, he strode to the door, his wife hot on his heels.

So, Ellie, it seems my hunch was right and the Fortesques may have known Randall before they came here. And they're definitely short of money. And I definitely need to talk to Clifford about their bedroom.

Their path was blocked by Henderson in the doorway bearing a coffee tray.

'Out of the way, man!' Sir Edward bellowed, barging past him. His wife followed him out of the room.

Eleanor rose and tipped the edge of the stunned footman's tray upright to stem the trickle of milk dripping onto his shoes.

'I think Sir Edward no longer requires coffee, Henderson.'

25

Castle Ranburgh was silent. *Too silent,* Eleanor thought. Outside, the threatened storm had yet to break and inside not a whisper could be heard. Since Inspector Lockhart had dragged Baron Ashley away, Baroness Ashley had only surfaced briefly to make sure, as much as she could, that her guests weren't being completely neglected. Then she'd locked herself away again in her room. Doctor Connell had retired home, making excuses about needing to get back to his patients early the next morning and the Laird and his son were nowhere to be seen. As for the Fortesques, they were avoiding Eleanor as if she had scarlet fever.

Dispiritingly, Clifford too had bid her goodnight with a finality she knew meant the minute his many duties were finished, he needed to retreat into his private sanctuary – solitude.

Eleanor lay in bed staring at the ceiling unable to sleep until a bone-shaking rumble overhead made her jerk upright.

At least something is up and awake with you now, Ellie. Even if it's only a wild Scottish storm!

She slid out of the huge four-poster bed that made her feel more alone than ever. Built for two, if not more, her slender frame failed to warm more than the minutest part of it now the bed warmers Polly had slipped in half an hour before Eleanor retired had lost their heat.

Wrapping the blankets around her shoulders, she shivered her way over to the narrow, arched window in her two pairs of woollen bed socks. The fire Polly had laid in the grate had long since gone out and the once cosy room was now freezing. She rubbed her hand over the leaded glass panes, trying to clear the crystals of half-frozen condensation. Peering through the pane, she gasped. Even though it was night, the snow lying on the hills seemed to give off a magical light.

Another crashing roll of thunder made her jump. A moment later, she stepped back as three forks of lightning split the sky.

Wow, Ellie! That was the brightest ever.

Having cycled over a host of mountain ranges around the world, she was no stranger to spectacular storms. But this one! This felt different. Even in her room, the electrified air made the hairs on her neck stand up. Despite the thunder and lightning, there was still no rain. When the next flash came the following rumble of thunder sounded further away.

Dash it, Ellie! The storm's receding.

In the flickering candlelight, she peered at her late uncle's pocket watch on the ebony bedside stand. One a.m. Another rumble of thunder had her heart skipping. She threw on her tweed trousers and thick wool coat over her pyjamas, grumbling at the folds of fabric that refused to tuck in anywhere.

Torch, Ellie, torch. Shoving it in her pocket, for a split second she hesitated. She'd promised Clifford she would be cautious. But staying in her room, being driven mad by her jumbled thoughts, was not an option. And the promise of more spectacular lightning was too enticing. Anyway, it was hardly likely anyone else would be up at this hour. Or in this weather. She'd given him her word not to be alone with another guest only. Torn, she seesawed her head. Then her eyes fell on the perfect thing.

That'll do nicely!

Fire iron in hand, she hurried from the room.

. . .

Inside the fort the Laird had taken her to, she scrambled up the uneven steps and swung her torch ahead as she climbed swiftly but carefully to the top. If there was going to be more lightning at all, that was the place to see it. And if it should by any chance light the straits her mother had been the only one to navigate safely... she nodded to herself.

Admit it, Ellie, you're looking for a sign.

Her hand strayed to her pocket where the velvet bag containing the stone she'd picked up on the beach lay safely cocooned. She rubbed her forehead so hard it left a pink mark, not convinced she hadn't made the whole thing up. The encounter with the young woman – if there had been such a thing – had left her feeling more hollow than comforted the more she'd run over and over it. Clifford hadn't said he didn't believe her, but he hadn't exactly said he did. She feared in truth he thought it had been nothing more than a mental aberration. A hallucination, made real by her twenty-plus years of longing for a chance to connect to her parents. And to her mother in particular.

She remembered that the last three steps of the curved staircase were particularly pitted and bent down to shine her torch. When she straightened up again, she was staring into a set of fierce eyes. She backed down a step and swallowed hard. The scowling face of Gordon Cameron looked all the harsher in the flickering light of the dim, glowing brazier on the wall behind him.

'Mr Cameron. What... what a surprise.'

'Nay surprise to me, Lady Swift.' He wore no coat, only a knitted woollen tunic, his kilt swapped for trousers.

She considered backing down the rest of the steps. *But he was here first, Ellie. He didn't follow you. And, anyway, if he has ill intentions, you'll be at a disadvantage with him above and you on the stairs. Better to stand your ground.* She gripped the fire iron harder and held it out of sight against her leg.

'Well, how right you were, Mr Cameron. Here I am. Good evening, by the way.'

'Witching hour left more than a wee while back, Lady Swift. Morrow's long upon us.' He half turned away. 'And may it bring something better.'

'Better than?' She steeled her voice, not wanting to appear unnerved.

'Just better.' His tone quelled part of her anxiety. He sounded more melancholy than menacing.

She advanced enough so she was on the same level as him. 'Your little fire there's almost out. Don't you feel the cold, Mr Cameron?'

'The brazier's for light, nay warmth, Lady Swift. Wind. Rain. Snow. Bit o' sun. It all comes and goes as it pleases here. Nothing's gonnay change just cause I take notice.' He glanced at her again, his eyes dark pools. 'Nay many come up here. Especially at night.'

Common sense began beating at her door again, along with Clifford's cautionary voice in her thoughts. 'I've interrupted you enough, Mr Cameron. I should probably get back to bed. I was hoping to see the lightning better up here, but it seems the second storm missed us altogether.' She turned towards the stairs.

He stepped around her, blocking her way. 'Dunnay go, Lady Swift. Another'll be along shortly. You can sleep when you're old.'

Assuming one lives long enough to be old, Ellie!

She hastily scanned his clothing. The gloom made it hard to be sure, but unless he had a miniature pistol or a small cosh tucked in a sock, he looked unarmed.

He seemed to sense her thoughts. 'I'm only asking for a moment's company, Lady Swift. I'm nay here to hurt you. You're the one who's come armed.' He nodded to her hand that held the fire iron.

Blast, Ellie!

She cast around for something to say. 'You're not much like your father,' she blurted out.

A fork of lightning lit the sky, chased by a clap of thunder. The sound rolled around the valley. He waited for it to die down.

'And you're nay much like an English lady.'

She laughed. 'I was brought up abroad and I've travelled a lot, as I believe you know, Mr Cameron.' She struggled for something to say again. 'Have you ever travelled?'

He seemed to consider the question. 'Nay for a long while. But I've been and seen Hamilton, Bannock and Bonnie Claire. That was enough for me.'

'I meant outside of Scotland.'

He looked at her oddly, then shrugged and looked up at the sky.

This is going nowhere, Ellie. Besides, you've a murder to solve and the man in front of you is a suspect. He openly disliked Randall and the scheme he was supposed to be funding.

'Mr Cameron, forgive my forthright question, but why are you so opposed to Lord Ashley's scheme? Is a ski resort really going to do so much damage?'

He laughed curtly. 'A ski resort? Nay so much.' His eyes darkened. 'But you have no idea of what will happen here.' He pointed out across the loch. 'The storm proper is coming. I'll leave you to it.'

He turned and was swallowed up by the darkness. She listened to the sound of his stout-heeled boots on the stone steps, making sure they were really receding.

'Well, that was interesting,' she muttered.

'Indeed, it was, my lady,' Clifford's measured tone came from behind her.

She spun around and made a face at his stern look. 'I'm armed. Look.' She waggled the fire iron. 'I could have called on my Bartitsu training and dealt with him with no trouble.'

'And if the gentleman had produced a gun?'

'You'd have knocked him out with that torch-cum-cosh you're carrying. And you can stop with that reproachful look. I knew you were here.'

He arched a questioning brow.

'Well, after a while.'

Seeming somewhat mollified, he cleared his throat. 'The lightning was spectacular, my lady. However, the next round will likely be accompanied by rain and more. Although' – his tone softened – 'also perhaps by the augury one might be hoping for?'

'Dash it, Clifford! If you learn to read my mind any better I'm going to have to think indecorous thoughts just to dissuade you from venturing in there.'

His face filled with horror. 'Dissuasion noted.'

He picked up the fire iron she'd put down and lifted the lid of the brazier Gordon had left behind. Throwing in several handfuls of dried leaves and an old bird's nest, he stoked the embers back into flames.

They stood without speaking, watching the storm approach. The wind picked up and the lightning and thunder increased until it was directly overhead.

She leaned towards him and shouted above the noise. 'It was just a silly thought. I don't believe in superstitious signs... really.'

'Then what are we doing up here, my lady?'

At that moment, an almighty clap of thunder broke overhead as a blinding bolt of lightning streaked across the sky and down the straits.

She gasped and stared down the channel, now in darkness again.

Was that a sign, Ellie? She shook her head. *You don't believe in signs, remember.*

As ever, Clifford had read her thoughts. 'Whether it was a portent or not, my lady, it will have woken Mr Drummond's monster. Shall we adjourn back to the relative safety of the castle's interior?'

'I suppose so.' She frowned. *You don't believe in monsters, either, Ellie. Except the kind that go around murdering people. And they're inside the castle, not outside. So, what are you really doing up here, then?*

She stepped to the brazier, spreading her hands out to warm them. And, if she was honest, to delay leaving for just a moment longer.

She blinked. *Of course!* Grabbing the fire iron again, she lifted the lid of the brazier and hooked the flaming contents out onto the flagstones.

'Put it out! Quick!'

Without hesitation, Clifford whipped off his coat and laid it over the flames.

She gaped at him. 'Clifford. Your coat!'

He looked at it and then her. 'Indeed, my lady. Yours was too combustible. Mine, being of a thicker weave and cloth, was more likely to cut off the oxygen to the fire and thus put it out as opposed to actually feeding it and bursting into flames itself. Which, I fear, in the case of your coat, would have been a waste of a fine garment.'

She shook her head. 'I know I said put the fire out, but I didn't expect you to sacrifice your coat. I'll buy you a new one the minute we get home. But for now—'

He held up a hand. 'For now, I have a spare, my lady. It may not be quite as robust, but it is serviceable until our return to Henley Hall.' He cleared his throat. 'If it is not too much of an imposition, may I enquire exactly *why* you felt the need?'

She grimaced. 'Well, I hope your coat hasn't been sacrificed in vain. But you see, I was thinking what exactly *was* I doing up here? And then it flashed into my mind, what exactly was *Mr Cameron* doing up here? At the top of a tower? At night? At the outset of a storm. In winter?'

Clifford glanced at his coat again and then nodded slowly. 'Because it is somewhere you would not expect anyone else to be.'

'Exactly!'

'Except, my lady, Mr Cameron did not allow for a visiting insomniac with an overactive imagination and little regard for her safety.'

Seeing as he'd ruined his coat for her, she let it go. 'Anyway, as you've no doubt worked out, our Mr Cameron wasn't here watching for signs.'

'Indeed he was not, my lady.' He leaned down and carefully lifted his coat off the extinguished remains from the brazier. 'Mr Cameron was, perchance—'

'Burning the evidence of a murder!'

26

Despite its vastness, after the freezing tower, the kitchen felt almost toasty. Clifford had lit one of the medium-sized ovens in the first range and now pulled a chair up to it. He held out a thick tartan rug and a pair of warmed socks to Eleanor before disappearing. Returning a moment later, he arranged Gladstone's quilted blanket around her feet. Even though he was panting, the bulldog refused to let her remove his Christmas jumper.

'Soppy old thing.' She looked up. 'Clifford, it's the small hours. You really can pause being a butler and at least partake of a warming brandy with me. You would have with Uncle Byron. And it is still Christmas.'

'As you wish, my lady.'

They raised their glasses and ruefully toasted to 'better times'.

Eleanor sighed. 'What a mess.'

'I agree, my lady.' He held her notebook open, shaking his head.

'You terror! I meant this whole business of Randall's murder. Not my enthusiastic, if spidery, note taking.'

He gestured over the pages. 'I had no idea arachnids were known for such zeal. Nor their propensity for trailing ink so liberally.'

She took her notebook with a mock huff. 'And yet, somehow, my untidiness hasn't hindered us too badly on each of the other cases we've been dragged into, has it?'

'On the contrary, I concede. That aside, this affair is, as you say, quite the mess. In all our previous excursions into such murky matters, the deplorable deed has never been committed whilst you or I were in such immediate or near proximity.' He bent and opened the oven door. A waft of something delicious tickled her nose. 'A jammy fruit bun, my lady?'

'Yes, please! They look too good for words.' She took one before he could reach the tongs.

He watched in horror as she licked the raspberry jam from her fingers, then turned back to her notebook.

'Now, as we said, despite any damning evidence against him, Clarence deserves an impartial investigation. So, let's to business again. The Fortesques.' She wrinkled her nose. 'I don't imagine for a moment that they are the successful society couple they pretend to be, especially after my last chat with them. Lady Fortesque has one set of jewellery and Lord Fortesque goes around the castle helping himself to as much of Clarence's free drink and cigars as he can lay his hands on. Though they try and hide it, they act as if the only chance they get to experience the high life any more is when it's at someone else's expense. In fact, I got the feeling they'd invited themselves to Castle Ranburgh despite their disapproval of Clarence's matrimonial choice, so they didn't have the embarrassment of not being able to afford to entertain over Christmas themselves. What do you think?'

'I concur, my lady. They are trying to hide it, but they have all the hallmarks of a couple in straitened circumstances.'

'Unfortunate investments or the war?'

'Likely both.'

'But then you'd imagine Sir Edward would be chomping at the bit to get in on Clarence's scheme, yet he's been nothing but dismissive. Or... do you think he might have killed Randall so he could sweep in as the saviour and bail Clarence out? At a hefty premium, of course.'

'The thought has struck, my lady. As you said, Sir Edward was close to apoplectic at news of your friend who was keen to finance the deal after Mr Randall was murdered.'

'You're right. Although you know my friend is completely fictitious, Clifford?' He nodded. 'And,' she continued, 'your theory would explain why the Fortesques invited themselves up here. Except—'

'If they are as *re pecuniaria*, or financially challenged, as we suspect, from where would Sir Edward obtain the money?'

'And why not just wait until Randall left? Unless they didn't know that he had refused the deal?' She chewed this over for a second, scanning the page of scrawled notes. 'Maybe Hugh will turn up something. I'm sure I hit a nerve when I suggested they knew Randall before they met him this Christmas.'

Clifford nodded. 'Chief Inspector Seldon has never let us down before.'

'And there's one other thing I haven't mentioned that I discovered about the Fortesques. Or Sir Edward, to be precise.'

Clifford arched a brow to show he was listening.

'When I was coming down to dinner the night we arrived, I spotted a man coming out of the second bedroom from the main stairs on the second floor. I thought he looked a little... jumpy, you know, looking this way and that. Well, I just put it down to an overactive imagination after the fatigue of a long journey and forgot about it.'

Clifford looked puzzled. 'That room is... *was* Mr Randall's. I assume it was he you saw?'

She shook her head. 'That's just it. I couldn't see who it was, but I could see when they hurried away that they had a slight limp. The same limp I observed on Sir Edward at breakfast! I checked which room was theirs and, as you just said, it wasn't the room that I saw him emerging from. It was Randall's! And I suddenly realised why I thought the man's actions so suspicious that night.

Apart from his demeanour, it was the fact that he hurried off towards the *staff* stairs. But I knew he had to be a guest because the only male staff apart from yourself, Clifford, is Henderson and he's much taller than Sir Edward.'

Clifford looked thoughtful. 'Very interesting, my lady. For the moment, however, I can only suggest we await the chief inspector's call to see if it throws any further light on the matter.'

'Agreed. In the meantime let's move on to Gordon Cameron and our other recent discovery.'

'I must say, my lady, along with Sir Edward surreptitiously visiting Mr Randall's bedroom, it was *your* discovery. I can take no credit for it.'

She smiled. 'Well, it was your coat that saved it from destruction.'

She carefully turned the notebook over and lifted the back cover. Underneath was a single piece of charred paper. She laid it carefully on the table. Clifford produced his magnifying glass and scrutinised it again.

'Despite the fire damage, the word "survey of" is clearly visible.'

She nodded. 'The night we arrived, when I was coming down to meet the other guests, I heard Randall accusing Clarence of trying to pull the wool over his eyes. I didn't hear the whole conversation, but what I do remember is Randall said, "No survey! No deal!"'

'I see, my lady. And you believe this is what remains of that missing report?'

'It seems likely, doesn't it? We know how opposed Gordon was to the scheme. So, he steals the report knowing Randall won't finalise a deal without it.' She frowned. 'But why wait until now to destroy it?'

'I imagine it would have been hard to do so with the police everywhere and everyone being so vigilant, what with a murderer running around the castle.'

'Of course! Since Lockhart arrested Clarence, everyone has

stopped watching everyone else like a hawk. It would have been next to impossible to get rid of it before now.'

'Although, Mr Cameron could have burned the document in the fire in his room.'

She shook her head. 'Come now, Clifford, you know that's often the first place a good policeman will look. But not in a brazier at the top of a rarely visited tower!'

'True, my lady. However, it would surely have been possible for Lord Ashley to have got hold of another copy of the survey.'

'Perhaps. But perhaps not before Randall had returned to America. We know he was due to leave on Boxing Day.'

'Which begs the question, my lady, if Mr Cameron stole the report so that Mr Randall would refuse to recommend Lord Ashley's scheme to his board back in America, why then having succeeded—'

'Would he kill Randall?'

27

Clifford thought for a moment. 'I don't know the answer to that, at present, my lady.'

Eleanor sighed. 'I wish my recent chat with him up the tower had revealed as much as our raking through the embers of that brazier.'

Clifford coughed. 'Forgive my contradiction, but I believe it did.'

'It did?'

'Yes, my lady. When you asked Mr Cameron if he had travelled, he replied in the affirmative. To Hamilton, Bannock and Bonnie Claire I recall.'

She flapped a dismissive hand. 'So? Even I know they must be in Scotland. I meant, *had he been abroad.*'

'I realise that. And so did Mr Cameron.'

She looked at him quizzically.

'Hamilton, Bannock and Bonnie Claire, my lady, are also the names of towns in *America*. Nevada to be precise.'

'Really? That *is* interesting.'

'Indeed. And what is even more interesting is that Mr Randall was from that area. I overheard him grumbling that nothing here was like Reno.'

'More and more interesting! But what do they all have in common, I wonder? The towns, I mean. Why mention them at all?'

'They are all former mining towns.'

She whistled. 'I need to call Hugh first thing, then. Which is probably only a few hours away now. He might be able to find out if Gordon Cameron actually met Randall.'

'A long shot, but worth pursuing. Although, the telephone line is temporarily down again. The storm has seen to that.'

'Blast!' She sat up straighter and took another sip of her brandy and then another bun. 'You suspect him most now then? Of killing Randall?'

Clifford rose and stepped to the long ceramic sink to fill up one of the large copper kettles, which he then placed on the top of the stove. 'Mr Cameron is certainly high on my list at this point due to the revelations we have just been talking about and his fierce opposition to Lord Ashley's scheme. However—'

She groaned. 'I know. That's all too neat and obvious for it necessarily to be the answer. In our previous dealings in these "murky matters" as you called them, the murderer is usually more discreet about shouting that they hate the person they are about to kill. Gordon made no bones about what he thought of Randall to his face and in front of all of us.'

'Well observed. However, Mr Cameron might be using the oldest ploy of all. Hiding in plain sight.'

She shook her head. 'I can't cope with double bluffs at this time of the morning. Or is that a single bluff? Anyway, let's move on. What are your thoughts about Henderson?' She waggled her pen at him. 'In regard to the murder only. Not his shocking disregard for fulfilling his duties.'

He shuddered. 'I have to confess I find it hard to separate the two. Of a man capable of performing his duties in such a criminal manner, I can imagine anything. However, in the interests of impartiality, I have yet to discern a motive for Henderson to have murdered Mr Randall. Means, yes, since he is obviously aware of the castle's armoury and its contents, assuming the dirk was from the collection. Opportunity, perhaps.'

'I know. It's eating me up that neither of us can be sure of the exact timing when he dipped back into the great hall to retrieve the key to the generator room. At least, that was what he professed he was doing. If he isn't the murderer, he certainly might be an accessory. We both believe he had the best opportunity to cut the lights.' She circled his name and added a quick doodle beside it – long spindly legs topped off by a pair of sneering lips. Clifford hid a smile and glanced further down the page.

'Ah! I see you have the Laird next. Thoughts, my lady?'

Eleanor tapped the pen on her chin. 'Hmm. He's a tricky one to fathom. His demeanour is delightful, his manners impeccable and his presence has been the only real highlight during this whole hideous excursion in the Highlands. Present company excepted, of course.'

'Thank you. Are you precluding him as a suspect then?'

She mulled over a few of her conversations with the Laird. 'Honestly, no. I mean, that money to Lockhart smacks as a bribe. I shall give him a mask for a doodle, since it feels like he's wearing one. A dashedly handsome one, mind. For his age, he's still quite the head turner. What is it about the rugged Scottish Highlander type that appeals to the ladies, do you suppose, Clifford?'

'I really have no idea, my lady. But, shamefully, your other staff would be most eager to render an opinion.'

'Ha! Has Mrs Trotman been up to her usual naughtiness in that regard?' As her butler's cheeks coloured, she waved a hand. 'It's alright, I shan't press you for the details.' She lowered her voice. 'Until our drive home, anyway.'

He coughed. 'Perhaps back to his lordship, the Laird? A possible motive?'

'None at all. Quite the opposite, you probably agree.' At his nod, she continued. 'He's been openly vocal with his support for, and involvement in, Clarence's ski-resort scheme. And if they needed Randall's money for the next phase, to have done away with him would be an act of lunacy on the Laird's part. Although Randall's refusal to put up the readies probably wasn't the end of the world for him. He seems to be doing fine, as far as one can tell. Not that you ever can these days. But I assume the resort is only of interest because it's on his... oh what's that expression Americans use?'

'His "home turf",' Clifford said with a sniff.

'That's it. So, no motive for the Laird then. Or Doctor Connell.' She seesawed her head. 'I think we definitely need to talk to him soon, however. He's sort of the invisible suspect at the moment.'

'Invisible?'

'I mean, I don't consider him when staring at the ceiling unable to sleep. After all, we only have that cushion business, not really that damming compared to the others.' As Clifford poured her a cup of tantalisingly rich roasted coffee, she rubbed her eyes. 'Tired now. But we must press on. Wilhelmina next.' She stared at the doodle of a delicate English rose. Something tugged at her memory. 'I say, Clifford, did you overhear what the Laird said about her when I first met him? Something about her having a backbone of steel and being one to fight the dawn or some such.'

'"The bairn that survived the hillside night", perchance?'

'Exactly! What did he mean?'

'It is said that in ancient times Scots would leave a sickly looking newborn child on a windswept hill overnight. If it survived, it was stronger than had been thought. If not, well... Forgive my forthrightness, but I concur with the gentleman that Lady Ashley is eminently capable of taking the dawn to task, metaphorically speaking.'

'I'm sort of with you on that. But I got a hint that she was uncomfortable about Randall being here. Not because Clarence was paying him too much attention, but—'

'Because Mr Randall was paying her too much attention?'

She threw her hands up. 'Honestly, Clifford, it's uncanny how you understand women. I thought confirmed bachelors were supposed to find us a completely unfathomable mystery. Don't tell me you'd guessed that Wilhelmina was with child as well?'

He stiffened. 'It is not my place to conjecture on such things.'

'That's a yes, then. But I agree. Randall's attention was far too liberal for it to be proper. Oh, gracious! You don't think...'

'I have tried fervently not to.'

She waved a relieved hand. 'Of course, it's impossible. I—' She frowned. 'What is it, Clifford?'

He cleared his throat. 'It would be impossible, my lady, were it not for the fact that I found out from young Lizzie that Mr Randall was here at Castle Ranburgh around six months ago. Apparently, the whole thing was very hush-hush. One can only presume that he was here on a forward-scouting mission for his board, and that having proved satisfactory, he then returned this Christmas to check on progress and, hopefully, seal the deal as it were.'

'Blast the deal, Clifford! That means Wilhelmina might have been referring to Mr Randall's *previous* visit. It's too awful to contemplate, but if Randall had forced himself on her then and now she's carrying his child—' Her hand flew to her mouth.

'That would be sufficient motive for Lady Ashley to have plunged the dirk into Mr Randall's back without a doubt.'

Desperate to shake the thought from her head, Eleanor slapped her temples, but it refused to budge.

'But she wouldn't have been able to carry on being civil to Randall and pretending up till his murder, would she? And, surely, she'd have told Clarence. Oh no!' That made her flop back in her chair.

'Who, my lady, being a true gentleman, would likely have taken every step to avenge his wife's honour.'

'Which might have been the real reason for the "blazing row" Clarence had with Randall only a short while before he was killed. Oh, Clifford, we've got to see Clarence and hear his side of the story. At the moment I feel all the evidence we have simply condemns Wilhelmina or Clarence to the gallows!'

28

Clifford pulled the Rolls to a stop outside a long squat building built of sombre grey granite, which contrasted with the white of the snow piled up around.

'We are here, my lady.'

Eleanor let out a sigh of relief. She'd waited all day for this. 'Not exactly homely.'

'Police station designers so rarely consider such important details as chintzy curtains in the cells and ample soft furnishings, my lady.'

'More's the pity when they're incarcerating who we hope is an innocent man.' She squared her shoulders. 'Now, we need to be prepared for Lockhart who will, I imagine, make us about as welcome as influenza.'

'Most assuredly.' Clifford's eyes twinkled. 'Yet, it is heartening that Detective Chief Inspector Seldon agreed to your request with such readiness.'

Her hand strayed to her stomach as the butterflies started up as she thought back to Seldon's rich, deep voice on the phone. She shook her head. 'Enough of that! Come on. Into the dragon's lair!'

The immediate and unmissable first impression on stepping over the police station's threshold was all-pervading damp. It made her nose wrinkle of its own accord. She looked around the stark, low-ceilinged and once whitewashed space that held nothing but a forlorn wooden counter bearing a telephone and a dog-eared ledger. On the opposite wall, an iron-rimmed clock was unreadable due to the condensation running down the inside of its glass.

A short, weathered policeman appeared and leaned his slight frame on the counter. *Constable Magoon, Ellie! He's a pushover compared to Lockhart. Maybe we're in luck.*

The policeman looked over his shoulder and then hissed, 'I'll thank yer to be as quick as the lightning of yesternight, Lady Swift. I'm alone, but Inspector Lockhart will be along wi'out a bagpiper's herald anytime before the clock strikes four.' He glanced around again, furtively. 'You see, he dunnay know that I'm letting yer see the prisoner. Yer detective fellow rang while I was on duty and the inspector were nay here.'

Clifford approached the counter. 'And her ladyship is most grateful.' He pulled a slim bottle of whisky from his jacket. 'Purely medicinal, Constable.'

Magoon licked his lips as he hesitated for a second. Then his hand shot out and took the bottle. 'The best chest rub for warding off a chill.' He nodded towards Eleanor. 'Thank yer, m'lady.' He leaned forward conspiratorially. 'I'm nay in the know as to why yer've braved the snowstorm that's a galloping o'erhead to see the prisoner. And I dunnay want to be.' He tapped his nose. 'Seeing as neither of yer are here. Clear?'

Eleanor smiled. 'Perfectly, Constable. Mr Clifford and I are at this moment strolling around the loch, enjoying the sights.'

'Och, yer'll nay find any sights out there.' The policeman jerked a thumb towards the front door. Fleetingly, his face took on a haunted look. 'Save the monster. He's a sight yer'll ne'er forget. This way to the prisoner and dunnay tarry about it, if yer will.'

In the dark narrow corridor they hurried down, their footsteps echoed on the stone floor and bounced off the grim, slate-grey walls. Two bare light bulbs along the corridor's length lit little more than the flagstone beneath which they hung.

At the second to last door, Magoon stopped and pulled an enormous ring of keys from his uniform's sagging jacket pocket. 'I'll have to lock yer in.'

'Most responsible of you, Constable,' Eleanor said.

'In yer go then.'

As the door slammed behind them and the sound of footsteps faded, Eleanor blinked in the gloom of the tiny cell. An iron bed frame took up the entire width at one end. On it sat Baron Ashley.

'Clarence!' She rushed up and reached for his hands.

He stood up in confusion. 'Eleanor?'

She stared at his dishevelled dress shirt and jacket, rumpled suit bottoms, and the dark shadow along his jaw that matched the circles under his eyes. 'Gracious, you look terrible.'

Baron Ashley grunted. 'Hardly my main concern, Eleanor. And what the dickens are you doing here?' He suddenly seemed to remember who he was. 'I say, that's terribly rude of me. Where are my manners? Won't you take a seat, er' – he glanced around and shrugged – 'on the bed. Apologies, it isn't much.'

She shook her head. 'I'm fine, thank you. And there's simply no time for niceties because Lockhart is on his way. And he doesn't know we're here.'

'Good Lord! He'll lock you up as well if he finds you.'

'Probably. But the thing is, Clarence, Wilhelmina asked me to help you.' She raised a hand as he opened his mouth. 'Listen. Tell me about the row you had with Randall and the truth about his involvement in your ski-resort scheme. And... and anything else. It's your only chance to get out of here.'

He hesitated, and then collapsed on the bed and let out a deep sigh.

'Oh alright. The long and the short of it is, Randall turned out to be a complete bloated shirt with his head in all the wrong trousers.'

She'd ask Clifford to explain what that meant later.

'Okay, so you argued because he wouldn't recommend your scheme to the investors he represented?'

He shook his head wearily. 'No. Not that. Well, yes, that as well. I hoped I could bring him round by cutting my margins to the wire so it would be impossible for him not to endorse it. But he somehow got it into his head that I was trying to cheat him. And then everything blew up when the blasted survey on the feasibility and cost of the whole project went missing.' He ran a hand through his unkempt hair. 'But it was no reason for me to murder the blaggard. Not that Lockhart sees it like that.'

'Does Lockhart know that your finances are a little... tight?'

'Of course he does. The first thing he did was call my bank and get the full damning picture. It's bleaker than I can bear to contemplate, if I'm honest.'

'Clarence, I need to be frank, because we have a few minutes at best. Your future looks just as bleak. To every logical-thinking person, after the blazing row you had with Randall, it's natural to jump to the conclusion that you killed him in a fit of rage.'

'Don't you think I know that already?' Baron Ashley snapped.

Eleanor's face flushed. 'But we both know we're not talking about that. Are you prepared to tell me why you *really* almost came to blows with Randall? Or not?'

Baron Ashley stared at her for a moment and then shook his head again. 'Not! It will have to stay undivulged because it will merely tighten the noose around my neck. Although, Wilhelmina will be better off when that happens. I failed her in the most unforgivable way.'

Eleanor was running out of patience. She threw out her hands. 'We've come to help, but you still aren't being totally honest with us. Clifford, it's time to leave.'

'Very good, my lady. I shall call Constable—'

'Wait!' Baron Ashley's voice came out as a croak. 'I'll... I'll tell you.'

'Finally,' Eleanor said. 'Now, what happened?'

'He...' – Baron Ashley balled his fists – 'he made a highly indecent pass at my darling, innocent wife when he was disgracefully drunk the last time he was here.' He looked up at her.

'I know Randall was here before, Clarence. Go on.'

He hung his head again. 'I never knew about it until Randall returned this Christmas. I noticed Wilhelmina seemed... withdrawn at the time, but I was so preoccupied with my financial worries, I just let her be.'

'So how did you find out when Randall came back? Did Wilhelmina tell you?'

'No. I... I saw it myself. And it made me sick to the stomach. Wilhelmina then told me that he'd done the same thing previously but she'd said nothing because she knew we were facing financial ruin and Randall was our only real hope of salvation.' He groaned and shook his head. 'I should have given him a thrashing and thrown him out immediately, the odious leech. But I was at my wit's end and' – he avoided Eleanor's eye – 'I behaved like a coward because I feared I'd lose everything. Including Wilhelmina.'

Wishing they had more time, Eleanor turned to Clifford. 'Show Lord Ashley what we found.'

Clifford shone his pocket torch as Baron Ashley examined the jagged piece of metal he'd dug out of Randall's chair.

'We think this might be part of the dagger or dirk that killed Randall,' Eleanor said. 'Or something to do with the murder weapon, anyway. Do you recognise it?'

Baron Ashley grimaced. 'Something is knocking on my thoughts but I can't... no, wait. Henderson!'

Eleanor and Clifford shared a look.

'Henderson?' said Eleanor.

Baron Ashley nodded. 'He had a metal thing this sort of unusual colour a few days before it all happened. When I glanced at it, he acted as though he was stealing the family silver. But he's never taken anything to my knowledge. And I was so distracted trying to work through the ski-resort scheme, I dismissed it as nothing.' He handed it back.

'Did you get a clear view of the object?'

'No.' Baron Ashley slumped at the sound of a key in the lock.

'Time's up, Lady Swift,' Magoon called from the doorway. 'I've got word Inspector Lockhart has left the records office, which is only five minutes from here. Haste yer both!'

In the Rolls, Eleanor couldn't contain herself.

'It must be Henderson, Clifford. If only I could think straight.'

Clifford's brow furrowed for a moment. Then his eyes lit up.

'The armoury room! In one of the cases an item had been removed.'

She nodded. 'The dirk that killed Randall, we now suppose.'

'Exactly, my lady. But there was a small cut where it would have been. At the time I thought it most odd. The other knives were all displayed lying flat. And the indentation suggested that the dirk had also been displayed in such a manner.'

She scanned his face. 'And your point?'

'That only if the dagger had been placed sticking up, blade downwards could it have cut the velvet so.'

Eleanor caught up. 'Of course! Clarence gave the Laird a tour of the weapons before Randall was murdered. Henderson had access to the display cases. So, he plunges the dirk into the velvet as if stabbing someone and leaves it there. Clarence comes along with the Laird, sees the dirk, thinks "what the—"'

'And grasps the handle and pulls it out. Then lays it flat as it should be.'

'Which means his fingerprints would be on the handle in exactly the same place as if he were stabbing someone.'

'More or less, yes, my lady.'

She frowned. 'But how did Henderson manage to stab Randall without obliterating Clarence's fingerprints? And not leaving any of his own?' She slapped her hands over her eyes in frustration.

Clifford stroked his chin. 'That problem aside, what was his motive?'

She threw up her hands. 'I don't know, dash it! That's what we're charging back to establish. Oh, why is Castle Ranburgh on a blasted island only accessible if one shares a rotting rowing boat with a man always draped in dead animals?'

Twenty minutes later, as they hurried over to the rickety jetty, Drummond approached with a dim lantern in one hand and a rod across one shoulder, a line of woodcocks hanging from it by their necks.

On board, Eleanor kept churning the same thought over in her mind.

It has to be Henderson, Ellie. But what was his motive? And how are we going to prove it?

She was shivering by the time they disembarked on the island at the tiny landing stage. It was a moonless night, the snow falling soundlessly. Clifford clicked on his torch and pointed it down the rough, unlit track to the castle. She waved away his proffered elbow. Almost at the entrance to the castle itself, he tried again.

'Please take care, my lady. Like the path, the cobbled entrance square is most uneven and covered in snow—'

'Oh, stop fussing, Clifford. I'm freezing. Let's— ah!' Eleanor stumbled.

'See!' He helped her up. 'Prudence is— oh!' He gently turned her away by the shoulders.

'Whatever are you doing, Clifford?'

'Keeping you from yet another unpleasant shock, my lady. Over what caused you to trip.'

'Why? What was it?'

'Not what. *Who*. It's Henderson, my lady. And I very much fear he's dead.'

29

'Eleanor!'

She shook her head. It must be the shock. Or the cold. Or both. But now she was hearing things.

She had refused to leave the spot where Henderson lay, so Clifford had headed inside to get help. But not before slipping something into her hand.

A pistol, Ellie! Oh gracious, whatever happened to Christmas?

Then standing there in the fresh snow, staring down at Henderson's body, she heard it again.

'Eleanor!' A deep, gruff voice tickled her ear. A flurry of butterflies swarmed from her stomach to her chest as she spun around.

'Hugh! But you can't be—' She blinked hard as Detective Chief Inspector Seldon's warm hand gently brushed the snowflakes from her eyelashes. His far too handsome, if weary, features almost broke into a smile. She stepped back to look him over, biting her lip at the sight of his broad-shouldered, athletic frame in evening wear. 'I don't understand. We spoke on the telephone just—' She peered up at his lean face, noting the lines under his usually bright brown eyes. 'How did you get here?'

'By train to Edinburgh, then another to Oban, followed by an interminable snow-ridden taxi ride. All topped off by a hair-raising expedition across that icy pond out there in a wooden bathtub by a disconcertingly silent man draped in—'

'Dead animals. That's Drummond. He's really quite harmless.'

Seldon grimaced. 'And charmless.'

'Actually, he's alright when you get to know him.'

'Unlike the Fortesques.' He jerked his head in the castle's direction. 'Honestly, Eleanor, dead bodies aside, I can't see what on earth possessed you to come up to this godforsaken place for Christmas.'

'Ah, yes. Speaking of which.' She indicated the body at her feet. 'It's Henderson.'

Seldon stared in disbelief. 'What? The young chap who greeted me an hour ago at my arrival as cheerfully as if I were a bout of chickenpox?'

'That would be him. He was the footman. But, Hugh, what I really meant is, why are you *here*?'

He gaped at her as if she'd lost her marbles. 'Because you asked me to come. Why else?'

'No, I didn't. I would never have dreamed of imposing upon your Christmas, especially since you're supposed to be resting.' She sensed a presence behind her. 'But I know a man who would have.'

'Clifford!' they chorused, spinning round to stare at her butler.

'My lady? Detective Chief Inspector?'

'You are—' she started.

'Incorrigible,' Seldon finished for her.

Clifford held out two powerful torches and an umbrella, which he passed to Eleanor.

'We need to have words,' she hissed.

'Naturally, my lady. Conversing would otherwise be a protracted and confusing affair.'

'No, I mean... oh, you are a total monster!'

'No,' Seldon said. 'I was reliably informed *that* actually lives in the loch.'

'Oh, stop it, both of you. In case you hadn't noticed, we've got a dead man at our feet.'

Seldon shook his head. 'Again.' He crouched and bent over Henderson's face. He inhaled sharply several times. 'Whisky.'

'Everyone drinks whisky up here,' Eleanor said, holding the umbrella out to shelter Seldon and the body. Despite her time serving as a nurse during the war and the unnerving number of murders she had become embroiled in, lifeless eyes still made her insides ache with sadness.

'Not while on duty, they don't,' Clifford said stiffly.

Seldon looked up. 'On duty or not, if he was drunk, he could easily have fallen' – he leaned back and covered his eyes from the fat falling snowflakes to scour the castellated battlements – 'from up there.'

Eleanor and Clifford glanced at each other.

Seldon grunted. 'Blast it, you two. What are you thinking?'

Clifford cleared his throat. 'Her ladyship and I had returned to Castle Ranburgh with information that led us to believe that Henderson was responsible for murdering Mr Randall.'

Eleanor nodded. 'And the timing of his death is just too... convenient.'

Seldon sighed and ran a hand through his hair, his chestnut curls soaked from the layer of snow already framing his head. 'Small consolation, but we at least have a fairly accurate time of death since he was the one who let me in, not more than an hour ago. Now, how do we get up there?'

'I believe the steps leading up to the battlements are over here, Chief Inspector.'

Eleanor looked at him in concern. 'Hugh, you haven't even got a coat on.'

If the wind had been bitter down below, it was the epitome of spiteful as Eleanor and Seldon neared the final section of the battlements. At least Seldon had consented to borrow the coat Clifford had worn since his other had been ruined by putting out the brazier fire.

She felt peculiarly protective as she watched Seldon's tired face study the scene before them.

She nudged his arm. 'We haven't got long. That oaf Lockhart will probably be here in less than half an hour. Clifford was right to telephone the moment we found Henderson's body since you aren't here in any official capacity, but I wish it was anyone but him coming.'

'Really?' He shook his head. 'No improvement on your lack of respect for authority then, I see. Including the police.'

'I respect you.' Her cheeks burned.

'Sometimes.'

She fought her way against the wind and snow back to the central point of the crenellated wall. Heaving her top half up on to it, she peered down to where Clifford was resolutely standing guard over Henderson's body.

'Eleanor! No!'

The dizzying drop to the ground would have been enough to make her head spin, but the sensation of Seldon's arm grabbing her around her waist was far more unsettling.

'Honestly, have you no sense?' He held her tightly. 'How Clifford makes it through a day of your recklessness, I daren't think.'

She turned to him, their faces almost touching, her eyes straying to his lips. 'Um, Hugh?'

He pointed over her head. 'Clifford's talking to someone down there.'

Sighing at the lost moment, she pushed herself off the wall. 'Is it one of the guests?'

'Portly chap with...' He leaned forward. 'Really? Is that a satchel?'

Eleanor was doing her best to listen to Inspector Lockhart without peeping at Seldon to see how he was taking the policeman's pompous theatricals.

With poorly disguised incredulity, Ellie!

Like the other guests, they had been ordered to gather in the same drawing room as before. The inspector delighting in resuming the position he evidently felt commanded the most authority, straddling the rug in front of the fire. Only Baroness Ashley had been given a dispensation, it seemed. Something Eleanor felt sure Clifford must have artfully engineered without giving away any hint of her condition.

'And what makes you think anything is amiss?' Lockhart barked at Eleanor, looking disparagingly over the fiery curls stuck to her forehead and her frostbitten red nose.

'Aside from the fact that Henderson is lying dead at the base of the entrance steps, you mean?'

He rolled his eyes. 'What else?'

'The distinct aroma of whisky on what would have been his breath, were he still breathing. Which he isn't because someone appears to have murdered him.'

'Supposition is a dangerous card in the game of detection, Lady Swift.'

'Then perhaps it might be wise to stop playing at it before anyone else is dispatched,' she muttered.

Seldon coughed to cover his chuckle.

'And you.' Lockhart shot a finger at him. 'Who are you?'

'I'm Hugh, actually.' Seldon rose and held out his hand. 'Hugh Seldon. A... friend of Lady Swift's.'

Lockhart's eyes narrowed as he ignored the proffered hand, making a show of resting his arm on his satchel instead. 'And you've suddenly arrived because?'

'Because I invited him,' Eleanor said. 'Hugh and I haven't seen each other for ages and it *is* Christmas.'

Lockhart scowled. 'Nay up here it isn't. And I've got to say I'm mighty tired of being dragged out here. Especially' – he threw out an arm towards the snow-covered window – 'in conditions like this when it's a complete waste of time.'

'Waste of time, Inspector?' Lady Fortesque said. 'Well, that's reassuring. Isn't it, Edward?'

'Certainly, my dear,' her husband said quickly. 'We've said all along Clarence showed terrible judgement when he hired that shambolic bunch he calls his staff. This dead blighter's clearly been stealing his whisky.'

'Aye. Easy enough to swipe a bottle and sneak away in a castle this rambling,' Gordon Cameron said.

Lockhart nodded. 'The boy could nay hold his drink and fell from his unwise hiding place up on the battlements, that is clear. 'Tis nay a job for the police.'

Eleanor couldn't help herself. 'If that were the case, Inspector, and he had stolen a bottle of whisky, mightn't he have been more likely to be hiding indoors? Out of the snow and bitter wind, you yourself were cursing earlier? As Mr Cameron noted, the castle is vast with a great many hidey-holes.'

'There's nay accounting for the foibles of men.' He glared at her. 'Nor of women, for that matter.'

Seldon tapped his temple. 'Will there be one of those... oh! What are they called? When a deceased person is examined?'

'Post-mortem. No! I'll nay waste more taxpayers' money on that foolery.'

The Laird nodded at Lockhart. 'How efficiently you have been able to draw your conclusion, Inspector. Mind, such is your reputation.'

'Aye, sir. And thank ye for reminding others of that.'

The Laird rose, swigging his whisky back in one go. 'A word, Inspector.' He ushered Lockhart into the adjoining room.

Eleanor, Clifford and Seldon shared a look.

'Lady Swift.' Lady Fortesque's nasal tone pierced Eleanor's eardrum.

'Yes?'

'You seem awfully interested in a servant's death.'

Her husband nodded, clearing his throat. 'Not usually the thing.'

'Perhaps not,' Eleanor said. 'But as I explained, I was just curious as to why Inspector Lockhart would think Henderson would have been out in such conditions. It's a veritable blizzard.'

'I would have thought you'd be the one to know.' Lady Fortesque arched her brow. 'Since you're the one who ventures up towers on this island in all weathers. And all times of night!'

30

'But what about Mrs McKenzie, Clifford?'

Eleanor, Clifford and Seldon were halfway down the stairs to the kitchen, Lockhart having departed, taking Henderson's body with him. Despite the lateness of the hour, they'd all three decided they needed to run over recent developments.

Seldon rubbed his hands over his sleep-deprived cheeks. 'Who's Mrs McKenzie?'

'Suffice to say, the scariest woman to ever wield a rolling pin. Or a meat knife,' said Eleanor.

Her butler gave an involuntary shudder. 'But neither is a match for the weapon that is her tongue. However, the lady is no longer on the premises. She resigned instantly on hearing of Henderson's death.'

Despite the late, or by now, early hour, the kitchen was a hive of activity. Mrs Trotman was kneading dough while Mrs Butters had her head in a huge wicker hamper, a flurry of linen tablecloths and napkins beside her as she counted aloud. Lizzie was washing a variety of pots and pans, while Polly's long willowy frame was precariously balanced on a tall stool. She seemed to be reaching for something at the back of one of the high oak cupboards. On seeing Eleanor and her guest, she tried to curtsey. Seldon caught her as she tumbled forward and gently placed her on her feet on the ground.

'Thank you kindly, sir. Oh, good morning, 'tis you, Inspect—'

'Polly!' Clifford said. '*Mister* Seldon is here purely as a friend of Lady Swift, as I mentioned before. Remember?'

'Yes, Mr Clifford. I do, now. We're not to mention he's a polic —' She clapped a hand over her mouth.

Seldon smiled at the young girl and put his finger to his lips. Eleanor bit back a chuckle as her cook and housekeeper surreptitiously cast admiring glances at him. Clifford turned and frowned at them, while taking the tray of teacups and saucers Lizzie brought. She bobbed a curtsey.

'Fairest morning to you, your ladyship. And to you, sir.'

'Thank you, Lizzie,' Eleanor said. 'I suppose it is morning now. We'll serve ourselves.'

Seldon tried to cover up the hungry gurgles from his stomach as the smell of frying bacon drifted over to them. 'I see, yet again, you have brought your entire staff on holiday with you. Including a new one, it seems.'

'Actually, Lizzie is one of Clarence's maids.' She sighed to herself as Clifford materialised beside her with her notebook, pen and a tray of mini delectables. She wished they didn't have to spoil the conversation with talk of death and murder.

Seldon looked at the food with the eyes of a starving man. 'Before we get into that.' He pointed at the notebook. 'I intend to devour a goodly amount of what I take is Mrs Trotman's wonderful pre-breakfast fare. After all, as a guest, it would be rude of me not to. And anything resembling a decent meal feels like days ago.'

Eleanor accepted a selection of hot savouries from Clifford. 'But I thought you'd been off work?'

'Yes. However, cooking doesn't seem to come naturally. I usually make do with toast.' He savoured a bacon and tomato triangle and sighed. 'Criminally good! Now, I might not be on duty, but I'm uncomfortable beyond all measure at what's been going on here. And how it's being handled.'

'By Lockhart?'

Seldon shrugged. 'I don't wish to speak ill of a fellow colleague I haven't exchanged more than three words with, but, yes. You made such a good point to him earlier, Eleanor, and it was totally brushed aside.'

'I did?' Her cheeks coloured at his unexpected praise.

'Absolutely. Why Henderson would have pilfered a bottle of whisky and then elected to drink it outside in a blizzard.'

'Which Clifford and I don't believe he pilfered or drank of his own accord anyway.'

Seldon nodded through his mouthful. 'I'll go with your joint judgement on that for the moment.' He held up the triangle. 'This is too good, by the way.'

'Try the eggy bread fingers with the red sauce. Or the cheese and bacon soufflé fellows, they're sublime.' Eleanor turned to Clifford and tutted. 'I know you won't, but I do wish you would sit and join us. But since you're respectfully abstaining, tell us, have any new theories come to you as to why Henderson might have been killed?'

'Only that despite our conversation with Lord Ashley and recent conviction that Henderson was the murderer, we were wrong. Perhaps, as we previously thought, he might have been an accomplice? One likely planned to be expendable from the outset perhaps, unbeknownst to him.'

'You did hint that he wasn't the sharpest tool in the box,' said Eleanor.

'In truth, my lady, the bluntest of bricks would not have been uncharitable, without wishing to disparage the deceased. What I cannot fathom, however, is why the murderer would have dispatched Henderson when he did.'

'Hmm, me neither. Perhaps if you could tell Hugh what Clarence told us in prison, he might have a theory?'

Having topped up their tea, Clifford relayed the conversation about Lord Ashley seeing Henderson with something resembling the colour of the piece of metal they'd found stuck in the dead man's chair. When he'd finished, he pulled his magnifying glass and the piece of metal from his inside pocket and handed both to Seldon.

Eleanor frowned.

'Hang on! You said you would make sure that got to Hugh safely.'

'As' – he gestured at Seldon scrutinising the piece – 'I have.'

'By handing it over in person! As you intended all along, perhaps?'

'Perhaps, my lady.'

'One day...' She slapped her forehead. 'Oh gracious, Hugh, I haven't thanked you for getting us in to see Clarence in prison. Whatever you said worked wonders, thank you.'

'Actually, it was what you said about Inspector Lockhart that let me get it right,' Seldon said.

'What did I say?'

'A great many unrepeatable and unladylike utterings. But they were enough to make me realise I needed to go around him, even without having met him.' He looked up at her. 'You realise, by the way, that Lord Ashley might simply have said all that about seeing Henderson with something made of the same metal as this simply to deflect suspicion from himself.'

'I know,' she said glumly. 'We've both thought as much but not been brave enough to articulate it yet.'

'We'll never get to the truth if we're not subjective, Eleanor.'

'I do know that.'

'So.' He put the magnifying glass and piece of metal down. 'You've dragged yourself and all your staff up here to partake of a forbidden Christmas in an icy castle. Why, for God's sake?'

'Because someone, not a million miles away' – she jerked her thumb at Clifford – 'badgered me endlessly about socialising with others in my, er... class.'

Seldon frowned. 'Nice going, Clifford. What an introduction to high society!'

'Let him alone,' Eleanor said. 'Poor chap's suffered enough

with being up here already.' She nudged Clifford's elbow. 'Besides, he's still got at least nineteen hours of being locked in the Rolls with me all the way home to apologise.'

Clifford bowed. '"Oh, for hindsight!" is so oft the cry of those in penance.'

Seldon laughed. 'Well, I have no idea what this piece could be from. Or how it could have helped Henderson – if it was him – to murder Randall and yet leave no fingerprints except Lord Ashley's.' He wrapped the shard of metal in a handkerchief and pocketed it. 'Now, let's put aside Henderson's death for the moment, as all talk of his murder is purely speculative, and concentrate on Randall's, which we can be certain *was* murder.'

Eleanor nodded. 'Hang on though, Hugh. You said last night on the phone that you had some news for us. You were going to tell me up on the battlements, but we got distracted.'

Seldon pulled his leather notebook from his pocket.

'Yes I do. About the Fortesques. Let's start with Sir Edward.'

'What did you think of him and Lady Fortesque, by the way? Objectively, of course,' Eleanor said.

'A pair of tired muttons masquerading as filet mignons.'

Even Clifford failed to stop his amusement from showing.

'Objectively speaking. However, I detected an unwavering devotion between them.'

Eleanor opened her notebook and flipped back and forth until she found her doodle of two clasped hands that she'd drawn for them. 'I did too. It's quite mesmerising to watch.'

'And encouraging.' Seldon avoided her gaze. 'Anyway, after pulling a horrible number of strings, I did uncover that Sir Edward had invested in a scheme some years back and lost a sizeable sum of money.'

'Ah! Which probably accounts for their, oh what's the polite word I'm supposed to use, Clifford?'

'Perhaps "impecuniosity", my lady?'

'That's it.'

'But' – Seldon lowered his voice – 'the deal was an

international one. And you won't believe the person who headed up the American side!'

'Eugene Randall the Third?' Eleanor breathed.

'One and the same.'

She glanced at Clifford. 'Well, there's a motive right there for the Fortesques murdering Randall that we hadn't fathomed.'

'Quite.'

'And, Hugh, you've reminded me of something. Clarence loudly proclaimed that the Fortesque family home was in significant hock just before Lockhart started.'

'Started what?' Seldon said.

'His "farcical perfunctions" as her ladyship described them,' Clifford said. 'Or "interviews", as the gentleman himself considered them.'

Seldon grunted. 'Given last night's performance, I can only imagine.'

'And, Hugh,' Eleanor said, 'the Fortesques weren't invited up here. They invited themselves. When I grilled them on it, Lady Fortesque tried to brush it off as them having a mutual open house policy, since she and Clarence are cousins.'

Seldon's face clouded over. 'Grilled them? Clifford, I thought you were going to keep your mistress from getting involved in investigating this until I got here?'

Clifford raised an eyebrow. 'Chief Inspector, have you ever managed to keep Lady Swift from investigating a broom cupboard, let alone a murder? Because, if you have, a few pointers on how to achieve this wondrous feat would be much appreciated. I said I would try, but truth to tell, there was an element of investigation even occurring before you rang.'

Seldon opened his mouth and then paused. Shaking his head, he sighed.

'Forget it. As should I. So, the Fortesques are certainly leading contenders for Randall's murder. Now, the Laird's son, what's his name?' Seldon looked down at his notes.

'Gordon Cameron.'

'That's him. He was definitely in America, supposedly visiting some far-flung clan members. But, interestingly, Eugene Randall was also in the area at the same time, although I can't confirm that they actually met. It could just be a coincidence. It's a big place, after all.'

Eleanor raised a finger. 'Hang on.' She hurriedly wrote out a new suspect list with the extra information under each name.

The Laird

Motive? No motive. Supported Clarence's scheme, so needed Randall alive!

Evidence? Lizzie saw the Laird give Lockhart an envelope full of money. For what?

Gordon Cameron (Laird's son)

Motive? Wanted to stop Clarence's scheme that Randall was financing.

Evidence? Was in same part of America at same time as Randall – did they meet?/stole and burned report on Clarence's scheme.

Fortesques

Motive? Revenge? Had lost sizeable amount of money in scheme Randall ran a few years before and now almost broke.

Evidence? Saw Sir Edward coming out of Randall's room the night of the murder.

Doctor Connell

Motive?

Evidence? Removed cushion from behind Randall that might have saved Randall's life just before his murder.

Clarence

Motive? Randall assaulted his wife.

Evidence? Standing behind Randall's chair when lights came back on/fingerprints found on murder weapon/rowed with Randall night of his death.

Wilhelmina

Motive? Randall assaulted her.

Evidence? She might have signalled for the lights to be cut just before Randall's death?

Henderson (footman)

Motive? None. Also now murdered.

Evidence? Clarence says Henderson had metal object possibly made from same metal as piece embedded in Randall's chair/as accomplice in best position to cut lights.

Clifford frowned. 'I did not hear the conversation. Perhaps I was fetching more drinks?' He clicked his fingers, the sound muffled by his pristine white butler gloves. 'I wonder though, Chief Inspector, if it really was a coincidence that Mr Cameron and Mr Randall were in the same part of the country at the same time? You see, Hamilton, Bannock and Bonnie Claire, the towns Mr Cameron mentioned to his ladyship as having visited, are also all American ex-mining towns, now abandoned. Gold mining towns to be precise.'

Eleanor started. '*Gold* mining towns? Wait a minute. Doctor Connell mentioned gold mining too! But here in Scotland. At dinner, before Randall was murdered, actually. But the Laird said only fool's gold and a few flecks of the real stuff had ever been found.'

'Interesting.' Seldon turned to Clifford. 'How in blazes do you know about gold mining by the way?'

'Alas, discretion forbids telling the full tale but suffice to say, Lord Byron, her ladyship's late uncle, engaged in some, er, gold mining of his own during our time out there.'

'Before you rode off into the sunset like cowboys?' Eleanor recalled Clifford had told her of her eccentric uncle's passion for everything cowboy.

Clifford's expression remained impassive. 'Indeed, my lady.'

Eleanor laughed. 'How I wish I could have seen you both.'

Clifford cleared his throat. 'Perhaps it is best you did not. Anyway, my point is it is odd, for one would think the Laird of all people would know the history of Scotland better than anyone, and this area in particular. Gold mining has taken place around here since 1500 and hundreds of thousands of pounds worth of gold extracted. However, no rich seams have been found for centuries. And, as far as I recall, no mines opened either.'

Eleanor looked puzzled. 'But Clarence's scheme is for a ski resort, so what—'

'Could that possibly have to do with gold mining?'

31

Eleanor watched Seldon's tall athletic frame as he marched away down the corridor. How could she dare hope the awkward relationship they had could ever blossom into anything consistently harmonious, let alone amorous? They were chalk and cheese. She had a deep-seated mistrust of authority, the very thing he represented. Added to that, they had actually only met when she'd unwittingly become involved in a murder. And this time was no different. Even if he'd felt in any way inclined to greet her romantically last night, he would have needed to embrace her with a dead man cosied up against his dress shoe.

Dash it, Ellie! Hardly the setting for a first kiss.

She closed her eyes and groaned. He'd looked too delicious in his evening wear. But even thinking that he might one day hold her tenderly in his arms and brush his lips over hers brought a smile to her face. Glancing after him once again, her heart skipped as he spun around and gave her an awkward wave. He ran his hand through his chestnut curls, as if unsure of what he'd done. With a hasty stride of his long legs, he vanished down the corridor.

Clifford materialised at her elbow. She held up a hand.

'I know. You've come to chivvy me into tackling the Fortesques again, seeing as they now appear to be among our chief suspects.'

'To quote the renowned Mark Twain, "If it's your job to eat a frog, it's best to do it first thing in the morning."'

'And if it's your job to eat two frogs?'

He winked. 'It's best to eat the biggest one first.'

'And which of the Fortesques is the bigger frog, do you suppose?'

He pretended to think this over for a moment. 'I am unsure. But do let me know. Once your unwelcome task is completed, and you've finished... assessing' – he nodded down the corridor in the direction Seldon had taken – 'a certain gentleman, of course.'

'Clifford! One's aged aunt traditionally plays the self-appointed family matchmaker. Not,' she said, pointing a finger at him, 'one's butler.'

He bowed. 'Apologies, my lady. I shall procure an aged aunt, forthwith.'

The breakfast room had but one redeeming feature, Eleanor concluded as she slid past Clifford without meeting his still twinkling eye. As well as containing two frogs, it also contained a large amount of Mrs Trotman's delicious breakfast fayre. She greeted the Fortesques brightly.

'Good morning! Just the three of us. How fortuitous.'

The look that passed between husband and wife suggested they didn't share her delight.

Lady Fortesque's gaunt hand strayed to her strings of pearls. 'Fortuitous, Lady Swift? And why is that exactly?'

Eleanor gestured to the salvers. 'More sausages to go round.'

Ignoring Clifford's horrified sniff, she slid into the seat he held out for her.

'Well, really!' Lady Fortesque muttered.

'What I really meant,' Eleanor said, 'is that I've been hoping for an opportunity to get to know you both better.'

'And yet I doubt our paths are likely to cross again,' Lady Fortesque said acidly. 'Since we appear to move in rather different circles.'

'Hmm.' Eleanor nodded. 'Truth be told, I'm still looking for my circle. I'm not terribly at home with formality.'

Sir Edward grunted. 'You don't say.' He quickly buried his face in his newspaper.

Eleanor ignored the quip. 'And I don't really do business, so I don't move in the same circles as you do, Sir Edward.' The newspaper stiffened. Eleanor waved at it. 'Christmas and still the financial and trade news needs to be devoured. I do wonder how businessmen like yourself manage to keep up *and* keep your wits about you? I mean, there are so many unscrupulous people about. Especially, I should think, when doing business abroad. And doubly especially, when doing a deal with *him*.'

A disconcerted cough emanated from behind the newspaper. Sir Edward's shoes scuffed against the floor. His wife adjusted the outdated lace of her high-necked blouse.

'Who is *he*?' Lady Fortesque finally said.

'You know, the poor chap who found himself on the wrong end of a dagger at dinner,' Eleanor said.

Sir Edward slammed his paper down.

'Lady Swift! The murder of a man is hardly a suitable topic for breakfast.'

'Absolutely not, Sir Edward. But I imagine the topic of Mr Randall's questionable business methods has been more than suitable conversation for the two of you over breakfast, lunch and dinner for a good many months now.'

Sir Edward glared at her. 'What precisely are you inferring?'

'Edward!' Lady Fortesque turned to Eleanor. 'Lady Swift, what is this nonsense?'

Aware that Clifford had done his usual magic trick of disappearing out of view without leaving the room, she held her hands up. 'Nonsense? So, it wasn't Mr Randall who swindled you so devastatingly in your last international business deal, Sir Edward?'

He groaned and put his head in his hands. Lady Fortesque's thin lips flapped like a fish but no sound came out.

Eleanor folded her arms. 'Now, come clean or I might just have to impart this information to a certain Inspector Lockhart. You're not here for Clarence and Wilhelmina's well-being. Nor solely to avail yourselves of their hospitality or Clarence's rapidly diminishing wine and cigar supplies. No, you invited yourselves because Clarence mentioned that Mr Randall would be here. Innocently mentioned, because, of course, he has no idea that it was Randall you lost so much to.'

'We... we...' Lady Fortesque set her shaking cup back on its saucer with a clatter. 'We thought we could warn Clarence off getting involved with him. My cousin is as stubborn in such matters as both our fathers were. We wanted to... help him.'

Eleanor shook her head. 'Help the very cousin you condemned the moment Inspector Lockhart arrested him? Let's be honest, you came to Castle Ranburgh to get revenge on Randall, didn't you?'

'It's no use, Fanny,' Sir Edward said. 'It will only look worse for us if we don't confess.'

His wife folded her arms defiantly but her hands trembled. 'That man was an unprincipled scoundrel! When we heard from Clarence that he was to be here, we knew it could only be because Clarence had some scheme he needed Randall's backing for. Edward and I came to catch him in the act of tricking Clarence, that we might... expose him.'

'Really?' Eleanor turned to Sir Edward. 'Is that what you were doing in his room the night he was murdered?'

Sir Edward's mouth fell open. 'How... how did you know?'

'I saw you. Now perhaps you would be good enough to answer the question. Or would you prefer Inspector Lockhart asked you? Were you trying to find evidence with which to blackmail him into repaying you the money you lost or not?'

Sir Edward's cheeks turned red. 'How can claiming back money that blaggard stole from me be in any way akin to blackmail!'

'Perhaps it can't. Inspector Lockhart can work that one out while he's charging you with Henderson's murder as well.'

Lady Fortesque gasped. 'How dare you suggest we would have

any dealings with a member of Clarence's ragtag staff. That fool couldn't even hold his drink well enough to cover his disreputable actions.'

'One moment, Fanny,' Sir Edward said in a voice that suggested for the first time it had once marshalled a regiment to attention. He threw the newspaper onto his seat behind him as he rose. Beckoning his wife to his side, he addressed Eleanor. 'Whatever your fanciful imagination tells you, do not for a moment think my wife or myself played any hand in Randall's murder. Or that idiot servant, Henderson's. It's not that I wouldn't happily have stabbed Randall in the back for the way he stabbed us in the back.' His wife gave a grim nod. 'It's just that I didn't get the chance. First because I found nothing in his room with which to force the scoundrel into giving us our money back and secondly because some other lucky blighter got there first and stabbed him for us!'

Lady Fortesque nodded. 'Exactly, Edward. We really must remember to thank Cousin Clarence at the trial for making sure the wretch got what he deserved.'

With that, they stalked off. The door closed loudly behind them.

32

Seldon's leather-gloved hands gripped the bench seat as the rowing boat pounded into the waves, his face a greenish tinge, the occasional groan escaping his lips. Since leaving the jetty, he hadn't torn his glassy gaze off the dead dogfish in the bottom of the boat. Eleanor brushed the fast-falling snowflakes from her coat and fixed Clifford, who was sitting stiffly upright next to her, with a stern stare.

'Very remiss of you not to tell Hugh he needed to pack his sea legs when you tricked him into dashing up here. Supposedly at my request too. He's positively bilious, poor chap!'

Her butler adjusted the perfectly aligned knot of his thick grey scarf. 'My lady, "tricks" are for music hall illusion artistes. I did not tell the chief inspector that you had requested his presence. I merely did not contradict the impression he drew during our conversation on the telephone.'

'Really? Well, at least I know where you learned to be such a scallywag now. In the music halls pulling rabbits out of hats, aided by a bevy of indecently clad female assistants, I imagine.'

He ran a horrified finger around his collar and brushed the snow from his neck. 'Looking to the positive, after the chief inspector received that second call last night, we now have a possible motive for Doctor Connell.'

'True. Hugh's contact told him that while Doctor Connell was practising in London, he had been struck off for prescribing the wrong dose to a patient. A patient who subsequently died. The medical board stopped short of suggesting that the dose had been prescribed on purpose, but Hugh's source believed it was certainly inferred to some degree, although as there was no proof, no further action was taken. I'm still amazed, though, if that is the case, how he came to be practising here in Scotland?'

Clifford waited for the rowing boat to settle down after a particularly choppy section before replying.

'Doctor Connell was struck off before the war and the influenza outbreak, my lady. Afterwards, as you know, there was, and in some parts of the country there still is, a dearth of medical staff. I doubt if the local medical board would look a gift horse in the mouth and bother to check too thoroughly a doctor's credentials if they wished to practise up here in the wilds.'

'Even if they had, I doubt they'd have made the connection as it seems Doctor Connell was practising under another name.' She glanced at Seldon again, just as the boat pitched particularly violently. He blanched and groaned hideously. She leaned sideways and whispered in Clifford's ear.

'I think the real problem is whether Hugh will survive long enough to reach our destination. He looks close to death's door as it is!'

In the back of the Rolls, Seldon folded his long legs into an untidy tangle and propped himself up in the corner of the back seat. With his sickly pallor and wet chestnut curls stuck to his forehead, Eleanor barely stopped herself from reaching out to take his hand. He rubbed his face and groaned as Clifford eased the stately vehicle out of the stone barn.

'Sorry. Not many choppy waves on the streets of London where I grew up.'

'Nor where you live now, I'm guessing.' She fiddled with the wool fringing of her scarf. 'I'm guessing because I have no idea where that is.' She bit her lip. She hadn't meant it to be intrusive. But aside from a couple of trips to Oxford Police Station where he was sometimes stationed, he had always come to her.

Actually, Ellie, be honest. You're aching to glimpse the real Hugh in his home surroundings.

He managed a wan smile. 'Suffice to say there are no three-foot snowdrifts blocking the roads or monsters lurking. And I don't need to call on fierce-looking men, draped in dead animals in unseaworthy buckets, if I require transportation.'

At that moment, the car lurched violently left. Clifford corrected it, only to have the car lurch right equally violently.

'My apologies. Ice on the road.'

From the back seat came another groan. 'Is there no form of transport that goes in a blasted straight line around here! Would someone remind me why we need to undertake this dratted trip at all?'

Eleanor tutted. 'We discussed this before we left. But perhaps you forgot during the crossing. After your revelation about Doctor Connell being struck off over a suspicious death in England, coupled with him having removed the cushion behind Randall's back just before Randall was murdered – the cushion that would probably have prevented the killer plunging the dirk far enough in to actually kill Randall – he's now moved up our suspect list. We also don't know where the Laird is, so Doctor Connell is the only other guest who might know *and* he mentioned something to do with mining and gold.'

She peered at his sallow complexion. 'And we're going to see Doctor Connell because I really do want someone to examine you properly.' This wasn't a lie, she was genuinely concerned about him. 'Why exactly were you given medical leave?'

Seldon rubbed his face with his hand and peered at her with

bleary eyes. 'My boss said I looked awful and was making too many mistakes. That and I fell asleep at the wheel while driving to interview a suspect in a robbery.' He held up his hands. 'I was fine. Not that my boss cared. He was more interested in the cost of repairing the car. And the wall. Anyway, he sent me to the police doctor, who said I was suffering from exhaustion and needed a week's rest.'

Eleanor shook her head. 'One week! You need at least two. You shouldn't have come up here, Hugh. Not in your state.'

Clifford turned his head towards them on the back seat. 'I am most sorry, Chief Inspector. Had I known, I would not have—'

Seldon held up his hands again. 'Look, I would have come whatever. I'm fine. This is no stress compared to my usual routine.'

Eleanor leaned back in her seat and said nothing, but her eyes betrayed her concern.

Twenty minutes of increasingly treacherous roads brought them to their destination. Eleanor rang the bell in the freezing reception area. Doctor Connell appeared from a low doorway in the whitewashed walls. Wearing nothing but a pristine white shirt underneath a plain bottle-green waistcoat, the sight made her shiver at the thought of not being wrapped in her thick sage coat.

'Doctor Connell, forgive my not having telephoned ahead for an appointment.'

He smiled at her. 'Don't mention it, Lady Swift. There's nay a soul in the village who has a telephone, save Constable Magoon and myself. Everyone simply walks in.' He waved a hand. 'If their ailment permits them, o' course.'

'Or they can manage it after crossing that blasted loch!' Seldon muttered.

Eleanor felt a wave of guilt at taking up the time of a potentially innocent doctor who might be needed elsewhere. *Unless, Ellie, he had killed Randall because the American had also found out about the doctor's shady past and threatened to expose him?* She became aware that Doctor Connell was staring at her oddly. She threw him a smile.

'I say... what a delightful surgery you have. And in such a...
pretty village.'

Doctor Connell continued to regard her quizzically for a
moment, then pulled a pocket watch from his waistcoat. 'I'd nay be
here on a Thursday morn of a regular week, Lady Swift, as I also
treat some folk in Craigstown, nine miles yonder. But the state o'
the roads has put paid to that today. So, you're lucky to find me in
my "delightful" place of practice. What is it I can do for you or
your' – he looked past her and nodded at Seldon and then Clifford
– 'companions?'

Eleanor stepped back and looped her arm through Seldon's
before pulling him forward. 'You haven't met my friend, Chief— I
mean Mr Seldon. You see, I'm concerned about him. I had to drag
him here since he is terrible about never making a fuss.'

She felt his arm stiffen.

*Boys, Ellie! Why do they always consider it so shameful to be
anything other than stronger than an ox?*

Doctor Connell's eyes flicked over Seldon's face. 'Then, you'd
best step this way. Both of you. Then we can attend to all the business in one go.' They both hesitated, sharing an awkward look.
'Ach, it'll be more than proper. There's no need for this gentleman
to e'en remove his coat. Come along.'

As he closed the door behind them, leaving Clifford to wait
outside, Doctor Connell shook his head. ''Tis common-a-day for
me to see a man and his wife in here together.' He looked between
them and smiled. 'Or two good friends, if that is what they prefer
to be. Sit, please, Mr Seldon.'

He pointed to the table dressed in an immaculate white sheet.
Eleanor glanced at Seldon and shrugged apologetically. She had to
bite back her smile as he perched on the edge, looking like a small
boy as even his long legs dangled off the floor.

Doctor Connell took Seldon's pulse before shining a pinprick
torch in each of his eyes.

'Hmm, as I thought. Your pulse said so. Eyes confirm it.'
Scooping up a tiny metal hammer, he stood to one side and tapped

Seldon's left knee, nodding at the weak kick this produced. 'You'll nay like it, nay will yer boss I've no doubt, but you need to rest, Mr Seldon, or all manner o' ailments will soon be your best friend. Exhaustion is fatigue's elder brother, sickness be their parents. Two weeks of rest minimum, though you need more.'

'I told you,' Eleanor blurted out.

Doctor Connell laughed. 'Hearty meat stews twice daily. Beef and liver is best. And all the fruit and vegetables you can fit in too. You're as run down as if MacAlister rumbled o'er your bones with his coal cart.' He pushed his spectacles further up his nose. 'I would say avoid the Munros and stroll only on the loch side and to switch from spirits to ale but you're nay an exercise nor drinking man I can tell.'

Eleanor saw her cue. 'That's amazing, Doctor. All your many years in medical practice really shows. Have you always practised in such a remote area of Scotland? It seems odd, a man of your obvious energy cooped up in this tiny village. Such a waste of talent.'

Doctor Connell eyed her coolly. 'It's nay on account o' examining folk o'er the years that I can tell what ails a person. It's studying human nature that informs a proper diagnosis. And my diagnosis for you, Lady Swift, is that your natural inquisitiveness will do you no good.'

Seldon jumped off the table, his eyes blazing. 'Are you threatening—?'

Doctor Connell held up a hand. 'And your inquisitiveness, Mr Seldon, is all part of your job I warrant.' He eyed them both for a moment. 'As you obviously know why I chose to practice in this' – he looked around the spartan surgery and out of the window at the grey, snow-laden sky – 'godforsaken place, I assume you came here, in truth, to find out if I killed Mr Randall?'

Eleanor smiled sweetly. 'It would be a help if we knew, Doctor Connell. At the moment an innocent man may well hang for the crime.'

The doctor smiled back grimly. 'Whether Lord Ashley is innocent or not, I dunnay know. That's up to the courts to decide. What I *do* know is, I'm nay about to take his place. Whatever circumstantial evidence you may have against me, you'll find no motive. For I have none.'

Eleanor pursed her lips. 'Perhaps you haven't, Doctor Connell. Or perhaps you have. Perhaps Mr Randall found out, like we did, that you were struck off in England and maybe he threatened to tell the local Scottish medical board?'

Doctor Connell shook his head. 'Why then would I murder him in public? And in such a theatrical manner? I'm sure you know that as a doctor I have access to many substances that would have killed Mr Randall discreetly without a trace, his death put down to say... a heart attack?'

Eleanor shot a look at Seldon who nodded imperceptibly in agreement. After all, that was what had been rumoured when he'd been struck off in England. She tried another approach.

'Did you pay Henderson to cut the lights? And then kill him when he tried to blackmail you? Or was it part of the plan to get rid of Henderson all along? No loose ends?'

Doctor Connell shot her a scathing look.

She held his gaze. 'Well, if you didn't kill Henderson, as you must have been his doctor, tell me, what did you think of his death?'

The colour drained from the doctor's face. He turned away and busied himself tidying up a couple of items of medical equipment. After a moment he spoke.

'I... I thought it was a tragedy. He was barely more than a boy.'

'I agree. But I meant about *how* he died.'

'He fell. Thankfully his injuries on impact from that height were sufficient to ensure it was o'er and done quickly.'

Seldon grunted. 'Strange, though, wasn't it? That he should have got so drunk out in a blizzard that he toppled off the battlements?'

Doctor Connell rounded on him. 'Henderson was ne'er drunk. He believed alcohol was the devil. If you'd seen the hell that poor boy lived through, with his father addicted to the bottle until it killed him when the boy was only nine, you'd nay question that. And, yes, I was his doctor. And as much else as I could be when he was orphaned by his mother, then succumbing to the troubled comforts of gin before he reached eleven.'

'Oh gracious!' Eleanor said. 'But why didn't you tell Inspector Lockhart that Henderson was teetotal?'

Doctor Connell, ignoring her, strode out through to the waiting room, past Clifford, and threw open the surgery door. An icy blast rushed in, accompanied by a flurry of snow.

'I should be getting on with medical matters, Lady Swift. I have *genuine* patients waiting.'

She followed him out. 'And I should probably be lounging about on a chaise longue like a proper lady. But, instead, I shall soon be clinging to the sides of Drummond's boat to get back to Castle Ranburgh where two men have died in the space of as many days.'

He silently gestured towards the door.

As they reached the Rolls, Doctor Connell called out to them. 'A word of warning. Watch your step. Not everyone takes as kindly to strangers in these parts as I do.'

As the door of the surgery closed behind him, Eleanor turned to Clifford.

'You have my full permission, next time I suggest Christmassing somewhere other than home, to call *our* doctor and have him confine me to a mental institution for the duration of the festive season. Even that would be an improvement on this year's Christmas so far.'

Clifford opened the door of the Rolls for her and Seldon and bowed as they climbed in.

'Very well, my lady. I shall make the arrangements in advance for next year. I'm sure the chief inspector will be happy to recommend a suitable institution.'

33

Back in the kitchen at Castle Ranburgh, Seldon looked far less peaky after their smoother return run across the loch. He helped Eleanor shrug out of her coat, then blushed as she fumbled to untie the tightly plaited bootlaces knotted around his wrists. Catching the small round pebble this released from each one, he shook his head.

'What a marvellous trick for easing seasickness, Clifford. Thank you.'

He bowed. 'My pleasure, Chief Inspector. A simple matter of engaging a natural pressure point in the body.'

Satisfied that the table was furnished with enough tea, fruit cake and other treats to feed an army, Clifford took up his usual post, that being three steps to Eleanor's side, his white-gloved hands behind his back. Gladstone chose that moment to struggle up from where he was sprawled against the range and let fly a round of sleepy, but husky barks.

She shook her head. 'That's done it.'

The bulldog heaved his heavy top half up into Seldon's lap, his stumpy tail wagging. Seldon ruffled the dog's ears.

'Hello, old chum. Nice jumper!' He turned to Clifford. 'Now, was Doctor Connell right?'

'Indeed, Chief Inspector. Having just checked Henderson's room, the two bottles of beer from Lord Ashley's supply I gave him on Christmas Day – regrettably, now we know Henderson's unfortunate background – are still untouched.'

Seldon choked as he savoured a mouthful of cake.

'From Lord Ashley's supply? Should I caution you for pilfering, Clifford?'

Eleanor tutted. 'As if! Clifford was merely ensuring Henderson had a good reason to stay in his room so we could all party down here with no one knowing. Of course, we didn't know he was teetotal then.'

Seldon laughed. 'Partying with your staff? Again?'

'It's Christmas!'

'Not that you'd know it!'

Eleanor sighed. 'Anyway, now we know what we do, it seems almost certain that Henderson was pushed off the battlements.'

'And,' Seldon said, 'as Lockhart has decreed there will be no autopsy, we won't know the level of alcohol in Henderson's blood. But I think it's safe to assume that someone forced him to drink enough and then tipped him over the battlements. Or they merely swished a godly amount down his throat once he was dead, before they tossed him over, so it would be detected on him.'

Clifford placed Eleanor's notebook and pen beside her. She opened it and hovered her pen over the late footman's name.

'Well, I don't believe Henderson was the murderer. For one thing we haven't been able to find a motive.'

Clifford nodded. 'Also, if Henderson had cut the lights, he would have had to then make his way swiftly from the switch by the door to Randall's chair in the dark, further than anyone else.'

Seldon grunted. 'So, let's assume Randall and Henderson's murderer is one and the same, otherwise there are two murderers running about the castle, and that isn't usually the case in my experience.'

Eleanor crossed Henderson's name off the suspect list. She stared at it for a moment.

'So did he know the plan was to kill Randall, or not?'

Clifford frowned. 'I believe I mentioned before that Henderson was not the sharpest blade in the room. And that would apply no matter what room one was discussing. It would have been quite easy to get him to carry out a series of actions without him realising what was going on.'

Seldon nodded slowly. 'So, we figure he was paid to cut the lights. And afterwards when he realised what he'd been dragged into, he was just too scared he'd be arrested as an accessory to murder to confess what he'd done to Lockhart.'

'Or,' said Eleanor, 'the murderer threatened him if he did.'

Seldon grunted. 'Either way, as he's dead, it doesn't matter much.'

Eleanor stared at her notebook, willing something they'd missed to jump out at her. Mrs Trotman flustered over, wiping her floury hands on her apron.

'Chief Inspector, sir, there is a telephone call for you, on the apparatus in the butler's pantry.'

'Thank you.' He leaped up and turned to leave, then spun back around and took another slice of fruit cake. 'This is too good, Mrs Trotman. The best I've had.'

Eleanor chuckled as Mrs Trotman's cheeks coloured. Clifford gave a sharp cough and waved the cook away.

Eleanor flapped a hand at him. 'Oh, come on, there's no harm in the ladies getting a thrill out of a handsome policeman being in their kitchen. How often is that going to happen?'

'I really couldn't say, my lady.' He leaned in and whispered, 'Since that is entirely up to you. However,' he interjected at her gasp, 'were the gentleman to become more of a... regular visitor at Henley Hall, I shall need a plan to deal with the shameful giddiness below stairs.'

A few moments later, Seldon returned. 'Eleanor, Clifford!' He waved his notebook. 'News.'

She tutted. 'What happened to you pretending not to be a policeman, Hugh?'

'Never mind. This is big. My source in London has excelled himself on' – Clifford stepped closer as Seldon dropped his voice – 'digging into the Laird's affairs. We already know the Laird's been supporting Lord Ashley's scheme. You said he's been quite open about it. But, it seems, he's got his fingers in myriad other pies.'

'To be expected,' Clifford said, 'of a man of his standing in the area.'

'Of course, but this is different. It transpires that the Laird was linked to a competing bid in an auction for a plot of land near here. The same auction that Lord Ashley eventually won. I'm assuming this is the land where the ski resort is planned to be built. The Laird's bid was placed through some, until now, all but impossible to trace company. But my man uncovered the details, and it seems the Laird is a director.'

Clifford's left eyebrow rose a fraction. 'Most surprising, Chief Inspector.'

Eleanor let out a long whistle. 'So maybe we have found a motive, or at least the beginning of one, for the Laird to murder Randall?'

'*And,*' said Seldon firmly.

'Oops! Sorry, Hugh, I didn't realise there was more.'

'*And* my man also found out that the Laird came down to London several times this year to visit R.H. Mining. They own and lease precious-metal mines all over the world.'

The three of them pondered. Clifford broke the silence.

'Why would the Laird secretly bid for the land and lose, only to then very publicly support the man who won? And what did he want with the land in the first instance?'

Seldon spread his hands. 'What he wanted with the land aside, it's highly suspicious that he would be so keen to invest in the very project that trounced his.'

'Perhaps he was just trying to make the best of a bad deal,' Eleanor said. 'If he couldn't get the land, at least he salvaged something?'

The men looked at her as if she were a small child.

'Pride, my lady,' said Clifford, 'would never allow a gentleman of the Laird's standing to take second best in a business deal.'

She frowned. 'It wasn't public knowledge that he'd bid and failed, though?'

'No. But *he* knew, my lady.'

Seldon rubbed his chin. 'Tell me, how did Lord Ashley come by this unwelcoming pile of rocks of a castle?'

Eleanor thought for a moment. 'I seem to remember he told me that the Scot whose family had owned it for decades went bankrupt. Clarence's uncle bought it for a song.'

'Along with the entire collection of weapons, I assume?'

Eleanor shrugged. 'I suppose so.'

'So,' said Seldon. 'As the original Scot's neighbours, the Laird, or Gordon, would have known about this armoury, which you must, by the way, show me later. Which means either of them could have paid Henderson to slide in and take the dirk.'

She slapped the table. 'It all adds up!'

She explained about the cut in the velvet in the weapon display case and their theory as to how Baron Ashley's fingerprints came to be on the dirk's handle.

Seldon whistled. 'Very impressive deduction, you two.'

Eleanor sighed. 'It would be even more impressive if we could deduce how the murderer – assuming it wasn't Clarence – managed to stab Randall without getting his, or her, fingerprints on the dirk.'

'And while still leaving Lord Ashley's unblemished. I know.'

'Robert Burns,' Clifford said slowly. '"On a Bank of Flowers".'

They both stared at him. Eleanor shook her head. 'It's no time to go all poetic on us, Clifford. We've a murderer to catch!'

Without a word he strode over to one of the wooden dressers and picked up a rectangular clock. Back at the table, he pulled a slim black tool roll from his inside pocket, along with his pince-nez. Whipping off his gloves, he selected a screwdriver no thicker than a mattress needle and turned the clock over. As he unscrewed the six tiny screws holding the backplate in place, Seldon leaned over to watch closely.

'I'm beyond intrigued.'

Eleanor said nothing, equally transfixed.

The back of the clock removed, Clifford held it with the fire tongs in the flames while he counted under his breath. One... two... three...

34

'Amazing!' Seldon cried ten minutes later. He held up a dirk, 'borrowed' from the armoury, the handle now swathed in a roughly made sheath, formed from the thin copper sheet of the clock back. Jamming the blade into a crack in the worn table again, he slid the sheath off a third time, leaving the knife behind. 'That's so obvious. Now.'

'Indeed, Chief Inspector,' said Clifford. 'The murderer or his accomplice tricked Lord Ashley into grasping the dirk so his fingerprints would be on the handle. The murderer then had a sheath made, similar to the rudimentary one I fashioned here. On the night of the murder, he slipped the sheath over the dirk handle, stabbed Mr Randall in the dark at the dinner table and pulled the sheath away, leaving the dirk behind in poor Mr Randall's back with Lord Ashley's fingerprints still on the handle.'

Eleanor tugged Clifford's jacket sleeve. 'Well done, you clever bean! What on earth made you think of that?'

He bowed. 'I have been reacquainting myself with Robert Burns' works while in his home country and I recalled the line, "Her closed eyes, like weapons sheath'd" from the gentleman's poem, "On a Bank of Flowers". I believe the jagged piece of metal extracted from Mr Randall's chair is part of the sheath made to fit the dirk. Even after being annealed, it can be brittle when faced with force.'

'Like being whacked against the unforgiving black oak of Randall's carver chair.' Seldon examined the rough sheath Clifford had made again. 'So, it seems we now know *how* the murder was committed and that Henderson was the murderer's accomplice. What we don't know is *who*, among our remaining suspects, is the murderer. Let's start with the good doctor, who we've just come from and who we were discussing before we were interrupted. He's right about the manner in which Randall died. As a doctor he could have poisoned him in any number of ways, as he was basically accused of doing with a previous patient.'

'And.' Eleanor swallowed the last bite of her fruit cake. 'I believe Doctor Connell's distress at Henderson's death was genuine.'

Clifford placed a new slice on her plate. 'Even if Mr Randall had found out about Doctor Connell's unfortunate past, why would he threaten to expose him? And I cannot believe that Mr Randall was trying to blackmail Doctor Connell. A local doctor in these parts makes but a pittance.'

Seldon accepted another coffee from Clifford and sighed. 'I hate to eliminate suspects without definite evidence, but I'm not sure we're going to get that in this case. Certainly not for every suspect.'

Eleanor leaned forward. 'So, eliminate Doctor Connell?'

Seldon shrugged. 'The method of murder. The motive. None of it fits.'

Eleanor crossed the doctor's name through. 'Well, that's two down. That only leaves the Laird and his son, the Ashleys and the Fortesques. And as we're assuming the Fortesques would have acted together – Sir Edward would have been the one to administer the fatal blow I'm sure – then in effect that's only five suspects.'

Seldon took a swig of his new coffee. 'Gah, that's hot!' He dabbed at his lips with a napkin. 'And I think that's as far as we can go for the moment in eliminating suspects. Of those remaining, the Fortesques are the best bet. They are the only ones whose motive stands, whether or not they knew Randall had declared he wouldn't back Lord Ashley's scheme.'

Eleanor picked up another forkful of fruit cake. 'I can see that for the Laird. And Gordon. They only had a motive to kill Randall if Randall was going to finance Clarence's scheme, whereas the Fortesques simply wanted revenge on Randall for him duping them out of their money. But Clarence might still have wanted Randall dead whether he supported the scheme or not because Randall possibly assaulted Wilhelmina. And she would have wanted him dead for the same reason.'

Seldon took a careful sip of his coffee. 'True, but take Lord Ashley. He knew that Randall had behaved' – he coloured and looked away – 'inappropriately with Lady Ashley way before Randall was murdered. In fact, he had a row with him over the matter. However, he didn't give him a sound thrashing and throw him out of the house as he told you he should have done. Why? Because he needed Randall's backing so badly that he still hoped to change the man's mind before he returned to the States. He told you so himself.'

Eleanor thought about it for a moment. 'You're right. All that points to the unpalatable but unavoidable conclusion that Clarence decided he needed Randall's money more than he needed Wilhelmina's love. His only saving grace is that he seems to have bitterly regretted the decision ever since.'

'Enough to try and put it right by murdering Mr Randall?' Clifford said.

Eleanor shook her head. 'It's possible, but that sound thrashing and throwing him out of the house Hugh mentioned would surely have been a better plan? And more likely to win Wilhelmina back rather than murdering a man in cold blood.'

Seldon finished off his now cooled second coffee. 'I totally agree. So, you'll be pleased to hear Lord Ashley goes below the Fortesques in our remaining suspects.'

'As does Lady Ashley, my lady.'

Eleanor and Seldon gave Clifford a quizzical look.

He continued. 'Even though Lady Ashley still had a motive whether Mr Randall supported Lord Ashley's scheme or not, it seems improbable, just like Lord Ashley, that she waited so long to get her revenge. And to do so in such a way that would have risked her going to jail or worse while...' He coughed discreetly.

'While with child?' Eleanor nodded slowly. 'I think you're right, Clifford. What do you think, Hugh?'

Seldon hastily finished his next slice of fruit cake and cleared his throat. 'I think that's an excellent point, Clifford.' He turned to Eleanor. 'I leave the final say up to you, as you know Lady Ashley better than me and I also feel you understand the female psyche better than me or Clifford.'

Eleanor laughed. 'Well, I'm not quite sure I understand the female *or* male psyche better than my butler, actually, but I don't believe Wilhelmina, no matter how much she wanted revenge, would risk her baby's life.' She crossed Lady Ashley's name off the list. 'So, it seems you were wrong, Hugh. We have reduced our probable suspects down to four – the Laird and his son, the Fortesques or, unfortunately, Clarence.'

She sighed and re-wrote her list.

The Laird

Motive? Needed Randall dead to regain land from Clarence.

Evidence? Headed secret rival company that wanted the land Clarence's ski resort was going to be built on. Also seems to have bribed Lockhart (envelope of money).

Gordon Cameron (Laird's son)

Motive? Wanted to stop Clarence's scheme that Randall was financing.

Evidence? Had stolen and burned Clarence's survey. Was in same part of America at same time as Randall – did they meet?

Fortesques

Motive? Revenge? Had lost sizeable amount of money in scheme Randall ran a few years before and now almost broke.

Evidence? Saw Sir Edward coming out of Randall's room the night of the murder.

Clarence

Motive? Randall had assaulted Wilhelmina.

Evidence? Standing behind Randall's chair when lights came back on/fingerprints found on murder weapon/rowed with Randall night of his death.

Seldon sighed. 'Sorry, Eleanor, but despite what we may think, it's still not looking that great for Lord Ashley. Even though there's a lot of circumstantial evidence that our remaining suspects could be the murderer, we've no proof. Especially without the sheath that preserved Lord Ashley's fingerprints. If indeed, we're right about that.' He tapped his chin. 'You know though, the Laird might have thought with Randall murdered, the investors would pull out, not wanting to get mixed up in possible adverse publicity. And with the deal as dead as Randall—'

'Given Clarence's parlous financial state, he would have had to sell the land to recuperate some of his debts.'

'Exactly. And the Laird could have bought it off him dirt cheap as Lord Ashley would have been desperate.' Seldon drummed the table with his fingertips. 'Mmm, it would have been a lot easier for the Laird just to have killed Lord Ashley, though.'

She nodded. 'And, besides, I'm pretty sure, as I mentioned, that the Laird knew Randall wasn't going to support the scheme, so why kill him?' She frowned. 'You know, I've never considered it before, but now we know that the Laird was supporting Clarence's scheme in public, but trying to derail it in private, perhaps—'

'The Laird and Mr Cameron are actually working together, my lady?' Clifford said.

Seldon paused, his cup halfway to his mouth. 'By jingo! You could be right! Both of you. It's the old con. In public Mr Cameron opposes Lord Ashley's scheme and his father's part in it. The fact that the Laird was willing to alienate even his son thus convinces Clarence of the Laird's commitment to the scheme.'

'But,' Eleanor said, slightly miffed that her idea had been hijacked, 'behind the scenes father and son work together to not only kill off the scheme so they can implement their own, but also to kill off Randall!'

Seldon stood up. 'We need to know if this is all just supposition or not.' He drove the dirk into the tabletop. 'And there's only one way to find out.'

35

Drummond turned the waxed-paper parcel over in his hand. Despite the thick falling snow, he wore no gloves or hat, his thin woollen jacket little more than a cardigan. He looked up at Clifford with a rheumy eye.

'Three more yer say, if I take ye all back?'

'And a wee dram of the finest in case you want to add a dash more to the gravy.' Clifford slid a bottle of whisky from inside his coat.

Drummond's eyes lit up. 'I'll nay add it to the gravy. I wouldnae mess wi' perfection. By the way, yer cook's nay looking for a ring on her finger, is she? 'Cos she's already paved the road right to me heart wi' that last hamper.'

'Allow me to be the bearer of your proposal on my return to Castle Ranburgh, Mr Drummond.' Clifford leaned in conspiratorially. 'But for clarity, would you prefer that I deliver your invitation on one knee?'

That drew from their oarsman a wheezy laugh that turned into a hacking cough as he bent over, slapping his leg.

'Yer a good sort, Mr Clifford. Three more o' her mouth-watering pies and that there whisky and it's a deal. I'll take yer all back when'er yer ready.' He tapped his weather-beaten nose, dislodging the shelf of snow that had settled on his bushy eyebrows. 'Mind, bring the lassie herself in her pinny along next time, and I'll row yer all for naught!'

Seldon and Eleanor stood listening with amusement to this exchange on the narrow strip of rocks next to the rowing boat.

Eleanor glanced at Seldon. 'Is the way to a man's heart really through his stomach?'

He shrugged. 'Depends on the man. But on the whole, I think, yes.'

'Then I'm definitely a lost cause. I can barely boil an egg.'

'I'd go hungry, no problem,' he said distractedly, watching Clifford help lash the rowing boat to a rock. Then he turned to her in horror as his words registered. 'What I meant Eleanor was, um... oh, blast it!'

She tried to smother her smile by burying her face in her scarf. 'Perhaps you meant going hungry is no problem because you do so most days on account of being overworked anyway?'

His face lit with an embarrassed smile of his own. 'Perhaps.'

Feeling awkward, they stepped apart, watching Clifford deftly swing a bulging rucksack with sturdy leather straps onto his back. A moment later, he joined them.

'Surely,' Seldon said, 'we could have split all that into two bags, Clifford, so we could carry one each? At least, you and I should take it in turns up that slope. It's steeper than anything I've ever scrambled up. Especially in this falling snow. It'll be treacherous.'

'Very good, Chief Inspector.'

Eleanor mouthed a heartfelt thank you to Clifford, knowing he had no intention of letting Seldon shoulder the burden, even for a minute. Not after Doctor Connell's diagnosis of near exhaustion. *Hugh shouldn't even be out in this weather, Ellie, let alone exerting himself by climbing a Munro to try to find the Laird and check out the land everyone seemed to want so badly.* She'd tried to reason with him, but he was as pig stubborn when he wanted to be as she was. He'd told her flatly that it was his idea to confront the Laird and she was lucky he was allowing *her* to come along.

From where they were standing, Eleanor had to agree with Seldon, however. The craggy, scree-strewn slope they needed to conquer would have looked formidable enough had it been the brightest of summer days. With the thick blanket of snow having blown into drifts, it would be hard to determine what the safest route would be. Assuming there was one. She slid her hands into the leather wrist straps of the ski poles Clifford handed her. Seldon stared at his.

'I can't ski.'

She rolled her eyes. 'None of us can. Not on this terrain of boulders and tree roots, you daft thing. They're just for balance and to test the depth of snow if we hit a patch that looks particularly deep. Come on!'

As her breathing deepened with the effort of climbing, the lungfuls of icy air felt as if they were peppered with shards of glass. Grateful for the two pairs of trousers she was wearing and even more so for her stout leather boots and double socks, she led the slow charge up the slippery path.

'If we had feet like mountain deer, this would be so much easier,' she called behind her.

'Hooves,' Seldon puffed. 'Even as a Londoner I know deer have hooves, not feet.'

Clifford gave a quiet cough. 'Their hooves are, in fact, two elongated toes. Encased in keratinous material for strength.'

Eleanor laughed as far as her lack of breath would allow. 'Thank you, Mr Encyclopaedia. But how is that use—?' Her feet sunk into a knee-high hole throwing her forward onto her face.

'It tends to assist them in not slipping, my lady.'

Scrabbling up with Seldon's help, she gave a mock huff and brushed her coat down. 'Touché, Clifford. But let's get a move on. We haven't been able to find the Laird anywhere else, so this is the last place to look. I'm sure he is up here somewhere. Between us we can force him to answer some difficult questions and we can finally see this land everyone seems to want. And maybe solve this case. How far is it do you think?'

Clifford looked up from consulting his pocket compass. 'Another mile or so, my lady.'

They both glanced at Seldon, then back at each other with a questioning look. Clifford patted his bag.

Ah, Ellie, a hot Thermos and some delectably sugary sustenance to keep Hugh's strength up no doubt.

Twenty minutes of sliding and scrambling later, however, she tuned into how much harder the going had become and how little progress they were making. That made no sense. The path had evened out and despite not having cycled long distances for some time, her fitness level was still high with all her walking, daily cycling and Bartitsu training. She rubbed her forehead and blinked hard. The horizon seemed to dip up and down as if she were back on Drummond's boat.

'My lady, stop!' Clifford inched hurriedly past Seldon on the narrow path and scanned her face. 'Hands.' He slid her gloves off by the fingertips. 'Hmm. Completely white.'

Seldon joined them. 'Eleanor, are you ill?'

'No.' She stared at both of them. 'Just a bit light-headed, for a moment. Ha!' She tried to laugh it off through chattering teeth. 'Can't be the altitude, I cycled over the Himalayas alright. Well, actually, I felt truly sick, but they're proper mountains.'

'As are these Munros, my lady. In terms of weather, at least. I noted you were swaying. Have you got wet feet by any chance?'

'No idea. I can't feel them at all now you mention it.'

'For Pete's sake,' Seldon muttered, pulling her gently down onto a large rock. 'Boots and socks off!'

Clifford rummaged in his rucksack. He pulled out a silver Thermos and a tartan blanket. Another short foray produced two pairs of thick socks.

'Thank you,' she slurred slightly, holding her shivering hand out. But that simple action made her topple sideways. 'Ah, maybe I'm a lot colder than I realised. Peculiarly, I have the desire to curl up and sleep.'

Clifford looked at Seldon. 'Her ladyship's feet need warming, Chief Inspector. And fast.'

'You mean you want me to be the one to—'

'If you will forgive me, Chief Inspector, it categorically cannot be me!'

As her butler turned his back, Seldon fell to his knees in front of her. Eleanor watched in numb amazement as he yanked her laces undone, pulled off her boots and then ripped her wet socks from her ghost-white feet.

'Apologies, Eleanor. No time for decorum.'

She gasped as he opened his coat, wrenched his thick jumper aside, and gently took her ankles. Sliding her feet up under his shirt, he tugged his clothing back down and set to briskly rubbing his hands over them under his jumper.

'Oh heck, they're freezing. Drink some hot coffee.'

'Um,' she mumbled into the Thermos' cup. He had always been so awkward with her. Yet here they were, up a mountain in a snowstorm, with her bare feet pressed against his taut stomach. Finally, a tingle of sensation came back after several minutes of his body warmth infusing hers. She wriggled her toes. This obviously tickled him as he doubled over. The ridiculousness of it made her laugh. 'Sorry, Hugh, it just feels a bit... a bit, um... nice, actually.'

His cheeks coloured. 'You are impossible. Thank goodness we all learned something useful during the war in the winter trenches, huh?'

Ten minutes later, filled with hot coffee and a sticky currant bun, she fended off any more offers of help. 'No, honestly, I'm fine now. If mortifyingly embarrassed for being so witless. And I can't believe you thought to bring me spare socks, Clifford.'

He bowed in response.

Seldon eyed Eleanor with concern. 'I can.'

Clifford stiffened. He lowered his voice. 'Chief Inspector, I believe we are being watched.'

Seldon nodded. 'Me too. There!' He pointed in front of them.

Eleanor peered into the swirling snow. 'Did someone just duck behind those rocks?'

Seldon nodded again. 'Yes, but there's not a lot we can do except keep going. We're safe as long as we keep them in sight and at sufficient distance.'

She stamped any lingering cold out of her feet.

'Then let's press on.'

As they were moving on after another brief stop, Eleanor held up a hand.

'Hold on. I think you've dropped something, Hugh.'

'Can't have. I haven't got anything in my pockets to drop.'

'Well, I definitely saw something glint.'

Clifford crouched down and scrutinised the snow. He stood up and dropped a pitted dull-burnished nugget the size of a large misshapen cherry into her gloved palm.

'Is that... is that gold!?' she breathed.

Seldon stared down at the nugget. 'It's fool's gold, I think. I remember reading something about it being less smooth than real gold. But you'll know best, Clifford, since you always do.'

Clifford examined it.

'I concur with your assessment, Chief Inspector. Fool's gold glistens. Gold shines.' Pulling the copper sheath he'd made earlier from his pocket, he ran it over the nugget's surface without leaving any trace. 'Plus, fool's gold or pyrite, being its mineralogical term, named from the Greek for fire "pyr", is harder than gold. It cannot be scratched with copper, whereas gold can.'

'Just a pretty bauble then,' Seldon said.

'Although it managed to excite a million men in the US to swarm to the gold-rush towns,' Eleanor said.

Clifford handed it to Eleanor. 'Notably, my lady, because the two minerals form in similar conditions.'

'What?' Seldon said. 'You mean—'

'That where there is fool's gold, there may well be real gold nearby.'

'I must say, you really are full of surprises, Lady Swift.' A voice hailed them from the head of the path.

Clifford and Seldon both stepped close to either side of her. Eleanor shoved the nugget into her pocket and spun around. She waved at the tall, thickset man swathed in heavy tweeds under a waxed overcoat.

'Hello, Robert. What are the chances of us meeting here, do you suppose?'

The Laird smiled. 'Evidently less slim than I anticipated.'

36

'Taking in our wondrous landscape while out for a stroll with your friends?' the Laird said with forced geniality. He pointed to the snow-laden sky. 'Perhaps you'd have done better to wait for fairer weather?'

Eleanor stood her ski poles in the snow. 'What better time to view the site of the ski fields you're planning with Clarence?' She tapped her temple. 'Wait though, "ski fields" doesn't sound right. What do I mean, Clifford?'

'"Slopes", my lady. I believe "fields" is a term usually reserved for places dedicated to other, quite dissimilar, activities.'

'Of course! Like mining gold.' She pulled the nugget from her pocket and held it up. 'Aren't they, Robert?'

The Laird gave a tight smile. 'Has your man packed you a shovel in his bag there? Because if you intend to pan for gold, you'll struggle. The burn, or stream as you would call it, is frozen.'

She shook her head. 'Absolutely not, Robert. You see, I've seen how everything that glitters is definitely not gold. And how greed can end for a person.'

The Laird took a deep breath, which he let out in a long, frosted cloud. He nodded at the nugget.

'You do know that's fool's gold?' He laughed mirthlessly. 'Of course, you do. You're no fool. But' – his forced smile crumpled as he ran a hand over his face – 'things were never meant to reach this ugly pass.'

'Just how did you mean for it all to end?' Seldon said.

The Laird shrugged his shoulders. 'With the fortune I should have rightfully made safely in my pockets. I'll admit that.'

Eleanor shook her head. 'You richer, but Clarence a great deal poorer.'

'Business is business, Eleanor.'

'It seems Randall was right, after all. He spotted underhand tactics in the scheme he was being pressured to champion. Only the underhandedness was all on your side, wasn't it, Robert?'

The Laird cocked his head. 'You shouldn't have come. None of you. Especially with a bulging bag of inaccurate accusations.'

Eleanor held his stare.

'I haven't actually made any accusations. I am merely stating facts. But perhaps if I fill in the details, it would make the conversation flow so much easier? And then I'll start on the accusations.'

His eyes narrowed. 'You want to be careful who you slander around these parts, Eleanor. I am Robert Cameron, Laird of Dunburgh. You do understand what that means?'

'Oh, absolutely. The power of your position affords you a most fortuitous privilege, doesn't it? No one dare touch you. And every man, woman and child in this region will automatically follow your lead on anything. Like sheep behind their Machiavellian shepherd.'

Seldon nodded. 'Just like on this ski resort scheme.'

The Laird laughed. 'So? That's good news for Clarence. He'd never get it through without my support.'

'But,' said Eleanor, 'you've been turning everyone against the scheme in the background whilst abusing Clarence's hospitality, haven't you?' Aware that the snow was falling more thickly, Eleanor knew they weren't far from a whiteout. 'It's no use lying, Robert. We know the truth about Clarence outbidding you for this land.'

The Laird stiffened.

'It can't have felt good,' she continued. 'The upstart Englishman muscling in on your territory. Not that Clarence knew he was doing so, since your connection to the bid was cloaked. But having lost, it was easy for you to secretly create enough obstacles that Clarence would have had to abandon his plan.' She looked at him in disgust. 'But to make sure you got what you wanted, Randall and Henderson had to die.'

The Laird's eyes blazed. 'I did not kill Randall. Nor the footman.'

She waved the nugget at him. 'Men have killed over a lot less than this, fool's gold or real.' She turned to Seldon. 'Despite being Lord of Dunburgh, the future looks bleaker for him than those mountain peaks over there, wouldn't you say?'

'Absolutely,' Seldon said grimly. 'As bleak as the long dark walk to the gallows.'

The Laird laughed scornfully. 'What would you know about things like that? You're a city man. Closest you've got to any of it is tutting over the newspaper headlines.'

Eleanor tilted her head. 'Hugh is a city man, you're right. But only since that is where Scotland Yard is based. You see, he's actually a detective chief inspector. And he's been investigating you and your questionable dealings for some time now.'

That took the wind out of the Laird's blustering sails. 'You've... you've no evidence of my part in those murders.'

'But I can find it,' Seldon said nonchalantly. 'Or embellish what I've got already. You've no doubt heard rumours of that happening in the force? Detective chief inspectors aren't called to question very often. If ever. I think you'll find that it will be considerably less damaging to your clan's reputation to come forth with the truth and shoulder the blame.'

The Laird raised his hands in surrender.

'Fine! But not because of your empty threats.' He hesitated for a moment. 'Alright, I met a fellow who found a gold nugget on this land before the war. Down there, no more than a few yards from the burn you cannot see for snow.' He pointed down the path. 'He had it valued at around eight thousand pounds and told me there was more.'

'Really?' Eleanor said. 'If that was true, why would this man have shared the news of his find with you? Why didn't he just sell the nugget and quietly get more?'

'Because war broke out and he was sent to France. He was under my command. One night, we none of us thought we'd make it out alive.' He sighed. 'Many of my men didn't. Anyway, he told me all about it. We made a pact that night that if somehow we survived, we'd come back together to establish a mine and find the rest. As you said, Eleanor, having the support of the most powerful man in the area meant he'd have had no bother staking his claim, undisputed. But the war changed everything. When we returned home, there were too many things needed doing just to keep life together. And then we found the land was to be auctioned.'

'And this partner of yours, did he make it back, too?' Seldon said.

'He did.' He hesitated. 'It was Doctor Connell.'

Seldon whistled. 'So, Doctor Connell was the one who originally found the gold nugget!'

Eleanor nodded to herself. It made sense. After all, Doctor Connell had told her himself that he had explored every Munro in the area, many twice. She folded her arms.

'We also know you set up a secret company to bid for the land when it came up for auction, Robert. The plan was to buy the land and then sell the rights to mine to an English company. R.H. Mining, if I remember correctly.' She glanced at Seldon who nodded.

The Laird said nothing, but his eyes glinted.

Eleanor shook her head. 'And for what? A fat percentage of the profits just for you and your partner? And when the mine was exhausted, the area would be abandoned just like Hamilton, Bannock and Bonnie Claire in America? Only how' – her brow furrowed – 'did you make sure the land came up for sale originally?'

The Laird's face darkened like a harsh storm. Clifford's hand slid inside his coat and pulled out the pistol he'd given her before as well as the torch-cum-cosh.

'Well?' Eleanor said.

The Laird's eyes switched from the pistol and cosh to her. 'This land came onto the market because old Gregor McFinley died after losing a long fight with illness. Amongst his loving family, mind. I don't kill people to get what I want, Eleanor. I don't need to. And I never planned to kill Randall to get this land.'

Seldon laughed curtly. 'So, what was the money you gave Inspector Lockhart for then if not to make sure you got away with murder?'

The Laird turned to Seldon. 'I'm impressed, Chief Inspector. However, it wasn't blood money. It was to allow certain... processes and inspections to be bypassed so we could get the mine up and running quickly, so there was something for the English mining representatives to see. It also included an advance fee for private security for the mine. Like a lot of the officers around here, Inspector Lockhart is not averse to bumping up his wages with some out-of-hours private work. Usually the local police authority has no objection – or no knowledge.'

As the Laird was speaking, Eleanor's eyes were focussed elsewhere, her brows knitted. As he finished, she jerked her head up and looked at Seldon.

'He's telling the truth.'

Seldon eyed her quizzically. 'How do you know?'

She frowned again for an instant and then nodded to herself before addressing the Laird.

'You can't have planned to kill Randall for one simple reason. No one did.'

'Eleanor?' Seldon's tone was quiet but urgent. 'What is this?'

She gestured to her right. 'It was Clifford who made me realise.

Although it hadn't sunk in fully until just then when he pulled *that* out again. Not the pistol, the torch.'

They all looked at the torch as Clifford turned it in his hand.

'But no one was hit on the head,' Seldon said.

'Exactly. No one was hit on the head, but—'

'The lights went out. Of course!' Clifford said. 'That is where events suddenly deviated from the murderer's carefully worked out script. Bravo, my lady. Beyond perspicacious deduction.'

Seldon gave her an enquiring look.

'He means well worked out.' She shrugged. 'Like I said, though, it was you who made me realise, Clifford. When we were re-enacting the dinner scene in the banqueting hall with the lights out, you were talking to me from the other side of the table. But then you turned on your torch and you were suddenly standing beside me.'

Like the Laird, Seldon was staring between them. 'You mean—'

She nodded. 'The darkness combined with the vaulted banqueting hall's misleading acoustics meant none of us could tell who was where.'

'Then Randall was stabbed by... accident?' the Laird said.

She nodded. 'He was never the murderer's intended victim. The murderer bumped heads with someone in the dark and lost his bearings.'

Seldon nodded slowly. 'So, now the murderer is slightly dazed, probably panicky, and knows he only has a few seconds before the lights come back on. He acts swiftly, but makes, for Randall, a deadly mistake.'

The Laird looked from Eleanor to Seldon, his brow furrowed. 'But why go to so much trouble to stab someone with a dirk?' He gestured to Clifford's torch. 'A well-timed crack to anyone's head would have done the job as effectively.'

'That,' Eleanor said, 'had me puzzled. But then the Fortesques gave me the answer. Sir Edward said Randall had stabbed him in the back when he'd stolen money from them in a business deal gone bad. And someone actually *physically* stabbing Randall in the back was poetic justice as it were.'

'I see!' Seldon said stroking his chin. 'Then who did the killer feel had stabbed him in the back so badly that he needed to avenge the wrong in such a poetic and dramatic fashion?'

'Surely, it's obvious?' the Laird said. 'If Randall was murdered in error, as the instigator and leader of the ski resort scheme, Clarence must have been the killer's intended victim.'

Eleanor shook her head.

The Laird threw his hands up. 'Then who?'

'*You*, Robert.'

All colour drained from the Laird's face. '*Me*? But who would want *me* dead?'

Eleanor looked him in the eye. 'Your son.'

The Laird stared at her uncomprehendingly. 'My... son? Go—' Then his face crumpled as understanding dawned.

Eleanor nodded. 'I don't know how but he found out about your scheme to betray your clan and sell their gold to the English. Perhaps when he stole and burned the original survey on the ski resort he stumbled upon another survey as well. One for the gold mine. But now I know that it wasn't the Laird and Clarence he was talking about when he said "but what you two have planned is more like dumping the two at the bottom of the loch". He wasn't referring to Clarence's ski resort, either. He was referring to you and Doctor Connell and to your plans to literally stab your fellow Scots in the back by selling their gold to the English. And after all that he believed, rightly or wrongly, the Scots had suffered at the hands of the English, his father betraying his clan to them was too much to stand.'

The Laird stood there, his head in his hands, repeating over and over. 'No, Gordon! No!'

Eleanor turned to Clifford. 'I think we should—'

'Get down!' Seldon yelled.

Eleanor spun around to see a figure emerging from the snow. And then the air was split by the crack of a gunshot.

37

She felt as if she were drowning. Her chest convulsed. She tried to breathe, but there was no air. Then the sight of the bright-red stain spreading across Seldon's white shirt brought her days as a nurse in the war flooding back.

You're useless to him like that, Ellie! Lock your heart away and use your head. Remember your training! It's his only chance.

Before she could speak, the sound of tearing cloth showed Clifford had anticipated her needs. She took the offering and pressed it on the wound, hoping against hope it would staunch the flow.

It didn't.

She looked under Seldon's already blood-sodden shirt. 'More wadding!' Pressing her fingers firmly around the ragged edge of the wound, she scrutinised the oozing crimson stain, praying she could at least slow it down. Otherwise...

At last! She removed the saturated fabric and replaced it with the fresh bundle of pristine white handkerchiefs and ripped shirt Clifford handed her.

'Pulse?'

She waited.

'Weak, my lady.'

She put her cheek to Seldon's. *Icy, Ellie. Deathly icy. Eyes vacant. No flicker of life. Breathing shallow.*

'He's going into shock!'

Clifford ran to the rucksack he'd been carrying. Tipping out the contents, he shot back, tartan blanket in hand. They ripped off their coats and scarves to add to the pile which she set about gently arranging under Seldon, leaving her coat last to place over the motionless man's lower half. Clifford tugged his jumper off.

'Mine too.' Without ceremony, he pulled it over her head. She cradled Seldon's ghost-white face in her arms.

'Hugh, you're going to be fine.' She bit her lip, hoping if her words reached him, they sounded more convincing than they did to her ears.

Clifford tucked her jumper around Seldon's chest, leaving her with just enough movement to press the remaining wadding onto the wound.

Something dawned. 'Gordon?'

'Gone, my lady.' He pointed to the pistol lying nearby. 'Unfortunately, I couldn't get a clear shot.'

'And the Laird?'

'He went to get Doctor Connell. He's waiting at their camp, further up the mountain.'

Clifford glanced at the still spreading stain on Seldon's shirt and then back at Eleanor and nodded at her unasked question. 'Yes, I believe we can trust him. He knows the bullet from Mr Cameron's gun was meant for him.'

For a moment she wished it was the Laird's body in her hands. That Hugh had never pushed him out of the way. He deserved it. Hugh didn't. She shook her head. No, there was only one person who deserved this. And locked away though it was, her heart told her when she found him, there would be another murder on this godforsaken mountain. Stroking Hugh's cheek, she grimly watched the life ebbing out of the man she now realised she loved.

Doctor Connell's voice broke into her dark thoughts. He ran to Eleanor's side and kneeled beside her. Without a word, he scanned

Seldon's face. At the same time his slender hands eased back the layers of warmth they'd lain over his torso. Briefly lifting the now sodden wadding, he took her hands and placed them back over the wounded area.

'You've done this man a great service. Now' – he yanked on his shirtsleeves until they ripped free – 'I need more dressings. And more pressure. I'll strap the wound as best I can, but I'll need more strapping for his chest too.'

'Trousers.' Eleanor jumped up.

'He's too weak to retain heat with just the coats and blanket.'

'Not his. Mine.' She tore at her waistband. 'I'm wearing two pairs.' In a trice, she pulled her extra pair over her boots, grunting as they caught and then stood up. 'I appreciate the gallantry,' she called to the backs of the two men who had instantly turned around. 'But for heaven's sake, can we just hurry!'

Her trousers were swiftly cut into long strips with Clifford's pocket knife. As Doctor Connell used them to secure the padding made of his shirtsleeves around the wound, Eleanor's breath caught at the tortured groan Seldon let out.

'Hugh, hang in there. You're in good hands.' She linked her fingers with his, trying to ignore how ghostly white and cold they were. 'Lots of hands. There are enough of us here to get you to somewhere with all the proper medical attention you need.'

His uneven, ragged breath had her praying her words were more than just an empty promise. She looked up at Doctor Connell questioningly. He lowered his voice.

'There's only one facility in this area with everything needed to save him.'

Eleanor frowned. 'So? We take him there. Now!'

He shook his head. 'That's the hospital in Craigstown. Seven or more miles from here by road.'

Eleanor's free hand flew to her chest. She kept her voice low. 'Seven miles away! But the roads must be close to impassable?'

He nodded. 'In a car, likely it would take two or three hours. Or more. *If* we can get through, which I doubt, even in that Rolls of yours. I wish I could tell you differently, but this man'll ne'er make it that long without treatment. I'm sorry.'

'You!' They turned as the Laird strode up to them. He pointed at Clifford. 'Conjure up a stretcher, man. Now!'

Without arguing, Clifford grabbed the rucksack along with the three sets of ski poles. Looking round, he spied the two snow-measuring poles in the Laird's hands and seized them in a flash. 'Coat, tie and belt! And help me string this all together. Quick!'

'Just what kind of butler are you?' Despite being addressed so informally, the Laird did as he was bid. With the addition of Clifford's belt, and Doctor Connell having thrown his over too, a rudimentary stretcher was soon created with the aid of Clifford's now empty rucksack.

Eleanor's mind was racing. 'But I don't understand. How are we going to get him to the hospital in time?'

The Laird stopped adjusting the makeshift strapping. 'We'll take the shorter route.'

Doctor Connell jerked around from tending to Seldon. 'That's nay an option to save this man's life, but one to end his and ours!'

The Laird's voice and look brooked no argument. 'This man saved my life. If I lose mine trying to save his, so be it. I don't expect you to risk yours.'

Doctor Connell returned his stare. 'You know me better than that, Robert. I'm a medical man. It's my sworn duty to save life if I can. But neither of us can navigate the straits. Nay at this time. They'll be at their fiercest. And if we wait until they calm down, t'will be too late anyway.'

'We don't wait. We go now. Neither you nor I could do it. But' – he pointed at Eleanor – 'she could. Our boat is only about fifteen minutes away if we can get our rhythm carrying the stretcher and manage the steeper of the two paths down.'

'Wait!' Eleanor looked at the two men, aghast. 'I can do what?'

'Get this man to hospital in time. Perhaps,' Doctor Connell said. 'It may be seven or more miles by road but by water the hospital is only a few moments away from the shore of the loch that joins this one.'

Her heart stopped for the second time. She rounded on the Laird. 'Robert, you think I can navigate the *straits*? Why? Because my mother managed it all those years ago? She was an expert sailor. I'm not. I've sailed, but...' She tailed off as he held up his hand.

'No, my dear, but your mother's spirit will guide you. And' – he pointed to where her fingers still gripped Seldon's – 'I believe you're the one who can do it because you have not yet had the courage to tell him how you feel about him.' His face lit with a grandfatherly smile. 'And he's never going to beat his nerves and tell you how he feels in return, if you don't give the hopeless fool a chance.'

They slipped and slid down the steep side of the mountain, almost dropping the stretcher many times, but somehow not. The three men had done a remarkable job of it, but Eleanor still prayed the poles and strapping would hold, and that the stitching of the ruck-sack wouldn't rip.

When they finally reached the shore of the loch, they had to tramp through drifts of snow to reach the Laird's boat. Eleanor groaned. The sails were furled and lashed tightly against their mountings. Setting to would take extra minutes they never had. Then she saw it – an outboard motor, secured in place on the boat's rear transom. And for the first time since seeing Seldon lying in the bloodied snow, she almost smiled.

'Nearly there, my lady.' Clifford leaped aboard, sweeping everything from the path of the Laird and the doctor as they placed the stretcher on the teak flooring.

'Not yet.' She ran her finger over the chart checking for hidden obstructions, but there were so many it was hopeless. Rocks, rocks and more rocks.

'Just let me stabilise the stretcher,' Doctor Connell called up to her. 'And someone find a thicker covering for this man. He cannay afford to be exposed to the waves that'll hit us.'

'Oh, come on, come on,' she muttered.

Clifford shot down the hatch into the cabin but returned almost immediately, empty-handed save for an enormous woollen cardigan, which he threw to her.

'No weatherproof coverings at all,' he shouted to the doctor.

'Time to cut and run,' the Laird called from the front deck. With two sharp strikes of a small axe, he spliced the ropes holding the smallest of the sails free. He delivered the sail to the stretcher where Doctor Connell arranged it as best he could over Seldon.

Clifford materialised at Eleanor's side as she finished pulling on the cardigan. She let her head fall against his shoulder for the briefest of moments. Without a word, he put something in her hand and rejoined the others at the stretcher. Looking down, she saw the pearly-grey quartz pebble that had called to her just before she'd seen the mysterious woman on the beach. She kissed the stone and slid it into a pocket.

Clifford started the motor and ran to the bow rail, ready to catch the front mooring rope the Laird was untying. Doctor Connell stepped up to her.

'His pulse is no stronger, but no weaker, either. You can only try, lassie.'

She nodded, swallowing hard.

'But,' the doctor said, glancing behind him, 'it might inspire you to know Mr Seldon just managed to rasp out your name.'

Her breath caught in her throat.

'And,' continued the doctor, 'he managed three other wee words after it. But I'll let him tell you those himself when he can.'

Three little words, Ellie! No. No. Focus. Breathe. It's just you and the boat. All you have to do is defeat the straits like Mother did.

But with the Laird having cast off the final rope, the boat instantly pitched violently in the swell only yards from the shore. She grimaced.

Or, as Drummond would say, all you have to do is defeat the monster!

Staring fixedly at the angry open water straight ahead, everything in her view blurred except the entrance to the straits at the head of the loch. She concentrated on getting a feel for how the craft reacted to the battering of the waves, allowing her body to roll and weave with every pitch and yaw. Just as she felt a ray of hope that she might master it, Doctor Connell semaphored to her with both arms.

'There's another boat bearing down on us!' He pointed behind her.

She darted a look over her shoulder, not daring to take her eyes off the horizon for more than a moment.

He's right, Ellie, it is another boat. But it's not coming to help. Not with Gordon at the helm!

38

Crouching down in case Gordon took a shot at them, Eleanor's view of the course she needed to steer was harder than ever to make out. Clifford grabbed the Laird's arm and pointed to the other boat. The Laird seemed to argue at first, but then pointed to the yacht's cabin, and made his way to the front. Clifford weaved his way to the cabin as swiftly as the wildly rocking deck would allow. Re-emerging, he darted to Eleanor's side, clutching a rifle. He dropped to his haunches beside her, hooking one arm through a lashed loop of rope to anchor himself. He cocked the gun, then gave her a rare smile. But it faded quickly.

'Mr Cameron's motor is considerably more powerful than ours, my lady,' he shouted above the noise of the outboard and the thrashing water. They both lurched violently to the left with the force of a rogue wave. 'He's gaining ground at a fair rate. Forgive my asking, but can you stay sufficiently focussed on navigating our course?'

She nodded. 'Gordon's tried to hit his mark twice already but failed. One man has died as a result and...'

Their eyes strayed to where Doctor Connell was doing his best to steady Seldon's limp form while hanging on himself. He caught their joint stare and opened and closed one fist against his chest to mime a beating heart. She let out a sigh of relief.

'... and another wounded.'

Clifford's tone was calm and measured. 'We still have a fighting chance, my lady. A Swift never gives up, however daunting the odds. I have personally witnessed that in the last year or so.'

She smiled grimly. 'The thickness of one's wedge of Stilton doesn't make it taste any less good.'

He arched a brow. 'Heartening news, I think, my lady.'

'We're just about to enter the mouth of the straits, Clifford. This is it.'

'Indeed, it is, since Mr Cameron is but ten lengths away.'

They stared at each other for a second, then over to the Laird where he crouched at the front of the boat, hanging on to the rail. Eleanor forced her gaze past him to check the course.

'It's too late, we can't outrun him. And there's no turning round. If we tried, we'd capsize for sure.'

As Clifford turned, braced himself and raised his gun, she grabbed his arm.

'If you miss, I'll jump overboard and find a way to kill him myself.'

He nodded.

For what seemed like an eternity, however, nothing happened. The choppy swell and the racing current meant neither boat made forward progress and neither man could get a clear shot at the other boat. Doctor Connell stood up and motioned down to Seldon.

'We need to speed up, my lady,' Clifford shouted. 'With apologies for stating the obvious.'

But she was already turning the tiller. 'BRACE!'

'My lady! We're going to broadside the—' Clifford's grip on the rope failed, and he slithered to the floor.

'Worst of the waves.' She finished for him a minute later. 'But it worked. I thought I spotted a faster stream in the pace of the water over here.'

'Bravo.' He regained his crouched position. 'Unfortunately, it seems Mr Cameron has followed you and is once again bearing down on us.'

A shot rang out. She ducked as Clifford returned fire. At the sound of the first shot the Laird had stayed down. At the second, however, he stood up and, hanging onto any available handhold, made his way to the back of the boat. Calling on every screed of concentration she could muster, Eleanor shut out the chaos around her and focussed on not capsizing them all into the icy loch waters.

'He's going to ram us!' Clifford shouted.

A moment later, the two boats collided. The impact wrenched the tiller from Eleanor's hand and sent her sprawling onto the decking. She scrambled to her knees. The other craft was still dangerously close. On the deck, Gordon was fighting to keep upright, his gun swinging in an arc. Out of the corner of her eye, she saw the Laird stagger to the side.

'Robert, no!' she shouted.

Ignoring her, the Laird held his arms out in surrender, seesawing wildly with the sway of the boat. 'It's me you want, son! Just me! Don't take these innocent people with me.'

Gordon regained his footing. His face contorted. 'Aye, it's you I want! Yer heart shot out, just like yer've been ripping the heart out a' everything our forefathers fought for.'

'You've got it all wrong. Son—'

'Dunnae you call me that anymore!' Gordon levelled his gun. 'I'll nay be any part of you and yer wicked schemes!'

Eleanor grabbed the tiller and steered them away from the other boat as Clifford braced himself against the mast and brought the rifle up to his shoulder.

'Prepare to meet yer maker!' Gordon yelled at his father, his face contorted with rage. 'And tell the devil it was me who sent yer back to him.'

Whether Clifford or Gordon would have fired first, Eleanor never knew. Gordon's boat was grabbed as if by an invisible hand and spun around. Then she saw it. A wall of water, twice as high as any other. It broke over the twisting boat, catching it broad on. The craft rolled over and disappeared under the breaking wave.

'GORDON!' As the rest of the deluge hit their boat, the Laird dived over the side into the frothing water.

Eleanor barely had time to register the Laird's action. The wave had knocked the tiller out of her hand and sent her sprawling a second time. The boat was corkscrewing in the maelstrom, moments from capsizing. She scrambled up, and as she placed her hand on the tiller, she felt another hand placed on hers. Not daring to turn around, she fixed her eyes on the spinning and bucking horizon and let the presence guide her.

The still choppy waters at the end of the straits felt millpond calm after the tempestuous waves of the rest of the channel. Finally, she allowed herself to relax. As she did so, she felt the hand that had guided hers release the tiller. She hesitated, then turned around slowly.

Her gaze was met by two berry-black eyes staring back at her. Her hand strayed to her pocket. She pulled out the pearly-grey quartz pebble. The seal blinked before sliding off the boat and sinking beneath the water.

'Thank you,' she mouthed.

A shout made her spin back. Clifford was pointing to the shore. She could make out a straggle of houses and beyond, further up... *It must be, Ellie, the hospital!*

'Doctor Connell!'

No reply. Her heart constricted. She'd beaten the monster, but Drummond had been right. It had taken Gordon and the Laird. *And maybe Hugh, Ellie.*

She was about to call again, when the doctor stood up with a smile as broad as the loch.

'Dunnae worry, lassie! Your man's going to make it!'

39

'Dash it! Why is composure so hideously difficult to master?' she muttered.

It had been several days since the awful events up the mountain and on the loch, and now she was waiting in the corridor of the hospital they'd brought Seldon to, hoping for good news.

Clifford pressed a handkerchief into her hand.

'Perhaps, my lady, because "the advantage of the emotions is that they lead us astray".' He winked. 'Oscar Wilde.'

'You total terror! You're forever chiding me for being a disgrace to decorum.'

'Not today, my lady. Not after history was made a second time by the formidable Swift ladies crossing the Straits of An-Dòchas. And not after the truly awe-inspiring fortitude you demonstrated in keeping those aforementioned emotions under lock and key long enough to get the job done.' He held up a gloved finger, his eyes twinkling. 'But tomorrow I will expect you to be the epitome of decorum and propriety.'

She laughed. 'I fear the reality may fall below expectations.'

'Steady now.' Doctor Connell's disembodied voice came from the other side of the white door.

'Thank you, but blast it, man. I'm going to be—'

'A terrible patient,' Eleanor finished for Seldon as he appeared in the doorway. 'Hello, Hugh. Welcome back.'

'Eleanor!' Seldon stepped unsteadily towards her, one arm strapped across his front, the other leaning heavily on a walking stick. He looked exhausted, his skin pallid, but to her, no less handsome.

'That's a policeman who's going to need a lot of looking after, Butters.'

'And fussing over, Trotters.'

Eleanor glanced sideways at her cook and housekeeper. Polly clapped her hands, her cheeks streaked with tears. Lizzie nudged her affectionately. Doctor Connell leaned against the door frame, sharing an amused look with the two nurses who had joined him.

Eleabor shrugged at Seldon. 'Everyone wanted to check that you are alright, Hugh.' She waved at her staff, who waved back.

Staring at the ring of faces behind Eleanor, he blushed and flapped a hesitant hand in return.

'Um, hello.' He shook his head and lowered his voice. 'Your entire entourage. Really? Now, listen. Before I work out how I'm going to get home, couldn't we go somewhere quiet for a moment?'

'Funny you should say that.' She looped her arm through his free one gently. 'Because it's all sorted.'

He stared at her in horror. 'What is? Blast it, Eleanor, what have you done?'

'Not me.' She jerked her thumb at Clifford. 'Him. I told you he was a total scallywag.'

Seldon turned to her butler. 'Clifford? Explain, please.'

He cleared his throat. 'Perhaps, it would be better to show you, Chief Inspector. A sedate ten-minute ride in the Rolls, perhaps?'

As if to celebrate that the horrors of their stay at Castle Ranburgh were truly behind them, the sun shone strong and bright. So strongly and brightly it had already turned the impassable snow of a few days before into slush. Nonetheless, Clifford drove sedately in case of ice, but apart from a few slips and slides – and one foray into a shallow, but easily escapable ditch – the journey went without incident.

Eventually they arrived at what passed for an airport in that region. The solitary runway looked as if it could do with immediate resurfacing, and the solitary brick building with immediate demolition. A massive battered wooden biplane with Royal Air Force decals stood at the end of the runway, its twin props turning slowly, engines humming.

The ladies tumbled out of another car with an exuberant Gladstone barking loudly. They were followed by Doctor Connell, who helped the women unload a raft of suitcases while repeatedly tripping over the excited bulldog. Eleanor and Clifford assisted a wincing Seldon out of the Rolls, where he turned and stared at the biplane.

'You've chartered an *aeroplane*? Tell me I'm dreaming.'

Eleanor tutted. 'I told you, my scallywag of a butler's behind it all. Doctor Connell wouldn't have discharged you until the middle of next week at the earliest otherwise. He made it quite clear you're not fit to endure a nineteen-hour trip in the Rolls, especially as you'd have to listen to Clifford and me bickering all the way. So...' She indicated her butler needed to finish the explanation.

He cleared his throat. 'Please forgive me, Chief Inspector. But I presumed, like her ladyship, you were keen to see the new year in, in comfort. And in a more congenial atmosphere than that of a spartan hospital bed and ward. So, I called in a favour on his lordship's sadly posthumous behalf to ensure you could stay at Henley Hall. As her ladyship's first guest, in fact.'

Seldon raised his eyebrows. 'An aeroplane?'

'A Handley Page Zero Four Hundred, Chief Inspector. Converted to carry passengers.'

Eleanor laughed at Seldon's bemused expression. 'As I'm finding out all the time, my late uncle Byron was owed favours by quite an eclectic assortment of people.'

'Our Wing Commander among them, Lady Swift. And willingly repaid.' A smartly uniformed pilot walked up to them and saluted. 'Flight Lieutenant Parnell-Jones at your service.' He nodded to Seldon and shook his hand. 'Chief Inspector.' He then shook Clifford's hand. 'And Mr Clifford, of course. Good to see you again.'

Seldon was still staring at Eleanor.

'New Year's Eve... at Henley Hall?'

The pilot pointed to the plane. 'If you'd like to board, we're ready for the off.'

'Thank you both, I think.' Seldon smiled. 'And Uncle Byron, of course.'

Doctor Connell took Seldon off to a discreet distance first to check the dressings and no doubt deliver words of caution not to take things too quickly. Eleanor knew he would struggle to follow the doctor's advice. *He's too stubborn, Ellie. Just like you. Well, you'll just have to make sure he does, that's all. You said he needed someone to look after him. Why not you?* Doctor Connell had been of the same mind, and had only finally agreed to release Seldon into her care because of her nurse's training.

Clifford passed her a couple of mint humbugs. 'To alleviate any discomfort to the ears during the flight, my lady.'

She took them with a fond smile and looked around. 'Happy to be leaving Castle Ranburgh, Clifford?'

'I believe when you first suggested coming here for Christmas I said it would be "woefully disagreeable". I was wrong. It was indescribably awful. I am happy to leave with every last fibre of my being. However, you are not of quite the same mind, perhaps?' He gestured to her coat pocket where her fingers were running over the pearly-grey quartz pebble.

'You know I'm not superstitious, Clifford, but—'

'But? Something that happened at the end of our trip through the straits?'

'The seal!' she blurted out. 'You'll think I'm mad, but I'm sure it was the same one I saw on the beach. The one that disappeared just as that young woman appeared. The one you didn't see.' She sighed. 'Maybe I am going mad with all the craziness we've been through.'

'Potential madness notwithstanding, my lady, I have no doubts about what you believe you witnessed. After all, it is not unknown for seals to board boats to escape predators.'

They both turned at the sound of a weathered voice. 'And right yer are too. But that's nay the reason yer saw her.'

'Mr Drummond!' Eleanor said in surprise. 'Are you here to enquire about the pies and whisky we promised you? Because Clifford has arranged a hamperful to be sent to you next week.'

That drew a hoarse chuckle from their faithful oarsman of the last few days. 'Nay, m'lady. I've come to ask the lassie in the pinny for her hand meself.' He gave Clifford a toothy grin. 'I'm thankful you gave her the message, but it must a' been the way you presented it that caused her to say no.'

'Undoubtedly.'

Clifford nodded, failing to hide his amusement as Mrs Trotman, having caught sight of Drummond, made a show of patting her hair and fanning her face. But first, Eleanor had a burning question to ask.

'Before you work your wooing charms upon my cook, Mr Drummond, how could you know what I think I saw?'

'Dunnae doubt yerself, m'lady. I know what you saw because I've spent ma' life on the loch.'

'Then please tell me. What *did* I see?'

'A selkie, m'lady, and nay mistake. I heard you talking to Mr Clifford about the woman on the beach on one o' our boat trips together.'

'A selkie? A seal woman. They're real?'

'If they weren't, I would nay be here. I took an injured seal aboard ma' wee boat one stormy night, but she was no ordinary seal.' He rubbed a calloused hand over his cheek, looking more misty than rheumy eyed. 'She rested at my wee home until one day she slipped into her silky grey pelt once more and slid back into the water.'

'When was this?'

'Enough years ago now. But she still looks after me. The monster's nay so much as tried a bite since.'

'The monster?' Eleanor scrutinised his face. *Is he playing with me?*

Drummond shook his head. 'It's no tale, Lady Swift. I seen him. His top half and his tail tip only, mind. But he's a fearsome beast. Nay one to be trifled with. He took the Laird and his son, God rest their souls. But the selkie saved yours and all those on board. Why, I dunnae know. Maybe, like Mr Clifford said, one jumped on yer mother's boat all those years gone by and she saved her from a predator. Maybe a shark or killer whale. We gets both here now and then.'

She nodded distractedly, her thoughts back on the rock with the mysterious young woman.

40

The ladies flustered over, Mrs Trotman struggling to restrain Gladstone as he spun in wobbly circles tangling his lead round her arm.

'Everything alright, my lady?' Mrs Butters said quietly.

Eleanor nodded and smiled. 'More than alright, thank you. I've just had a question answered that I shall take a while to digest. In truth, this Christmas has been quite the ride, hasn't it?' Wishing for the hundredth time it was acceptable to pull them all into a hug, Clifford included, she patted their arms instead and nudged Clifford's elbow.

Once her cook had gently but firmly turned down Drummond's offer of a hut on the shore of the lake – with as much venison and dogfish as her heart could desire no less – Eleanor marshalled her staff.

'Right. Are we ready?'

'To ride in an honest-to-goodness aeroplane?' Mrs Trotman said. 'You'd have to tie me legs together and chuck me in the loch to stop me, my lady.'

Clifford sniffed, but his tone was teasing. 'At least you would have a gentleman fisherman to gallantly hook you aboard and rescue you from the monster.'

Mrs Trotman put her nose in the air with mock affront. She

gave a resigned Drummond a farewell wave and let Gladstone drag her over to join the other ladies who were queuing up to be helped into the plane.

At the back of the queue, Polly was hugging Lizzie, tears streaming down her face.

'I'm delighted, but are you sure it's what you want, Clifford?' Eleanor whispered.

'For Lizzie, categorically. For Polly, absolutely. And for the chinaware of Henley Hall' – he let out a long sigh – 'most assuredly, my lady. Lord Ashley was very happy to agree. He intends, I believe, to engage entirely new staff at the castle.' He beckoned the two young girls forward. 'Lizzie, I am impressed that you did as you were bid and kept things a secret.'

'Thank you, Mr Clifford. It were terribly hard when Polly was so upset earlier though.'

'Polly.' He held out a handkerchief to Eleanor's tearful maid. 'There is no need for tears. Not since you will see Lizzie again.'

'I will, Mr Clifford, sir!' The young maid stared up at him. 'When? If it's not against the rules to ask, 'course.'

'Well, for starters, you will see her every morning when you both light the fires.'

Polly's lip trembled. 'I'm to stay on at the castle then, Mr Clifford?' She glanced at Eleanor, her eyes welling up again. 'If them's your wishes, your ladyship. Of course.'

'Oh, Polly!' Eleanor scooped the girl into the hug she'd always wanted to give her. 'You're not staying here. Lizzie is coming to work and live at Henley Hall.' She pulled back and dabbed at the girl's wet cheeks. 'I would never part with you. Ever.'

Seldon hobbled over, Clifford helping him.

'Eleanor, I, um... I need to say something to you before we're incarcerated in that flying box with your staff and over-enthusiastic bulldog.'

Clifford's lips quirked as he melted away, herding the two maids ahead of him.

'Eleanor!' Two voices called. 'Over here!'

'What now?' Seldon muttered.

The Ashleys stepped out of a car Eleanor had been too distracted to notice pulling up. Baron Ashley still looked haggard from his incarceration, but from the way his wife grasped his arm, Eleanor knew all was well once more in the Ashley marriage. They hurried over.

'We wanted to catch you before you left,' Baron Ashley said, 'but we arrived at the hospital too late. Some of the roads around the castle are still pretty snowbound. I, we, owe you an enormous debt.'

Eleanor raised an eyebrow.

'And Clifford, of course. Sorry, force of habit. He's an exceptional fellow. Chief Inspector too, we're in your debt.'

Baroness Ashley threw her arms around Eleanor. 'And you are an exceptional friend. Thank-yous will never be enough for what you all did for us.'

Baron Ashley nodded. 'You saved me from the gallows and a disastrous business deal. But we have ideas for new, more trustworthy, investors. Unlike the Laird!'

Eleanor held up her hand. 'I understand how you must feel about the Laird, Clarence. His actions in relation to your scheme were unforgivable. But he risked his life trying to do the honourable thing and save the man who saved his. And he never guessed Gordon's murderous intentions towards him until the day on the loch. And, despite that, he still sacrificed his life trying to save his son's. I feel whatever he did before, that day he put right any wrong he may have done.'

Baron Ashley raised his hands. 'I agree, Eleanor. In the end, it's our final actions that count and I cannot argue on that score. But on to more cheerful matters. We had hoped you'd stay for New Year's Eve. But, of course, you want to be home after all that nasty business.' He patted Seldon gently on the shoulder. 'You most of all, probably.'

'A weekend in London with us a little later in January?' Wilhelmina said. 'Both of you?'

With dates agreed for meeting in the new year and the good-byes finally over, Seldon tugged urgently on Eleanor's arm.

'What does a man have to do to get your undivided attention for just a moment?'

'Aside from pressing my bare feet to his shirtless stomach? And in front of my butler, too. Tsk, tsk!'

He smiled, but then his expression became earnest again. 'Seriously, I don't want to wait to tell you this. Eleanor—'

'All aboard please, folks,' their pilot called from the steps. 'We've got a short window for landing the other end.'

'Blast the window!' Seldon shouted across the tarmac. 'Clifford, for Pete's sake, help an injured man out here!'

A moment later, they were finally alone. Seldon shuffled his feet and ran a hand through his curls.

'I think I tried to say this when you were saving me from bleeding to death on a frozen mountain. But I don't suppose it came out right since I kept lapsing in and out of consciousness.' He winced. 'Or maybe it did?'

She raised a finger. 'First of all, Hugh, it wasn't just me. Doctor Connell, Clifford and the Laird played their part. And I really don't know what you said.' She bit her lip. 'But only because it wasn't me you said it to.'

'What!?'

'It's alright, Doctor Connell's been in practice for many years. I bet he's heard all sorts.'

He groaned and half turned his back to the plane. 'Nothing goes right when I'm with you, Eleanor. We're either up to our necks in dead bodies, arguing on that wretched telephone apparatus or—'

'Or what, Hugh?'

'Torturing ourselves that we might ever be able to make this work. Make us work.'

'We could try,' she said quietly.

He turned back around slowly and stared at her hands before scooping them up awkwardly with his bandaged one. 'I don't want to try. I want to *know* it will work. Agh!'

She scanned his drawn face. 'Hugh, let's get you on board. You're overdoing it. I need to attend to your wound.'

'It's not the bullet wound. It's you. Blast it, it hurts when I'm with *you*.' He held her gaze. 'But... but more when I'm not.'

'Oh, Hugh! You mean the three words you told Doctor Connell thinking it was me were—'

He pulled her against him with his one free arm, then lifted her chin to bring her lips within an inch of his.

'Yes. I said, "You are impossible!"'

On the plane, Clifford clapped his hands over his ears against the ladies' raucous cheers and Gladstone's barking as they watched their mistress melt into the arms of the man whose life she'd so recently saved.

'Finally,' he muttered as he pulled a handkerchief from his inside pocket. 'Bravo, my lady.'

A LETTER FROM VERITY

Dear Reader,

I want to say a huge thank you for choosing to read *Death on a Winter's Day*. If you did enjoy it, and want to keep up to date with all my latest releases, just sign up at the following link. Your email address will never be shared and you can unsubscribe at any time.

www.bookouture.com/verity-bright

I hope you loved *Death on a Winter's Day* and, if you did, I would be very grateful if you could write a review. I'd love to hear what you think, and it makes such a difference helping new readers to discover one of my books for the first time.

I also love hearing from my readers – you can get in touch on my Facebook page, through Twitter, Goodreads or my website.

Thanks,

Verity

www.veritybright.com

facebook.com/veritybrightauthor

twitter.com/BrightVerity

ACKNOWLEDGEMENTS

Thanks to Maisie, my outgoing editor, for all the fantastic work she did on getting the Lady Swift series to where it is today, and thanks to Kelsie, my incoming editor, for jumping into a difficult job and making *Death on a Winter's Day* so much better than my first draft.

HISTORICAL NOTES

Christmas in Scotland

At the beginning of *Death on a Winter's Day*, Eleanor is horrified to find that Christmas has been cancelled!

The trouble arose after the Scottish Reformation of 1560 when the Scottish Church split from Rome. Christmas and all its traditions – yule logs, decorating trees, kissing under the mistletoe and so on – were seen as pagan rites converted to a quasi-Christian festivity by the Catholic Church.

Thus, around 1580, the Presbyterian Church banned Christmas. This was followed up in 1604 by an Act of Parliament. So severe was the ban, that bakers were forbidden to make mince pies and encouraged to report anyone who tried to order them! Some rebellious bakers, rather than comply, reduced the size of their mince pies so they could be better hidden by their customers.

The ban on Christmas lasted until 1958 when it was repealed in the Scottish Parliament, thirty-seven years too late to save Eleanor's Christmas at Castle Ranburgh.

Castle Ranburgh

Castle Ranburgh is loosely based on Castle Stalker, which is located on an island in Loch Laich, near Oban. It was originally built by the MacDougall clan and then held by the Campbells and Stewarts. Castle Stalker is famous for being featured in the film *Monty Python and the Holy Grail* and now equally, if not more famous, for being featured in *Death on a Winter's Day*.

Gold mining in Scotland

You may not think of Scotland when you think of gold mining, but Clifford is, as ever, quite right. Gold mining has taken place in Scotland since at least 300 BC. It really took off, however, after a nugget weighing over 2lbs was found in 1502. Most of the mines were leased by James V to German miners who had greater experience than their Scottish counterparts.

Although in equivalent terms, millions of pounds of gold were mined, the seams eventually dried up. A few centuries later, in 1852, a second gold rush occurred around Fife and another near Sutherland in 1868.

Gold mining continues to this day and the first Scottish gold mine for centuries is due to open sometime soon.

Monsters

Drummond's monster in Loch Vale is only one of several monsters inhabiting Scottish lochs. Most people know about the Loch Ness monster, but only seventy miles away in Loch Morar lives Morag, rumoured to be Nessie's sister. In 1968, the barman of the local hotel reported a sighting: "I saw... something coming out of the water... The neck was about one and a half feet in diameter and tapered up to between ten inches and a foot. I never saw any features, no eyes or anything like that."

https://www.scotclans.com/scotland/scottish-myths/scottish-monsters/morag/

Selkies

In the final chapter, while waiting for their plane ride back to Henley Hall, Drummond tells Eleanor about the legend of the selkie, confirming what Clifford had suggested she might have seen. These seal creatures are capable of shedding their skin and taking human form. However, they have to return to the water.

One tale tells of how a fisherman saved a female selkie in a storm and then hid her skin so she had to remain on dry land with him. Many years later after having children, she found where he'd hidden her skin and returned to the sea. For years afterwards the fisherman's children would see a seal following them and looking wistfully at them. In another version, the selkie saved the fisherman in a storm, returning the original favour.

Seals (and therefore selkies) do have some natural predators in Scottish waters, notably sharks and killer whales (although the largest shark found in Scotland at thirty-three feet, the basking shark, is actually harmless). Most killer whales are migratory, but there is a pod, as they are called, that lives in Scotland year-round.

So, was the seal Eleanor saw on the rocks and then in the Laird's boat just a seal? Or a selkie? And was it repaying a debt for Eleanor's mother having saved it from predators or a storm years before? Or was the guiding hand which helped her save them all at the end, that of her mother's? I'll leave it to you to decide.

Outboard motors

The first outboard motor was actually electric and developed around 1870. Petrol-powered outboards followed later, but it wasn't until around 1906 that they were mass-produced. We don't know exactly what model the outboard on the Laird's boat was, but it probably was only around five horsepower, not much by modern standards!

Handley Page

Eleanor, Clifford, Seldon and the ladies are transported back to Henley Hall in a Handley Page o/400. For modern flyers, it would have been a terrifying experience. The plane had a hundred-foot wingspan and was made mostly out of spruce. It was developed as a bomber in WW1 and then converted to a passenger plane originally to ferry officials back and forth to the Treaty of Versailles.